Redeemed

Redeemed

Keshia Dawn

www.urbanchristianonline.com

Urban Books, LLC
78 East Industry Court
Deer Park, NY 11729

ISBN 13: 978-1-60162-830-5
ISBN 10: 1-60162-830-7

First Printing May 2012
Printed in the United States of America

10 9 8 7 6 5 4 3 2 1

Distributed by Kensington Corp.
Submit Wholesale Orders to:
Kensington Publishing Corp.
C/O Penguin Group (USA) Inc.
Attention: Order Processing
405 Murray Hill Parkway
East Rutherford, NJ 07073-2316
Phone: 1-800-526-0275
Fax: 1-800-227-9604

REDEEMED

Keshia Dawn

Dedication

This book is dedicated to those of you who inspire me, encourage me, and to those who pray with and for me. Everything I am is because of you.

Other Books by Keshia Dawn

Novels:
By the Grace of God
His Grace, His Mercy
Keeper Of My Soul

Short Stories:
The Triumph of My Soul *(Stroke of Purpose)*
Bended Knees *(Baby Boy)*

Acknowledgments

Being able to acknowledge those who have helped me get to where I am wouldn't mean anything if I couldn't thank God in heaven, first, for every writing opportunity He has afforded me; fiction and non-fiction.

To my daughter, Chayse. I know you are my number-one fan and I will forever thank you for being patient and sometimes understanding when it comes to me having to work (write). Thanks for being my everything and I hope and pray I am the same for you. Thank you to my parents, Elder Donald and Fannie Sauls for always having my back and supporting my endeavors. Packing up and moving to your city so that I could complete my degree wasn't an easy task. In the end it was only possible with your encouragement. And I did it! Thank you. To my sisters, Fanasha and Angel, I'm so excited you all are catching up in age with me! Lol. Love you two! Our best years together are yet to come. My brother-in-law, Kendrick, you are more like a brother and I love you for keeping watch over me and Chayse. I have nephews! Kayden and Langston. I'm so thrilled to be TT-Keshia. Love you, boys, and I'm going to enjoy watching you two grow into God-fearing, respectful young men. Without Urban Christian, I would not have had a platform to be able to share my stories, my thoughts, my ministry, and my gift with the world. I'm forever thankful to Carl Weber and my editor, Joylynn, for taking a chance on me in 2007. You've allowed me to continue dreaming. There

Acknowledgments

are way too many of my peers who have contributed in my literary endeavors for me to name. Just know I'm forever in debt to you for the words of encouragement, promoting, and vendor opportunities. And please believe my support is just as giving. I'm a reader, what can I say. To my support team: my readers. Thank you so much to those who through e-mail, Twitter, Facebook, my Web site, bookstores, and more have reached out to me. Your testimonies always touch my heart and I'm blessed to have been a part of your lives and the positive reaction my stories bring. I can't close my acknowledgments without being thankful for Temple/Belton Texas, Austin, San Antonio and I'll just say all of Central Texas. Again, too many people to name, but for those who supported my writing, even before I knew who you were, words cannot express the feeling in my heart. It means the world when those close to you can support you, but when there is support from those who believe in you and your ministry . . . priceless. Just know there will always be a "To Be Continued" version just for you. And yes, it all started with you Missionary Gladys Hawkins! Smile!

Until the next time . . .
Keshia Dawn KeshiaDawn@gmail.com
www.KeshiaDawnWrites.com

Prologue

"I'm full as a tick." Keithe chewed the barely there remnants of his hearty breakfast. There was nothing left of the blueberry pancakes, soft scrambled eggs, and sizzling bacon, which had melted away on his palate.

"Michelle, those cooking classes really have brought out the Southern woman in you." The forty-three-year-old dabbed his mouth. Placing his paper napkin on the table, Keithe reared back in his chair and patted his growing abdomen while trying to catch his breath.

"Ha-ha. Don't start none, won't be none." Michelle swatted at Keithe. "You act as though I'm just now learning how to cook. I . . . cook . . . well." Michelle stood from the table and began clearing her chinaware. Nothing but the best for Mr. Morgan.

Keithe was enjoying his morning. Having fun poking at Michelle, he knew good and well she would pay him back sooner rather than later.

"Dear, you cook . . . well . . . now! I will give you that," he said with a shrug of his shoulders. "But I suffered. I mean, suffered, from waaaaaay back." He put emphasis on his deep-voiced words while lowering his head and putting a scowl on his face, which spoke volumes.

"I mean, that one time when you tried to cook lasagna from scratch . . ." he explained as he shook his shaven-to-the-scalp head from side to side fiercely. "It did such a number on me that I . . ." Before he could finish the painted picture of his exaggerated experience, Michelle stood over the man she had exchanged vows with more than sixteen years earlier. Her eyes dared him to continue.

With the barely used dish towel in her hand, Michelle raised the pink and yellow–trimmed material and swatted the man she loved on his shoulder yet again.

"You had better watch it, man! Like I said, don't start none, won't be none." She laughed and belted out a cutesy cry as Keith grabbed her around her firm waist.

Being two years away from the big 6-0, Michelle only shied away from his hold because of the tickles she knew he would be issuing out. There was definitely nothing wiggly, juicy, or lumpy when it came to the judicial employee. And if there was, Spanx were her best friend.

"Stop! Keithe, you'd better stop tickling me. Quit it now," Michelle half demanded, and half wished he'd continue, as she tried her best to wiggle out of his grip. Kicking her legs frantically, it was a good thing she opted for a cashmere jogging suit for the January weather.

"Oh no! You asked for it, Sister Michelle. You tried to lay hands on a brother," Keithe continued to joke. By the time he placed Michelle in his lap, Mr. and Mrs. Morgan held a continuous laugh that just wouldn't stop.

After catching her breath, Michelle decided to remain seated on Keithe's lap. She figured the womanly weight she'd gained in her fifty-eight-year-old hips wouldn't dare hurt the hard legs of the forty-three-year-old. Resting the back of her head on his broad shoulders, Michelle's eyes watered as she wrestled with reality and her undying love for Keithe.

"This feels so right. It just feels so good to be here. Right in this moment. Don't you agree?" Michelle tilted her head. Taking her free hand, Michelle patted Keithe's chest and allowed her manicured hand to remain, feeling the muscles underneath his shirt.

Keithe debated if he should respond or allow Michelle a few minutes to wallow in her sensitive moment. He fought against being selfish and released a smooth moan of agreement from his voice box.

When his moan wouldn't suffice, Michelle whispered, "What about you, Keithe?" Still waiting, Michelle completely turned her head to the left. Close enough for a kiss.

With the layered portion of her bobbed hairdo lying across her right eye, Michelle didn't dare to move in fear the mood would be lost: the mood she hoped Keithe would become a part of.

There seemed to be no winning but Keithe wasn't going to allow it to happen again. He wasn't going to allow Michelle to sulk once more in his presence for the decision they both agreed upon, even if it had been his idea to begin with.

At least once a month Michelle played the "woe is me" card. Keithe thought the last two years would have been enough time for her to heal, to settle with the whole notion of what had happened between them. Obviously it hadn't.

Through all of the trials and tribulations their relationship had endured, his love for Michelle remained. For all they had gone through, nothing took his love for Michelle in a different direction. His love for the woman who grew him into a man overnight hadn't wavered. Being *in* love with her . . . that was a whole other issue.

Three years before, their marriage had been turned upside down. Being real with himself, Keithe knew problems had lived in their relationship for quite some time, but with the depth of things that had invaded their marriage, it had only pushed their union to the limit. Even when the end product left Michelle saved and living for God, having reconnected with a daughter that only she had known about, Keithe was still left bothered, unfulfilled, and asking God what the problem was. When it was all said and done, Keithe had asked Michelle for a divorce.

"Penny for your thoughts?" Michelle nudged, still sitting on her ex-husband's lap, yet waiting for some sort of verbal response.

He cared too much. "Too nice of a guy" was what he'd been told all of his life. At the very moment with Michelle waiting for an answer, Keithe knew he had to stop coming around his ex. But he felt obligated. She hadn't asked for the divorce, so Keithe felt it was his duty to keep some sort of relationship with her.

With a quick breath, Keithe shared, "Just thinking how much I don't want to rehash this each time I come to visit. I want you to know that I do love you and always will. But this"—he nudged Michelle from her leaning position so that she could look into his eyes—"we are going to have to stop revisiting."

When she received divorce papers, Michelle hadn't put up a fight. For one, she couldn't deny she hadn't noticed how Keithe's demeanor had changed, even when she had finally gotten her act together. She just figured she had been a day late and a dollar short. Michelle knew how emotionally, mentally, and physically disgusting she had been during their marriage and allowed Keithe to leave without so much as a fight.

If anyone ever thought it, Keithe knew for a fact Michelle's role as his wife had been catty, deceiving, and conniving. She had lied, cheated, and manipulated their marriage. She was even abusive when in actuality it was herself whom she hated. Michelle had taken Keithe for granted in their sixteen-year marriage. And she'd done the ultimate: keeping her past, that she had mothered a child, from Keithe.

Michelle didn't know what she was thinking. Maybe she hadn't thought things through when it came to not letting him know she had birthed a child. For a fact, she knew she hadn't, but that was even years before meeting Keithe.

Having a baby twenty-four years ago really hadn't been on her to-do list. A quick relationship developed with Stoney's real father, the Bishop Ky Perry, only after her desires to be with his friend fell through. Confused, devastated, and embarrassed, Michelle pushed her emotions to the side and made the decision she thought was best.

Dropping her baby with her mother, Michelle never looked back. Meeting Keithe years later and with her past out of sight, out of mind, Michelle never felt compelled to share what she had done. Even up until the day she was busted, Michelle had still found it hard to share all of herself with Keithe. Even when all he wanted to do was to love her.

And that was just it. Keithe only wanted to love God and his wife, as Christ loved the church. But finally, after sixteen years of marriage, it had been too late to make up for all of her wrong. Like all other days, today didn't stop Michelle from trying to show her ex-husband that she still loved him.

"Whoa. Do I need to come back at another time?" Stoney almost lost her footing as she made her way into the country decor–styled kitchen. "I mean, really, Mom?" Stoney gave off a questionable laugh as she placed her hand on her Southern eating–produced hip.

Having been reunited with her mom in the most unusual circumstances, Stoney was now settled in her role as Michelle's only child, albeit a twenty-four-year-old child.

Raised by her maternal grandmother, Stoney didn't meet Michelle until she was twenty-one. Even then it was a meeting that almost left Stoney psychotic and Michelle physically battered.

Since she could remember, all Stoney wanted was to know and be with her birth mother: a mother who literally dumped her into the arms of a schizophrenic grandmother. The mental struggle her grandmother, Michelle's mother, battled with was too much for a young Stoney to deal with on her own, and often pushed her to the edge of giving up. But she had survived.

"Oh hush it," Michelle said and threw the dish towel, she still held on to, at her daughter.

"Your mom was just getting up," Keithe said as he slightly pushed Michelle to her feet. "Trying once again to fill me to the rim so I can't leave." He patted his extended stomach. Keithe made a joke out of the truth as he stood from the table. Straightening the crease Michelle had inadvertently set in his cargo pants, Keithe stepped behind the chair.

Stoney walked over to her stepdad and stood in a ballerina's stance, on her toes, and gave him a kiss on the cheek. "Pops, you leaving so soon?" she asked, adding a sad face she hoped would convince him to stay a bit longer. Adding a sly grin to her lips, Stoney stood waiting for a reply.

Even with twenty-one years apart from her mother, having never laid eyes on her, except for one photograph, Stoney resembled Michelle to a T. With her brownish-caramel complexion, Stoney also held the signature eyes that popped, even without mascara. And with her size twelve, mostly in the hips, Stoney knew she was her mother's child.

"You two are gonna have to stop ganging up on me. Every month it's the same old thing." Keithe was tired of being made to feel bad, as if everything fell into his lap and he had been the bad husband, bad parent.

Two weeks off into the New Year, Keithe really did think it was a good idea to spend time with the two he still loved and called family. Now with all the badgering, he second-guessed himself.

"We wouldn't have this problem if you still lived here," Stoney said, tilting her head and allowing her ponytail to lie on her shoulder.

"Or at least in the city," Michelle chimed in, loving Houston as if it were her birthplace.

Pushing his chair in, Keithe said, "It's definitely time to go." Grabbing Stoney, Keithe held her in an embrace.

"Well, I know you only come home once a month now to spend time with your mother, and is it so bad that I want to share in the love?" He held open his arms, not letting on how he had also been overdue for a visit with his parents, who still lived in the city. "Plus, I'm only leaving because I want to leave some time for you two to do all the girly stuff I know you have planned for today."

"If you say so," Stoney retorted, always holding on to the ill feeling that she had been the straw that broke the camel's back in Keithe and her mother's marriage. In her mind, Stoney felt if she had never gone looking for her missing piece to a scrambled puzzle, her mother would still be happy and her stepfather would have remained her husband. No matter how many times Keithe had told her she had nothing to do with the divorce, Stoney could never be certain. That was one of the reasons Stoney chose to continue her college studies at a school an hour away; she had hoped her mother and stepfather's time together would fill the space that had grown between the two.

"Stoney, please don't. Especially since I see you more often," Keithe reminded Stoney of her visits to Dallas to spend time with her biological father.

"Okay. But you do have my graduation date on your calendar, huh?" Stoney wanted to make sure her stepfather planned accordingly for her graduation ceremony, which was five months away.

Before Stoney had connected with her mother and Keithe, she had gone through countless misfortunes her entire life. Once addicted to prescription drugs, most of the time the medication not being her own, but that of her grandmother's, Stoney had been labeled schizophrenic. In reality, her heart had been broken from her very beginning.

Wanting to know who she was and who she belonged to had been her main objective in life. Not knowing how to deal with the heartache had been her catapult to self-destruction.

Once connected with her past, Stoney was finally at a point where she knew who she was and where she'd come from. Having lost her focus and desire to do anything with her life, it wasn't until Stoney was settled with who she was that school had become a priority again. Only months stood in the way of her receiving a Bachelor of Arts degree in psychology, which she was determined to flip into a master's degree in no time.

With a side eye, Keithe didn't even bother to answer what he thought was a crazy and sarcastic question. Of course he would be there for Stoney. Placing another kiss on her forehead, Keithe then walked toward Michelle and made sure he squeezed her extra tight and kissed the cheek she offered.

"Okay, ladies. You have a good rest of the afternoon. I will call you when I make it home safely," the six-foot attorney assured.

"Really wish you could stay for church tomorrow." Michelle tried to convince Keithe to prolong his stay with a simple raise of her arched eyebrows.

With his mind set to exit through the kitchen's door, Keithe placed his hand on the doorknob before rejecting the two people who still meant the most to him.

"You know, if I didn't have to present this class at church in the morning, I probably would," he said with light emphasis on the "probably." Then he silently wondered what her latest beau would think about the invite. Obviously Michelle hadn't thought about that either.

"Um, huh," Michelle responded and turned, heading back to the kitchen sink.

"Oh. If you happen to talk to Bishop, don't forget to tell him I will be down next week." Stoney referred to her biological father by his title, so as not, she thought, to make Keithe feel lesser in the role he had played in her life. Even in the short amount of time of them being in one another's life, Stoney looked up to Keithe and happily accepted his role. Waving one last time, Stoney left the kitchen.

"Got it." Knowing he only spoke with Bishop Ky Perry from time to time, Keithe thought nothing of it and just labeled it as small talk on Stoney's behalf. With the twist of the knob and a backhanded wave,

Keithe was almost home free until Michelle made her move. It was obvious; by the stretching of her neck toward the kitchen's exit, Michelle made sure Stoney was out of listening range.

With a mumbled sound coming from Michelle, Keithe hated to turn around but replied with, "Huh?"

"Who is she?" Michelle sternly responded once more as she turned to face her ex-husband. "Only a woman can be the inspiration for a man driving all the way out of town one day with him turning right back around, headed home, not even twenty-four hours later." Michelle looked at her TAG Heuer pearl-diamond polished watch. "Who is she, Mr. Morgan?"

"Ahhh, there you go again," Keithe responded and took a step, placing one foot back inside of the house. "I told you. When I get serious with someone, I will let you know." With his body halfway in, halfway out the door, Keithe continued. "And not because you are entitled, but only because you're nosy. Because guess what, Michelle. We aren't married anymore."

Leaning against the kitchen sink, Michelle crossed her arms and squinted her eyes. "Touché. Okay, so you say. But I beg to differ. I'm a woman. Humph." She smiled. "Who am I kidding? I'm Michelle. I know, I know, I don't get down like that anymore." She gave a *Super Fly* gesture, curving her lips and all. "But I know it's someone." She turned back around to her awaiting suds. "Be careful. You know how some church women can be." She mainly spoke about herself rather than others.

Shaking his head and rolling his eyes, Keithe hoped Michelle hadn't let her former life cross over into her being born again. He decided to not respond but rather leave gracefully. He figured if he could handle Michelle for sixteen years, there wasn't anything he couldn't put up with. Obviously she was gonna give him a run for his money as far as his next relationship was concerned.

Finally easing the door shut, Keithe made his departure, ready to head back to his refreshed life as a single, saved, and searching bachelor.

Chapter One

His car was like a gigantic magnet pulling him. Or at least that's how he wanted it to seem. Keithe rushed out the kitchen's door to his car he had parked on the outside of the garage. He was ever so grateful to Michelle for allowing him to finally leave peacefully. The last time she had actually barricaded herself in front of the door.

Keithe was tired, very tired, of reinventing the wheel. No, he was sick and tired of taking all the blame. He partially did so, so that the questions, all of the small talks, would stop. Another reason was, well, he was to blame, or so he figured.

In all actuality, it had been his fault for staying in a marriage far too long, a dead-end marriage at that. It no doubt was his fault for putting up a front, thinking that if Michelle had done this, if she'd done that, things would be okay. But when it was all said and done and his wife had been born again, there was still a hole.

No matter how many sorry pouts Michelle had thrown his way, it was hard to believe he had sacrificed so much for her. One thing in particular was him being a father.

It had been clear from the beginning. It wasn't that Michelle couldn't have children; it was that she wouldn't. "I'm not mommy material," Michelle would reiterate each time Keithe asked about starting a family. After a while he just accepted that he loved her enough to believe his being a father just hadn't been meant to be. Now forty-three, single, and not even so much as a prospect in his life, Keithe got mad just thinking about what could have been.

He took nothing from accepting Stoney as his. Keithe had welcomed her with open arms and graciously became a father overnight. Literally. But with Stoney there were no first steps or late-night feedings to go along with his new role.

It was just the realization of how Michelle said she had never wanted to be a mother when in fact she had been one all along. She had worn the title for twenty-one years without acknowledging it at all. Keithe was still clueless about how someone could pull that off. But then he had to realize just who he was dealing with. There were times when he still felt he had been punk'd by Ashton Kutcher.

Even after the dust did settle and Michelle and Stoney reunited, there was that very image of the bond that had grown between mother and daughter, seeing Michelle glow in motherhood. Of course her child was anything but a child, but it didn't matter. Keithe held some resentment toward his ex-wife. While Michelle and Stoney had one another, Keithe felt as if he had no one. That's when he knew he didn't have closure with himself. That was what eventually led to the divorce.

Now with everything spilling over with him having to convince Stoney she hadn't come along and messed up their marriage, Keithe really didn't know if that was the truth. Would he have stayed if Stoney never made her entrance? Keithe thought over and over. Ultimately, he knew that was blame he couldn't put off on anyone but him and Michelle: himself for staying too long and Michelle for never being honest with herself; therefore, not being able to be totally honest with him.

After their divorce two years ago, it hadn't taken Keithe but a second to figure out a game plan. When realization hit like a ton of bricks after all the residue of their tumultuous marriage settled, Keithe found himself thinking beyond Houston. He didn't want to go far, leaving his parents behind, but he wanted to go far enough to start a new life. That new life for him now resided somewhere he'd only visited. Home for Keithe was now in Dallas.

Hours had passed since Keithe was finally able to leave the premises of the home he and Michelle had had designed and built from the ground up. After stopping and visiting with his parents, Keithe made his way on to the highway as he settled into the full-sized bucket seat of his upgraded Porsche. Having traded his two-door prized possession, the black-on-black Porsche of his dreams, Keithe knew he was getting ready for something new to fall into his life when he purchased the four-door Porsche Panamera: his new black. Whoever she was, his new lady, he was going to floss with her in style.

There was no doubt he was already a husband. Just because he was no longer married didn't mean he had given up on love. The desire embedded in him was what kept him going; that and his desire to be a daddy to a baby who would look just like him. He wasn't giving up on being a father. Keithe thought that surely if Hollywood stars could have babies in their mid-fifties and beyond, a child of God, a believer as himself, would be able to keep up with his kiddos.

Maybe a girl who looks like her mother . . . nahhhh. Who am I kidding? I need a little Keithe who looks just like his handsome daddy, Keithe often played over and over in his mind.

He had gone out on a few dates in the last two years but things were way different. Over twenty years ago when he was single and in his early twenties, Keithe's morals and desires for a mate hadn't been what they now were, as someone who had a relationship with Christ, was honest, trustworthy, and respectful. Back then, all a woman had to have were happy lips and healthy hips. Although he had no plans on turning down his wife-to-be, if hips were attached, now in his forties, he knew there was much more than what the eye could see.

Just as his mind soared back to Michelle and her comment about a love affair that didn't exist, Keithe shook his head at the courage of the woman he'd chosen as a wife and how she pulled out a low blow.

"Wondering what woman I'm running back to. Umph. The nerve," he said aloud. Especially when Michelle was dating a deacon from the church they used to attend together. Matter of fact, she was dating a brother who Keithe had actually liked and called a friend. But, regardless, he had given his blessing on their dating; anything to get her out of his bald head. Yet it appeared sweet Michelle couldn't seem to do the same.

Laughing at Michelle's antics, Keithe's thoughts were jolted when his phone rang in its holster attached to the dash. Although he didn't hesitate to answer, for a moment he felt guilty when he realized Michelle may have been more right than he wanted to let on.

"Hello," he greeted the caller.

"Hi there, Deacon Morgan. Did I catch you at a bad time?" Evangelist Clark, a hard worker and servant of the Lord who attended the same church he attended, rang through on the other end.

With an added smile to the smirk he held when he'd first seen her telephone number pop up on his screen, Keithe was ready for conversation. Or so he hoped.

"Uh, yes. No. Well, uh. No." He took a breath. Just like all the other times, anytime he was in the young woman's presence, even via the telephone, Keithe couldn't get his mojo to work. He may have been an award-winning attorney, winning a number of high-profile cases under his skilled title, but when it came to Evangelist Kenya Clark, his get up and go always sat down.

"I mean," he pouted, "I'm available." He winced and silently hit his steering wheel, hoping he didn't sound as though he was giving himself away to the highest bidder. But then again . . .

There was something about the saved thirty-something woman of God he had finally gotten to know within the last year. For the first year being at the church, he admired her from afar. When it came time for him to get more involved in the church and allow his own ministry to grow, Keithe took the first opportunity that presented itself.

The men and women of the church were asked to volunteer their time and efforts in helping to build a new support system for divorcees. Without hesitation, Keithe knew it was meant for him: helping other divorcees heal from broken marriages while healing himself at the same time. The group was titled Physically Divorced, Spiritually Married, and it just so happened Evangelist Clark had been attached to the opportunity. All Keithe could think was God was good all the time, and all the time God was good.

"What can I help you with?" he finally managed to get out.

"Oh, I wanted to remind you about Sunday School in the morning. We are going to officially kick off our once-a-month Sunday morning worship with the group." Kenya shared a smile through the phone.

And maybe I'll just have the courage to ask you out for dinner. Officially, he thought.

The two had gone on numerous outings, lunch and even dinner. But the divorce group was always the reason behind their getting together, or at least for Evangelist Clark it had been. Every time they'd met it was on Keithe's mind to ask her out on an official date, but he couldn't bring his nerves under submission.

"Sounds like a plan. I am driving in now from Houston, so I will no doubt be there in the morning."

"Oh?" Her voice held a question. "I didn't know you were going out of town or I would have changed the date." Kenya wanted to be fair. "Did you only come back for the group? You should have told me, I would have—"

"No. There is absolutely no problem. I was just visiting my wife, ah, I mean, my ex-wife and daughter. I mean, ah, stepdaughter." Keithe wished he could just hang the phone up and be done.

Another "oh" was all she responded with. Kenya bit down on her bottom lip and waited for his response. Always wanting to know the depth of who Deacon Morgan was, Kenya dared not ask or show any interest. Dealing with her own disclosed issues was enough.

Everything was still new to him. He didn't know what was politically correct and what wasn't when it came to bringing up his past. Hoping he didn't share too much, or disrespect his family, Keithe changed the subject.

"Well, while I have you on the line, Sister Clark, let me ask you—" Before he could finish his intro, his line beeped. "Can you hold, please?" Keithe asked as he rolled his eyes once he realized it was Michelle. Whatever it was she planned to lay on him, Keithe had his mind set to not even buy into it.

Chapter Two

"Hello?" Keithe threw out a hard and annoyed greeting toward Michelle. He didn't know if it was because she had possibly shortened his conversation with Evangelist Clark or if it was because it had been Michelle on the other line. Period. Switching his driving hand, Keithe repositioned his cell phone and waited for Michelle to give the reason behind her calling.

"Get over yourself, my brotha." Michelle snatched an attitude once she heard the tone of Keithe's voice. "I just wanted to check on you." No doubt she cared about Keithe's welfare, but there was something she had been meaning to run by Keithe. Sitting on the stool in front of her vanity, Michelle tried on one of five different shades of Bobbi Brown's new lip color she had bought while she and Stoney had been out for the day. She settled with the brightest shade and slid it across her puckered lips.

Keithe knew Michelle still cared for him, but with the phone call he felt she was over doing it. There was no doubt Michelle was still clocking him. Why else would she call him before he called her? Desperate, maybe.

"I'm good," he answered. "I'm on the other line, Michelle. Is everything okay?" Keithe had only departed Michelle's house hours ago, not days, and Michelle had to have remembered him telling her that he would call once he reached town. Even with him stopping at his parents' home to visit, Keithe was still making good time back into Dallas.

Concluding their shopping after a couple of hours, Stoney decided to hang with friends from church before she departed from her mother's house and headed back to her off-campus apartment. Michelle just decided she would retire early. She had actually debated picking up the line and calling her ex, but when she figured there could possibly be a chance Keithe would somehow be happy with her decision, Michelle's fingers did the walking.

She hadn't shared with Keithe how she and her latest beau, Deek, had called it quits. Cupid had come to do his job. Unfortunately it was her beau's ex-wife who had won him over. So with Stoney away from the house, Michelle felt she had way too much time on her hands and had no shame in flirting a bit with Keithe. As far as she was concerned, he was still her hubby. As what she'd read in the Bible said, he *was* still hers since neither of them were remarried or dead. She was ready to reclaim what was hers.

"All is well. I just wish you would have stayed a little longer. You know you can still spend the night when you visit, Keithe." Michelle ran the thought by her ex-husband, knowing it wouldn't happen. The last time she offered for him to sleep over and rest before his drive back, she had offered him herself as well. For Michelle, it had worked out perfectly. For Keithe, well, he had driven back in repent mode his entire ride home.

"Michelle . . ." Keithe urged Michelle to get to what she wanted. "Again, I'm on the other line."

"Oh, excuse me, sir." Michelle threw in her own attitude. Knowing Keithe's annoyance for her had been settled in even before the phone call, Michelle's decision to tell Keithe about her plans to move to Dallas were halted. She already knew he probably wouldn't wholeheartedly agree and would definitely be furious, but she still had hope.

Not knowing what else to do with her thoughts and feelings for Keithe, since he was all she thought about, Michelle decided to just hold off on her news.

"Okay, okay. I will . . . I will just speak with you later, Keithe. I wouldn't want you to keep the little missus waiting." Michelle tapped her phone with her nails and disconnected the call. She may have asked God to enter her life, but game still recognized game, and for some reason, Michelle just knew she would have to fight for her man.

"Oh, I'm gonna stay saved," Michelle declared as she puckered her lips and shifted on her seat. "It will just be . . . What do they call it? A holy war. Hey now." She pumped her hands in the air like she was getting happy for Jesus.

Before he could swap the call back to the other line on his BlackBerry, Evangelist Clark had disconnected her end.

"Dang it!" Keithe threw his phone in the passenger's seat. There was no way he could find the nerve to call back for the sole purpose of asking her out. He hadn't gotten that bold in five minutes.

"Michelle! What are you up to?" Keithe's right hand squeezed and remained on the leather-padded steering wheel as he slouched in his seat.

He couldn't put his finger on it, but Michelle had been a little bit too gentle on this last visit. No real clinging as she had done before. To him, that could only mean she was playing the whole reverse psychology bit on him.

For the past few months she had pulled all kinds of stuff to try to get him to return to her arms. He knew Michelle was a little off-kilter when she had the nerve to call him one afternoon after they'd reinvented their bedroom roles of husband and wife. When she shared with Keithe that she might be expecting, he quickly let her know if she was expecting anything besides a miracle she could hang it up, then showed her an example by hanging up his phone.

Not so unusual for Texas, the cool, not cold, January air pushed through his vents as Keithe relaxed his thoughts on Michelle and her antics. Decreasing the thermostat number to seventy degrees, Keithe needed to bring some comfort to his ride.

Replacing his thoughts of Michelle, Keithe grabbed at his brief conversation he'd held with Evangelist Clark and knew without a doubt she had been his motivation to head back to Dallas. He didn't know how or when, but Keithe knew soon enough that he would get Evangelist Clark to see giving him a chance could be just the start she needed for the New Year.

Chapter Three

Kenya was so happy to have eased her way off of the phone with Deacon Morgan. A minute longer and she was sure he would have found the courage to ask her out.

"Lord, that was a close one." She openly thanked God for call waiting.

To Kenya, Deacon Morgan was tall, dark, and definitely handsome. If he ever had hair, Kenya didn't want to see any pictures; that man oozed sexiness with the clean and clear scalp. And his goatee appeared as if it were painted on. Cold black.

There was nothing more Kenya would have liked than to go on a date with the handsome deacon to see if more could be established. She was sure it was possible, but she just didn't know if she was ready. As a matter of fact, she knew she wasn't ready. Kenya wasn't at all secure that a recent past would stay in the past.

"Oh to be wooed by a saved man of God," Kenya declared, shaking her head as she put her cell phone on its charging station. "And, Lord, you made him look so goooood." Switching her riding boots for her house slippers, Kenya pulled her wool sweater over her head and threw it over on her sofa.

The cool January's draft throughout her house chilled her body through her coffee-colored camisole. Grabbing for the back of her head, Kenya gave her hair a quick pull to make sure her ponytail holder was still tightly in place as she walked deeper into her home.

Deacon Morgan was hard on her mind. That man was godly, gorgeous, and going after her: a single, saved woman's dream. This was the reason Kenya wished she had called him first thing in the morning. There was no way she was going to sleep anytime soon. Not even a nap. Knowing all minds had to be clear before her head hit the pillow, Kenya wasn't going to take any chances. Either that or she'd find herself on some sandy white beach, wrapped up in Deacon Morgan's big black arms.

"Lord Jesus, help me." Kenya scooted her five-foot, seven-inch, 140-pound self from room to room, tidying up loose ends.

All it took was a thought to get one going in the wrong direction. And from where Kenya was struggling to come back from, she knew the symptoms all too well.

All in all, the saved, anointed, and sophisticated young woman kind of enjoyed the crush she had on the deacon; something that had been out of the norm for her for quite some time.

Ever since theology school, Kenya had been on the go for Jesus and His spiritual direction for her life. Yes, she had a desire to get married and to be someone's wife, but it just hadn't been a priority.

She'd dated here and there, but when she would share how she had no intentions of crossing the line as far as intercourse before marriage was concerned, her phone almost always stopped ringing. And that was just the so-called "saved men."

There was no doubt Kenya was playing cat and mouse with her copartner. She indeed liked the forty-something, but she knew that was only part of who she was. There was too much she was trying to figure out and deal with about herself. That was the very reason why she wouldn't dare try getting involved with Deacon Morgan until she knew for sure she was over all of her hang-ups.

Being anointed to speak God's Word over His people, Kenya didn't take her calling for granted. She knew even at the young age of twelve she had been different, set apart from the average teenager. She didn't have the desire to go out to clubs, smoke, or to drink. Boys were cute and she could even recognize the handsomeness behind their walk, but she just hadn't felt the need to disobey God. The feeling of the Holy Spirit giving her a natural high was all she had been concerned with. And because of that, she took life seriously. This was why she couldn't believe all she'd gotten caught up in at this stage in her life. Kenya was still on a mission to forgive herself for her own mishaps.

Kenya scooted around, almost leaving her house slippers behind, as she made her way toward the open kitchen. Even with the weather almost spring like, Kenya had a taste for hot chocolate. With a microwave-safe container, Kenya warmed her water for her beverage of choice. Leaning against her cabinets, watching the water come to a boil, Kenya grabbed at relaxation and knew she wouldn't be leaving her four walls for the remainder of the evening.

The only thing on her agenda for the rest of the evening was to prepare for the next day with prayer. Before she'd shield herself away for one on one with God, Kenya planned on sitting and reflecting on what she really wanted in her life. No doubt she would begin with relationships she had endured.

It was hard enough to dodge being set up on blind dates by family members, but most recently Kenya even had to dodge her pastor's hints of possibly getting to know Deacon Morgan better. She knew he meant well; for the fact of the matter, she knew everyone who tried to hook her up with someone meant well. But she just felt she couldn't bring someone into her world, a world she hadn't always been so proud of.

Sure she was getting older, in her mid-thirties to be exact. Kenya knew people were starting to question why she was still alone. She had been in the ministry since she was a teenager and, because of that, Kenya had been able to use her evangelism as an excuse. Now that she was semi-retired from missions work and was at her church home more often than not, the questions came without guard:

"When you gon' get married, Sis Kenya?"

"You need to get married and have at least one baby."

"Don't pass your child-rearing age . . . that ain't good on your body."

And when the questions arose from the bold, Kenya would be asked:

"Do you like women?"

"Girl, you ain't got caught up in some other kind of stuff, have ya?"

No matter how confident she had been and how she thought her ministry spoke for itself, Kenya always came back with, "God has called me to speak and preach His Word. When He is ready for me to be married, God will send my husband to come scoop me up." And then she would no doubt add, "And you can rest assure you will have an invite."

Reality let Kenya know that her desire to be and have a companion was just the start. She had believed and knew in her heart that someday she would add wife to her title as well. But "faith without works is dead," and if Kenya really wanted to share in God's ultimate testimony—marriage—she had to clear out her guilty excuses. Albeit, great excuses, doing God's work, but she knew God hadn't placed a Jeremiah spirit in her.

She just used the excuse to buy time. And from being around Deacon Morgan, it looked as though her time was winding up.

In the end Kenya knew she had only been fooling herself. She could honestly make time for the right one if she wanted to. She could even allow Deacon Morgan the opportunity to win her heart. That wasn't the issue. The matter of the problem was all about figuring out if what she had gotten involved in had become a part of who she really was, was just something that happened, or if it was indeed who she had been all this time.

Kenya wanted and needed to make sure the "old man" was indeed dead. She may have been saved since her childhood years and knew the Word as if she'd helped write the books of the Bible herself, but there was no doubt she was up against one of the toughest mountains of her saved life.

"What in the world have I done?" Kenya wished she had not crossed the line. She still couldn't believe what predicament she had put her relationship with God in. But if there was one thing she knew, Kenya knew it had been a spiritual battle. One she was unfortunately losing but was willing to fight for.

Sitting on her chocolate-colored suede sofa that faced the view of her lit back porch, Kenya sat with her favorite mug in her hand, settled in the warmth of her home. Just looking at the slight wind easing through the branches on her tree sent a brief chill up her spine. Picking up the remote control, Kenya clicked the electric fireplace on.

Sluggish in nature from the full day she'd had, Kenya slid from her sofa and onto the hairy rug that hugged her floor. Wiggling her toes from the heat the fireplace produced, Kenya leaned her back against the sofa. Thinking about how blessed she was to be able to live in her own home and not have to worry about where her help was coming from, Kenya shook her head of the mere thought of losing all God had blessed her with.

Being young, beautiful, and saved left room for joy beyond measure. God had shown Kenya how just by trusting in Him and doing things His way left peace. And it had up until she had moved without prayer and didn't take the way of escape that God always sets in place.

Only if she could trust herself again. Only if she could forgive herself.

She didn't know what she was going to do. There was no doubt that time was running out. Being the well put-together man he was and presented himself to be, Deacon Morgan was going to make a move. Kenya didn't know if she was strong enough to turn him down, and she certainly didn't want to drag him into her world until she knew the coast was clear: a world she hadn't yet closed the door to all the way.

Kenya had never been married but had been in relationships. Some she had been proud of, even when the timing was off; others, the timing had been perfect but she definitely hadn't been proud of. The next relationship, Kenya wanted God to be in the midst of, through and through. But first she had to make things back right with Him.

Thinking about the drama she had been able to steer clear from for so many years, Kenya rolled her eyes, embarrassed of having to repent for things she never would have thought she would have to confess to.

Bypassing finishing her beverage, Kenya placed her mug on her end table and turned to face the back of her sofa. Resting her palms against each other, Kenya began speaking directly to the Lord for things to come, and things in her past to remain in her past.

Chapter Four

When Keithe visited First Communion Baptist church it reminded him of his worship experience back home in Houston. It was like a fresh wind experience, just like what gospel artist Micah Stampley sang about. Whatever issues he had walking into the sanctuary he was able to praise and worship his way through, and leave his burdens there, under the guidance of the Holy Spirit and the sound word from the pastor.

After initially moving to Dallas, Keithe had visited other churches in the metroplex. He even visited his good friend Mike's church with the thought of joining. But with all the personal issues Mike had been having, he thought it better to make a fresh start somewhere else. He definitely didn't need his name attached to anything Mike had gotten involved in.

The medium-sized church had everything a believer needed to go higher in the Lord: worship, praise, and the Holy Spirit sitting in each and every pew. With the mindset of a well-organized mega church, First Communion prided themselves on God first and "family first and a half," as their pastor often reiterated. It was about having a relationship and allowing it to grow on every level.

Looking over at his digital styled clock on the glassed-topped nightstand, Keithe lay in his king-sized, platform-styled bed in the early hours of the morning. Thinking.

He was now forty-three, single, and living a totally different lifestyle than he had in almost two decades. The last time he had lived alone had been when he was twenty-four years old. And even then he frequently spent the nights with his parents for their food and company.

For the most part, Keithe had good days and bad days but he'd finally gotten the hang of doing things alone. If it weren't for being able to see Evangelist Clark later on in the morning, he knew today would be one of those bad days when he would second-guess his decision of divorcing Michelle.

Keithe had to watch himself. He loved God and all that was in Him and was excited about spending time in the spirit. But he also couldn't deny he was excited about just being in Kenya's presence.

With no engagement or wedding rings on her awaiting finger, Keithe was holding on to the notion that she wasn't attached. He didn't know if that meant much in this day and age, but it surely had to mean something for a woman of God. He hadn't asked anyone about her or put himself out there, but something must have shown through his glow because it was too frequent that their pastor made sure to always drop "Kenya nuggets" on him. Although he never confirmed one way or the other, Keithe mentally docked everything he was told.

Keithe felt somewhat played, though. With all the lunches he'd invited her to, surely she would have caught on that he was interested. *Surely* not all of his words had been stammered. Had they? It no longer mattered. No matter how hard it was to get his question out, Keithe was adamant in asking Evangelist Clark out on a date right after service.

With one hand across his chest and the other underneath his head, Keith lay in his blue and white striped Ralph Lauren pajamas and prayed through the quietness of his room.

"I'm so grateful for yet another day, Lord. Today I want your will to be done. No, I need your will to be done. I don't want self to get in the way. Lord, I thank you for placing a new ministry at my feet. I pray to do exactly what it is you want me to. As always, please go before me and lead the way."

He knew he'd be lying to himself if he didn't mention his heart's desire. Especially when it would greet him head-on in just a few hours.

"Lord, please prepare me. The desire you've placed in me to express myself as a husband, yet again, I pray it is your will. Help me to hear you loud and clear. And I pray for patience to see who she is," he added, hoping all the while it would be Kenya.

Knowing he had a few more hours until he had to physically get ready for Sunday School, being that he'd had his attire laid out for the day, Keithe allowed his eyes the rest they wanted.

It seemed as if the sun and his phone had planned to make themselves known at the same time. With one eye fighting to stay closed, Keithe greeted the caller in the midst of his sleep.

"Hello," he greeted the person on the other end, without bothering to look at the caller display screen. Hearing the rush on the other end, he wished he would have.

"You mean you're not up? Bro, how you gonna invite dude to your church and he beat you there?" Mike spoke in the third person as if he hadn't been talking about himself.

"Mike?" Keithe questioned groggily once he realized it was his childhood friend. "What are you talking
about, man? I'm up. Thanks for the call though." Keithe pushed to sit up in bed. "But I thought you couldn't
make it," Keithe said, recalling Mike's initial decline to
his Sunday morning invite.

"Oh, you can leave it right there. I'll get it later. Are
you leaving?" Mike spoke to someone in his company
in a more soothing tone. "I wasn't." His attention fell
back to Keithe. "But I got some inspiration this morning." He left the details out and winked as his company
made their exit.

Not wanting to ask any questions for fear his friend
would lie to him, Keithe continued the previous conversation and just hoped Mike would retire his old
habit of being "free."

"Okay. Well. Yep, I'm about to get up and get things
started." Keithe swung his legs on the side of the bed.
With his eyes closed he fished around for his slippers.
The original coldness that was housed in the month of
January found itself latched on to Keithe's hardwood
floors. Placing his feet inside of the gift that Michelle
and Stoney had given him for Christmas, along with a
robe and pajamas, Keithe set his pace in motion.

"Snap. Oh, well. I just wanted to let you know I was
coming to church, but I'm not going to be able to stay
the whole service. I'm going to sit in as minister of
music for this church around the corner from y'all and
they are having their anniversary at one o'clock. I need
to go over and talk with their music department and
get set up. Trying to get that next position, you know?"
Mike dared not speak of his no longer playing for
Bethel, the church he had been minister of music at for
more than ten years. His being fired two years earlier
still didn't sit well with him.

"I know," Keithe was careful to say. He didn't want to go off into the reasoning behind Mike's departure from the church he had headed the music department to for the last decade. "That's what's up. I guess I'll just see you there. And you have to let me introduce you to the sister I've been telling you about . . . I want to know what you think. Oh, and Mike?"

"What up?" Mike hoped Keithe didn't start in on him early in the morning.

"We still need to catch up from the other week, dude. I thought you were going to chill on all of that?" Keithe wanted to bargain. He didn't want an in-depth conversation, but he wanted Mike to know he was concerned about him.

Without even so much as a breath of response, Mike disconnected the call.

Keithe wasn't even in the mood to dial his friend up and ask what his problem was. Knowing Mike, he'd ask him the same thing. All in all, Keithe wanted to somewhat be the reminder Mike obviously needed to walk the straight and narrow. Literally.

Evangelist Clark was almost always the first to arrive to church to set up for Sunday School. Mostly it was because she was the teacher, but she couldn't deny loving to be in the presence of the Lord all by herself.

With Deacon Morgan calling her to let her know he had a flat tire and would be running late, Evangelist Clark put in overtime assembling the rest of the packets and setting them out for the students in their class.

"Good morning." Mike had followed the sound of someone singing a worship song and peeped his head through the door. Looking for someone to direct him toward Keithe, Mike stood at the door, wanting to make the lady feel comfortable with his presence since the two seemed to be the only ones there at the moment. "I'm Mike. I'm looking for Deacon Morgan."

Putting a halt to her tune as well as her preparations, Evangelist Clark laid down her pamphlets and walked toward the door with her arm extended, ready to greet the visitor. Not knowing him personally, Kenya scrunched her manicured eyebrows and knew she had seen his face somewhere before.

"Good morning. Come on in; the deacon is running late." Kenya used her firm handshake to welcome Mike into the large room. Releasing Mike's hand Kenya stopped to look at her accessorized watch for the time. "He actually had a flat tire this morning. Are you here for our divorcee class, Physically Divorced, Spiritually Married? I don't think I've seen you in our preliminary sessions before." Kenya grabbed her chin while thinking about where she'd seen him before.

"Um. I haven't even made it to marriage, and doubt that will happen anytime soon." Mike playfully shook his head and held his hands up in defense mode. After a flash of his pearly whites, Mike put one hand into his slacks' pocket and leaned against the threshold.

Giving Kenya a look over from head to toe, Mike thought how she should have gone for a higher heel since her skirt rested at her knees. Not daring to make his fashion expertise known, Mike snapped back to their conversation.

"Actually, I'm just coming to visit this morning." Mike waved toward Kenya without thinking about it. "Hmm, you look familiar." He grabbed at his own chin, wondering where he'd seen the smiling beauty before. Tapping his pointer finger on the bottom of his chin then pointing at her, Mike asked, "Did you happen to speak at Wayside Missionary Baptist Church the other week?"

"Yes, I did," Kenya said with a smile beaming across her face. In that instant she knew of Mike, even though she didn't know him personally. "Is that where you attend?" Kenya became comfortable with his presence once she realized she knew Mike had been a fellow Baptist.

Not letting on that she knew more about him then she cared to share, Kenya walked back into the middle of the classroom and continued to set up for her class.

"Come on in while you wait," she said. "By the way, my name is Evangelist Clark. Kenya Clark."

Taking a seat in two of the chairs, the two chatted another twenty minutes before anyone made their way into the classroom. They talked about people they knew from different churches and different church events they both unknowingly had attended together. Mike made Kenya laugh and he felt just as comfortable with her as she had with him. The two chatted like old church buddies.

Knowing he had no clue who she was and despite knowing his reputation before actually meeting him, Kenya felt relaxed in his presence; as if she didn't have to hide out while she dealt with her own battle.

There was no outright connection she felt with Mike, and vice versa. It would take someone with a keen spirit to know Mike had his own personality. It was clear to Kenya that Mike wasn't an "out of the closet" type of man who would just put his cards on the table. And because of that, knowing Mike was Deacon Morgan's friend, Kenya instantly had the idea to bring favor to her.

With people currently on her case about marriage and allowing "Mr. Right" to find her, Kenya believed getting to know Mike better could help her ward off those naggers. With a steady flow of Sunday School parishioners coming in, Kenya didn't want to allow the opportunity to pass her by.

"I have really enjoyed the Sunday morning talk." She grabbed at his hand, wanting to test the waters. "We should exchange numbers and talk more, Brother Mike." Kenya didn't want to seem as if she were coming on too strong.

"I would like that, Sister Kenya," Mike said. He really didn't have the guts to tell her no, thanks, but Mike went along with the smoothness of the conversation. Just as the two exchanged cards, Keithe walked through the classroom doors.

"Hey, bro. You made it after all," Keithe said, waiting for Mike to stand tall before they greeted each other with a brotherly hug. Feeling somewhat bad for bringing drama to Mike's Sunday morning, Keithe was happy his friend had made his way to church nevertheless.

"Hey. Yeah, I've been here about thirty minutes." Mike looked at his studded watch. "I wanted to come and let you know that I wasn't flaking out on you, but I got a call from the church needing me to play Sunday morning service for them as well. But you know I had to come by because I said I would." Mike really wanted to apologize for hanging up on his friend but knew it wasn't kosher to bring personal business for the world to know. Plus, if it hadn't been for Keithe bringing up his business, it never would have happened.

"Oh, okay. That's cool." Keithe leaned in and gave his friend dap. "Because I really think if you just busy yourself with God's Word, like you do the music, God can really speak to your heart and guide you from . . ."

Mike stood there with an "I know this man ain't bringing my business up in here" expression.

Welcoming others through the door, ready to start class, Kenya interrupted, "I kept him company . . . and of course he promises to return." She peered around Keithe's shoulders to make eye contact with Mike, making sure her signature smile was on display.

With a disgruntled look on his face, Mike wiped Keithe out of his thinking and happily said, "Of course. Plus, you know how to track me down if I don't." The two started chuckling, having already exchanged numbers.

Keithe jerked his neck back and smirked, wishing he knew the inside joke and hoping, wishing, praying that what he thought happened . . . hadn't happened.

"Okay. Well, I'm out." Mike turned without laying another homeboy-styled dap on Keithe's fist. Leaving his friend hanging, Mike crossed over Keithe and leaned in for a hug with Kenya. "I'll call you in a couple of days and set up that lunch date," Mike let it be known. Just that quick, he went from knowing he would never call Kenya's number, nor accept her phone calls, to making a mental note to call her as soon as possible. Even if it was just to get under Keithe's skin.

With a smile drawn on her parted lips, Kenya said, "I'd like that," as she turned and walked to the front of the classroom as Mike made his way out of the door.

"Date," was all Keithe could mumble.

Realizing what had just happened between his friend and his love interest, it took everything in Keithe to pull himself together for the class. He didn't know how, but he knew he would be wearing a fake expression for the remainder of the church day. Adding a plastered smile on his face, Keithe felt crushed as he made himself useful by greeting the students piling into the classroom.

"Ahmm. Everything all right, Deacon Morgan?" Missionary Gladstone walked through the classroom's door slowly, mostly because of old age, but mainly, as she said, because her cane slowed her down.

Keithe moved to the side in order to make room for the mother of the church to make her way farther into the room. Just as soon as he made space, she closed in the gap between them.

"Oh. H . . . hello. How are you doing, Mother Gladstone?" Keithe asked, adding a fake smile to his blood-drained face.

"Hmm. Look like I'm doing much better than you." She stood, leaning on Keithe and pointing toward the door with her cane. "Was that there your friend? That fella who just left?" The pastor's mother situated her right hand on her protruding hip.

"Um. Yes, ma'am. Mike." Keithe didn't know where the conversation was headed. Looking around the room at everyone getting situated, Keithe took a step, trying to walk around Missionary Gladstone.

Without saying a word, the mother of the church slammed the back of her nugget ring–clad hand in his chest.

"Go to God about it; you can't do it yourself." She looked past Keithe until her eyes landed on Kenya. "If you stay on your knees about it, God will show you the way and the truth. It's yours for the asking, but be patient, be gentle. Most of all, be understanding," she said while finally looking into his eyes.

"Let me get out of here and go get me some of this breakfast, 'fore all these young'uns get their li'l sticky hands all in the oatmeal. They mamas don't teach 'em nothing, I tell ya." Mother spoke her mind as she headed out of the classroom's door as she continued her breakfast rant.

Not sure he wanted to ask any questions beyond what she'd shared, Keithe opted to just pocket the information and go help out with the class.

Chapter Five

"Oh, really!" Keithe yelled throughout his car. "So that's how you're gonna do it, Mike? Why? To prove a point?" This was one of the rare times when Keithe couldn't wait until church let out. No longer being able to hold in his anger, and seeing he wasn't allowing any of the Word to seep into his spirit, Keithe called it a day and left service before the benediction.

Mike tried his best to hurry and turn down the latest Donald Lawrence song he'd been blasting. He knew Keithe would come out of the bag on him but he didn't care any longer. He shook his head to the drama Keithe brought.

He had gotten tired of Keithe questioning him about his own life, making him feel as if he were beneath him. What he did and who he did, he finally concluded, was no one's business but his own.

"Mad if I do, mad if I don't, huh? I just can't win with you, can I, bro?" Mike threw his voice into the phone, already knowing what the yelling match was going to be about. Although Keithe never gave "her" a name, laying eyes on Kenya, Mike knew it was she who Keithe wanted to get to know better.

Too many times to count had the two friends spoken about the saved and gorgeous woman, Sister Kenya, at Keithe's church. Mike had been the dating promoter. Never knowing when the right time would be, Mike all too many times tried to pump Keithe up to ask her out.

"Oh well," Mike said aloud about what he'd done. Having left the church for a quick bite to eat before the next service, Mike maneuvered his car into the crowded parking lot.

Removing his ascot with both hands as he steered with his knee, Keithe was furious. "Oh, well?" Keithe questioned. "It's not a game! Why do you think this is a game, Mike? I've been in your corner far too long, man. I try to pray for you, try not to question you about all you do, but you've been making that hard, too." Keithe had had enough of Mike and his happy-go-lucky way with life.

It had been no secret to those who were in their circle. Mike had always been who Mike was going to be. When Mike had come out of the closet in his late teens, Keithe had never left his friend's side, even with the knowledge of him living his life as he chose: as a gay black man.

To Mike, it used to seem as if Keithe was his best support system: not agreeing with him but, just the same, never questioning him about his lifestyle. But it was obvious that was before he moved to the same city Mike had chosen to reside in for decades now.

Keithe seeing his friend's lifestyle up close and personal rubbed him the wrong way. Especially when Mike still flirted with and dated women without letting them know all the facts: that he also dated men.

It was set in stone. Mike knew Keithe didn't like his homosexual lifestyle, but he was sick and tired of the little innuendos Keithe threw at him every chance he got. Just the same, Keithe was tired of Mike's nonchalant attitude about dating a Jack one day and a Jill the next. Keithe wasn't ready to accept Mike's lifestyle one way or the other, but being upfront with the women he dated was a start, Keithe thought, only if he didn't start with Kenya.

Yeah, sure it was wrong to date women without letting them know he didn't and couldn't gather feelings for them. In the end, Mike felt it was all in friendship, and that a woman would know that when he didn't try to take things further.

His best friend didn't get it. It wasn't like Mike was proud of what he was doing, because he wasn't. Mike had tried to live a life that could parallel what Keithe had made look so easy. He'd shouted from the rooftops about wanting to be a straight and saved man of God; he wanted to be a changed man, with a change of heart, and explain how a spiritual awakening had come over him. But from where he was now, he just couldn't. Right now he'd just be who he was: a gay man who still loved God and no doubt knew that God loved him.

Then there were times when he'd even begun seriously dating women . . . In most recent years, Vicky. At the time, to anyone who would listen, Mike let it be known his days of living his life the way he had wanted were over. But just as soon as he had started on his straight and narrow path, he had veered off from the spiritual fight.

The company he had run from, stopped taking calls from, stopped hanging out with, was the same company he chose to run back to. This left his girlfriend wondering why she had given him another chance to begin with. Then Keithe decided to move to Dallas.

For all the years the two self-proclaimed best friends had lived in different cities, there was never a strain on their friendship. Maybe it was because they didn't get to see the everyday ins and outs of one another's lives. But once Keithe divorced Michelle and decided to move to "his city," as Mike called it, things changed. The lifestyle Mike had picked back up and had tried to hide from Keithe had been exposed yet again.

It hadn't been until Keithe had actually "caught" Mike on a date a few weeks ago that Keithe had began coming up with more tough-love antics. It was his realization that Mike had slipped back into his old ways that set Keithe on a tantrum. From that day on, Mike had a constant guard up and tried his best to play off what he was sure Keithe already knew: Mike had lost his battle of giving up his gay lifestyle, a lifestyle that had turned into a down-low secret for the women he dated.

Now Keithe was put in the middle.

It was becoming all too common. Anytime Mike's back got pushed into a wall and questions started being tossed his way, he stopped fighting. When the going got tough, Mike took off the boxing gloves and threw in the towel. But this latest antic . . . Keithe had no idea what his friend was up to.

Pulling his vehicle into his garage, Keithe barely threw his car in park before he got out of his ride. When he walked into his living room space, Keithe allowed his keys to clash against the wood dining room table, and walked in the other direction. He was still going off on Mike, who didn't even know what to say simply because he didn't know how to choose. He just knew he wanted to be happy.

"This is real. You are playing with fire, dude . . ." Keithe growled through the phone.

"Why? Because you want her? Yeah. I saw the way you were looking at her. You should have asked Kenya out if you wanted to. I told you to." Mike shrugged his shoulders as if Keithe could see. "But because I did it's wrong, huh?" Mike no longer cared if Keithe was in his life. He wasn't going to lie to Keithe. He knew his friend liked a woman at the church and when Mike saw the way Keithe laid eyes on Kenya, there was no longer a doubt which one. "I can't have a good girl, huh? I can't get 'em like you can, huh? What? I'm not as blessed as you, Keithe? I'm not manly enough to have a woman like Kenya?"

He's disrespecting her title. Keithe thought about the ministry Kenya honored and didn't want her getting in the midst of a scandal.

"No . . . no," Keithe responded, although he wanted to fight for the right to have a chance to have Evangelist Kenya Clark as his woman. "You got it twisted." He calmed down. "It's because you haven't made up your mind. I just saw you at the restaurant last week, Mike. Did you forget you were wasted, slurring, hanging all over some young dude?" Keithe hated to even have to bring Mike's lifestyle up. "But today, today all of a sudden you know what . . . no, you know who you want?" There was silence.

It was an unspoken fact that Mike had reverted to his old lifestyle. The parties, the excessive drinking, and the crowd he'd started hanging back with. Even without sharing it directly with Keithe, who didn't dare to speak aloud about any of Mike's goings-on, inadvertently it was known. Mike had continued his lifestyle but for some reason cared what Keithe thought about it.

"Look. I'm here at the church and there are people walking up." Mike had gotten out of the car and opened the back door to retrieve his suit jacket. "It's really none of your business what I do"—he switched the phone to his other ear—"or who I do for that matter." Mike turned the knife that was emotionally in Keithe's heart. "Who I date and where it goes from there, it's none of your business. Matter of fact, you don't have to be concerned anymore, bro. It's all good," Mike said before he disconnected the call and walked toward the doors of the church.

Keithe had made his way into his own sanctuary and flopped on his bed. Not stopping there, he slammed his sweaty back on his mattress and just rested with his arms above his head. Right when he thought his life would turn toward a new beginning there was drama added with a little heartache.

What he couldn't figure out was how Kenya had been so ready to say yes when Mike asked her out. One thing for sure, there was no way he was going to allow Mike to ruin Kenya's life. He didn't know how or when but he knew he had no choice but to let her know the real truth about his best friend Mike.

Chapter Six

Sunday morning had come and gone. The anticipation of a great start to a promising group had been all Evangelist Kenya Clark had prayed for. Even members who hadn't initially signed up for the class had shown up for the Sunday School gathering to see what it was all about. Church members she wouldn't have ever fathomed having issues in their relationships had even added themselves to the medium-sized group, hoping for resolution.

Through all of that, accidentally meeting Mike had added a little hope to her plan of getting her loved ones off of her back. Mike's timing couldn't have been more perfect. She hated he had to be Deacon Morgan's best friend, because she really did like the gentleman, but with so much going on in her own spiritual and emotional walk, Kenya needed time.

Sundays were always set aside for family. With her mother having passed away just a few short years ago, her older sister, Kendra, had become even closer to her than ever before. With almost a twenty-year difference between the two, Kenya had always looked up to her older sister, even though she had been ten years old before she met her.

For years Kendra had been estranged from their mother, Herlene. With Herlene having a drug and drinking addiction for years, there were disturbing times Kendra had gone through under her care. The little guidance and care sent Kendra into a downward spiral in life. Feeling that she never received love and never knew love, the older sister had inadvertently allowed life to beat her up.

Grasping on to drinking, partying, and premarital and promiscuous sex, it was only after she'd hit rock bottom, close to the age of thirty, that Herlene reappeared: saved, healthy, and wanting to be everything Kendra needed. And she was. And now Kendra was doing the same for Kenya, which was why she hated to ditch Sunday dinner plans.

With Kenya being single and always her own dinner date, Kendra and her husband, Bishop Ky Perry, made it a point to share their world with Kenya. Sundays were never an exception to the rule.

With an overwhelming feeling of her personal battles, Kenya really wanted to be able to spend a day doing nothing so that she could hear everything. It was the peace in God she was yet looking for, feeling she had become unworthy.

Kenya was still trying to gather all of her thoughts together. She figured the best way to do so was to spend as much time with the Lord, alone, as she could. Pushing away from her dining room table, Kenya took her dishes to the sink and slid them into the awaiting water. Usually she'd clean her kitchen immediately following dinner, but being ever so worn out from the day's activities, Kenya opted to relax and free her mind instead. An advantage in living alone, Kenya was able to do her chores as she pleased.

With a flip of the switch, Kenya turned the kitchen light off and headed through the living area. The natural-colored family room was welcoming with smooth sounds of jazz floating out of her surround system her brother-in-law had finally gotten around to installing for her. Walking toward the master bedroom placed in the back of her three-bedroom, single-family dwelling, Kenya admired what she had accomplished.

Everything was cozy. Kenya opted for a suede/leather mixture of furniture that allowed for comfort in every welcoming spot throughout her home. The natural tones surrounding her constantly gave her the sense of not being alone when, in fact, she was 100 percent of the time.

Her hallway walls alone were filled with framed photos of her mission trips around the world. Her latest evangelistic excursion to Africa had been an adventure of a lifetime and there were pictures to prove it. Lives had been saved, children had been healed, and even monies were raised in order to help out villages. If only that had been all Kenya had brought back from the continent. The guilt traveled back as well.

Kenya removed the chopstick-style ornaments from her hair and allowed her tresses to unravel onto her shoulders. She had tried to forget as best she could the flesh-driven decision she had made when in what some called "The Mother Land."

It wasn't easy. Kenya had repented and asked God to renew the right spirit within her . . . and she felt He had, but she still felt unworthy. All that was left was for Kenya to forgive herself, which wasn't an easy thing to do. She no longer trusted herself and had even begun to doubt just who she was. Clarity was what Kenya hoped time alone with the Lord would give her.

She had tried her best to suppress her guilt and replace it with the elated spirits of the new group. In all actuality, Kenya couldn't help but be happy with the new activities at the church. The divorce ministry had been placed in Kenya's spirit after so many of her friends and God's people had fallen victim to the family destroyer.

Having never been married, Kenya had wrestled with the decision to even bring the ministry to Pastor Peters. But after many restless and praying nights, she had no choice. She knew when people were taught and encouraged, they usually went back to teach and encourage others.

There were support groups for single people, hoping they'd get things right the first time when it came to marriage; married people, hoping they could work out their troubles; but for divorced people, there was nothing but for them to try it again and, the majority of the time, wind up with a replay of the first results.

Some argued being single and divorced could fall under the same category. Kenya heavily objected. Those who were single, having never married, had opportunities to try to perfect their dating and choosing skills. Those who were divorced could easily be discouraged, disgusted, with no hope for the opposite sex, being their experience didn't succeed the first go-round. Mixing the two could confuse the parties involved.

Yet and still, there were those who objected to Kenya heading up the group, being that she was a single lady with no attachments. There was much doubt about what she would be able to teach. "No problem," she had responded to Pastor Peters when he had passed on the word that other church members didn't deem it appropriate for her to be over such a group.

"We will just need a saved and divorced man to partner with me," she happily suggested. Kenya had no doubt in mind that the women of the group were behind her demise to single-handedly call the shots. With an unattached man as her partner, she knew things would change.

Kenya was all for it. It was best to have opinionated yet open-minded leaders in the group. And definitely one male and one female. Watching Deacon Keithe with her spiritual eye, Kenya was secure hearing God confirm he was the partner she needed for the group. With the meetings, brainstorming, and the Holy Spirit being evident in his walk, Kenya hadn't thought twice about confirming the older and distinguished Deacon Keithe being the partner she needed.

"You may want to consider him as your partner on another level, too, Kenya," Pastor Peters had said, chuckling. Kenya had only put a scowl on her face and walked away.

If it wasn't her pastor, it was her sister, brother-in-law, her niece, or anyone else who wanted the best for her. And she wouldn't even start with Pastor Peter's mother, Mother Gladstone, wanting her to hurry, marry, and have little chocolate babies. There was no doubt Kenya wanted the same for herself. Her home was beautiful, but she was ready to share her life with someone who needed and wanted the same.

Kenya stood in front of her full-length mirror and disassembled her Sunday wear along with her jewelry. With her slip still on, Kenya walked over to her queen-sized bed and took a seat. Even with the joy in Kenya's heart running rampant about the group and her being settled in her blessed life, she didn't yet have the feel of completion.

It wasn't that being complete and knowing God was all she needed, but completion as in a mate specifically made for her. That's why if anyone was confused with the task she had on hand, being over a divorce group, it was her. But when God spoke to her heart, she knew she had to be obedient. There was so much she owed to God.

No one had to preach to her. They didn't have to tell her that Jesus was enough. She knew it. One reason why she hadn't shared her latest and greatest issue with anyone, not even her sister, was because she didn't want to hear, "Jesus is enough."

She didn't need a cliché prayer. Kenya needed clarification about what had gone wrong in her own thinking. Hadn't she been saved, sanctified, and filled with God's Holy Spirit? Didn't she believe God had her back and patience was what she needed? But the major question was, didn't she know that God had indeed created her for a man and a man for her?

God had been her morning, noon, and night. He had been her breath of fresh air when she needed Him most, which was why her past year doing mission work in Africa left her confused about her actions.

She had crossed boundaries she never would have thought she would have crossed. Just the blessing to be able to travel to a place where so much history had begun . . . Kenya had guilt all over her by her actions while there.

Kenya had led a lustful relationship she knew wasn't of God while in Africa. Even if she tried, Kenya knew she couldn't blame all of her sinful actions on the enemy. She knew it was wrong. The disgust she felt built in her loins let her know just that.

Crawling to the middle of her bed, Kenya pulled her hot pink blanket over the bottom part of her body. Hoping to get rest before evening service, in the back of her mind, all Kenya could think was how she no longer felt privileged. The call she had on her life reigned superior over whatever her flesh thought it wanted; nevertheless, she had taken a chance with her soul more than twice, and for that, Kenya felt God would strip her soul dry.

Closing her eyes and adjusting her pillow, Kenya prayed that all she had hoped for and was born for wouldn't be lost because of her inability to control advances she never saw coming.

Chapter Seven

Two weeks had passed since the stunt Mike pulled at the church. February had barely touched down and Keithe still hadn't talked to his best friend, not even once. Along with that, he had only spoken godly business with Kenya. Things still weren't sitting well with him and he just couldn't shake his attitude.

Keithe was furious and decided to take it out on the equipment he had set up in his home gym. His three-bedroom condo had enough room for him to have sleeping quarters, a home office, and a workout room. He didn't bother with having a guest bedroom, being that when his parents did visit, his mother insisted on going to the impeccable upscale hotels in town. She liked being pampered and knew a bachelor's pad just couldn't accommodate those needs.

With his iPod Touch connected to the sweat band around his bicep, Keithe turned the volume high while doing his first set of squats. Listening to the words sailing through Brian Courtney Wilson's voice, Keithe used the song for the strength he needed in the physical and the spiritual. "I am a Christian, do you know what that means? It means I'm far from perfect but simply redeemed. . . ."

Keithe never claimed to be perfect himself but just wanted a better life for Mike. He couldn't help that he cared about his friend the way he had. And Kenya, he hadn't even gotten a chance to show her just how much he could care for her. Thanks to Mike, that too was cut short.

He hadn't meant to be so drastic when it came to his blowup with Mike. But because Mike knew that Keithe had feelings for Kenya, it made the getting angry easier. Now it was him left with confused emotions . . . having to deal with it on his own.

After his full set of squats, Keithe moved on to the inclined workout bench he used for the sit-up and crunches portion of his exercise regimen. He was determined to become one again with the six-pack he had let go after his divorce.

Having always been in shape and priding himself on taking care of his inner man as well as his physical man, Keithe didn't think he would be affected emotionally after his divorce, but soon found out different. After his move to Dallas, and during his two-week vacation before starting his position as a senior lawyer at Sims and Sims, a prestigious downtown law firm, Keithe fell into a slump. There were days he couldn't get out of bed; or, rather, wouldn't. His time was spent stuck on reprimanding himself for being in an unyoked marriage all those years. The rest of the time was spent missing Michelle.

On one hand, he felt he gave up too soon. Honestly, he had prayed for years, a decade or more, for Michelle to seek and accept a relationship with God. He felt it was his godly duty to do so. Then she had. Yet, he still hadn't been settled. Too much had happened.

"This sucks," he blurted out of the blue. Wiping down the black plastic leather–mixed exercise bench, Keithe was ready to cool down. Giving himself a good stretch, he headed for the treadmill. Setting a steady pace, Keithe walked in stride.

Keithe always agreed with God, which was why he hadn't moved in haste. He knew he had to pray about his departure from his marriage before he had mentioned his thoughts aloud or even to Michelle. It was only when he felt a peace about his moving on that he opened up to his wife. When it was over, said and done, and he still felt the pull after his fasting and praying, Keithe moved forward.

After a fifteen-minute cool down routine on the well-worn treadmill, a vibrating notion on his hip grabbed his attention. Taking the white earplugs from his ears, Keithe hesitated in taking the call. "Of course," he muttered to himself.

It was always weird to him when he thought about her and then received a call soon after. It was as if God was telling him he had made a mistake leaving Michelle. Either that or they had been married so long their minds had meshed.

"Yes." Keithe answered his cell phone while walking at a very slow pace. He automatically grabbed an attitude and had no idea why.

"Hey, Keithe." Michelle spoke cordially over the telephone, regardless of the very dry and rude greeting she had just received.

Putting the finishing touches on her Sunday dinner, Michelle wanted to put in a quick call to Keithe before she finished preparing her Pampered Chef recipe—inspired meal.

With a quick switch of the phone to her left ear in order to get a better view of her creamed corn heating up on the stove top, Michelle questioned, "Are you busy, Mr. Morgan?"

Deciding not to play the Mr. and Mrs. Morgan game with her, Keithe only responded with, "No." Pushing the quick stop button on his treadmill, Keithe walked off the stationary track and left the room, headed toward the kitchen.

"What? No Sunday dinner for you and that special someone?" Michelle went off the subject, still wanting Keithe to confirm if he was indeed dating. When she only heard Keithe gulping down a beverage, she continued. "I just wanted to let you know that Stoney will be flying in to Dallas tomorrow morning. I wanted to give you her flight information for—"

"Wait a minute," Keithe said as he came up for air. Putting the cap on his Gatorade, Keithe walked toward his bedroom in search of his T-shirt once the drink had produced a cool chill throughout his body. "Why isn't she driving in? I have work, Michelle," Keithe responded, not liking the last-minute plans he had become a part of. Even though he was one of the top lawyers at the firm and could dismiss himself at a moment's notice, Keithe loved what he did and always enjoyed being at work. Plus he had only been there two years and didn't want to be a bad example to the younger attorneys behind him. He didn't want to break his dependable title. "Why are you just now calling me?" Keithe needed to know.

Hearing her doorbell sound in the background, Michelle wished she could go deeper into the need for him to pick up Stoney from the airport. She was sure it was just his ego that needed to be soothed. Even more she wished she now had the nerve to share her bright idea of uprooting herself from Houston and making her temporary home in Dallas. Home of NBA champions the Dallas Mavericks.

"Look, Keithe." Michelle wiped her manicured hands on her stylish apron. "Stoney *just* called me this morning and said her car did not start and she had it towed to the dealer." She walked out of the kitchen. "Of course she tried to call her father to pick her up tomorrow, but he won't be in until the evening himself." Michelle knew she was reaching, but wanting to throw a little salt in Keithe's game. "Now if you can't do it . . ." A silent attitude attached itself to Michelle's reasoning. Winding her way through the mini-mansion, with less than twenty feet from the door, Michelle snatched her apron off with vengeance. Keithe's harshness was all of a sudden getting under her skin.

"I got it." Keithe had calmed down. Picking up his shirt off the bed, Keithe clicked his BlackBerry on speaker and threw the phone on his sheeted mattress. "No problem. Just give me the flight information."

"Fantastic." Michelle claimed the victory. "I'll forward the itinerary over to you later this evening," she said. "Someone is at my door, so I will have to call you back to make sure you have received it. And if you can, dear, remind me to share some news with you as well. I have to run now. Smooches." She air kissed through the phone and disconnected the call.

Taking a seat on his bed, Keithe didn't bother to stop himself from lying flat. His bed had seemed to be his companion of late. Making no defined friendships as of yet, Keithe only wished there was someone he could call to vent to.

He needed to rant. He needed to cry. Keithe needed someone to tell him that things wouldn't always be this way. Without hesitation, Keithe rolled over and picked up his cell phone and pushed the number two button.

"Something told me it was you on the other end of the phone." Ladybug sat on her back porch with her iced tea in her right hand. Rocking the glass in a circular motion, the seventy-something mother of one enjoyed her days of not doing much. Sitting pretty, watching her husband drive the riding lawnmower over their manicured lawn, retirement had never been better.

"Oh yeah." Keithe automatically added a smile to his face. "Maybe that's because of the caller ID screen on your phone. Technology, Mom."

With the sound of the ice clinking ceasing, Ladybug said, "Oh, boy, hush," and laughed a deep belly laugh. "What you doing calling your mother in the midst of this beautiful Sunday afternoon, Deacon Morgan?" Ladybug Morgan, as everyone called her, asked, very proud of her son and his love for the Lord.

"In between Sunday services, Ma. I'm heading back in a little while. Just wanted to call and hear my beautiful mother's voice. How are you, Mommy?" He exaggerated his voice to sound like a young man again.

"You are a mess, son. Well. And how are you doing, really?" She set her drink on her glass outdoor table. Getting up from her seat, Ladybug opted to go inside the house to ward off the noise the lawn equipment made. "You sound kind of, I don't know, under the weather is it?" She took the first seat she walked up on, which was her husband's recliner. "Are you okay?"

"Hmm. I don't know. I'm not sick . . . just sick of people. Me and Mike got into it. Yes, a woman is involved. And then Michelle—"

"Uh-uh. You know I don't want to hear nothing about Michelle. Not gonna let you do it, Keithe." Ladybug had just started liking Michelle after her son had divorced her. "We are cordial and have even had dinner a few times. I don't want to be in the midst of it, son," the short, gray-haired, petite woman said as she rose from her seat.

"Ma, it's nothing like that. It's just that . . . she just called and dropped a bomb on me that I need to pick Stoney up from the airport. And Mike, he's back to his old tricks. Pushing up on the young lady I have feelings for, knowing good and well he's not stuttin' nobody."

"Um. That poor boy. He just needs to let go and let God," Ladybug said wholeheartedly.

"Exactly! That's what I've been trying to tell him, but he thinks I'm judging him. I keep telling him that he just needs to put his mind over matter and come up off this trip . . . but not with my woman," Keithe said.

"Your woman, huh? Keithe, hush." Ladybug pulled the lever on the side of the big brown leather chair and relaxed. "And how do you know he's not letting go and letting God the way he knows how to? Mike's getting over being gay you may think is an easy thing to do. That's not always the case, Keithe. People have battles, honey. You don't condemn them, you pray for them." Ladybug was sincere. "You know, how you prayed for that floundering wife of yours. And voilà. . . ." Ladybug rubbed it in.

"Ohhhh, so now you talking about your friend? Um, huh," Keithe joked.

"No. I'm just telling the truth. But seriously, I love Mike as if he were my own son. I do not like the sin, but I love him. We each have our own crosses to carry . . . our own deadly sins. I didn't like it when you used to do all that rump shaking stuff with all those little fast-tail girls when you were in college. God and everybody knows you were sinning up a storm. And then had the nerve to lie to me over and over again about what you were *not* doing. As if I were born just yesterday . . ." Ladybug was nonstop.

"Okay, okay, Ma. Geez. That was over twenty-some-thing years ago." He finally kicked his running shoes off. Keithe knew it was all the truth. It wasn't until his relationship grew with God and he read the Word for himself, without compromise, that he knew better. "I understand."

Keithe thought for a moment how at one time it had been extremely hard for him to stay away from the opposite sex. He equated himself to Lance, Morris Chestnut's young character in the movie *The Best Man*. It was like an addiction to him. No, it was as if it were second nature to him. One that had him sent to the dean's office, had his parents called in, and had counseling sessions set up for him. It was real. It wasn't that he had forgotten, but he just didn't see how Mike could even fathom doing the same with men. But he really did realize now that nothing had to make sense.

"I'm just saying, Keithe. You got to talk with Mike through love. It's not easy to understand why people do the things they do, or even why we do the things we do. But we can only hope that God can help us before we get too far gone. And again . . ." Ladybug knew she was pushing it.

"Let me guess . . . like my wife?"

"Exactly." Ladybug giggled.

Switching his phone to the other hand, Keithe knew he was on a limited time frame before night service. "I still love you though, Ladybug." Keithe admired his mother for being real and staying real.

"Of course you do. I made you. I love you, son."

"And I love you too. Tell dad I said what's up frat." Keithe loved the double bond he and his father had.

"And?" Ladybug waited.

"But of course. And tell my dad I love him. See ya, Mom."

Chapter Eight

With so much attitude coming from Keithe, Michelle still wasn't able to share with her ex-husband her plans to move to his city. Although she had no plans to permanently move to Dallas, Michelle knew in order to get her husband back she would have to be willing to leave her comfort zone and stay as long as it took. Still shaking her head from the conversation between the two, Michelle knew it would be hard to get Keithe to understand where she was coming from.

It hadn't taken Michelle but a hot minute to sign up with the best house/apartment locater in the Dallas–Fort Worth area. Having Keithe's address since the day he departed their shared quarters, Michelle had no qualms about lending his residence to the locator. She wanted to get close enough to Keithe in order to be the first one he'd call for dinner, but far enough away to have him miss her.

Dallas had initially been her stomping grounds. She hadn't been reared in the city but she arrived there as soon as she could. And when she had, she painted her name all over the town.

From the very beginning of her adulthood it was love Michelle had been looking for. With each new beau she had dated, Michelle hoped and prayed *he* would be *the one*. There had been a fling here and there three times over. Then she had met a handsome and honest man, Marcus, and knew without a doubt he'd be the one to change her last name. And he just might have, but just like the luck she was used to, Michelle hadn't been princess to the princess-cut diamond Marcus presented his bride, Gracie.

Ky, now the infamous Bishop Ky Perry, came along and presented Michelle with another chance at love. But the love had come too late and too narrow being that he was Marcus's friend. Still hanging on to the hope of eventually getting back with Marcus, even after his nuptials, Michelle cheated on Ky with Marcus and found herself pregnant.

Initially she hadn't known who the father of her child was. When she did find out, she fled town without sharing the truth: a truth that created darkness in her life. So confused, so heartbroken, and so alone, Michelle dropped her newborn with her mother, who she hadn't spoken to in years, and just as easily picked up her life and made a new beginning for herself in Houston.

And now with tape in one hand, and scissors and a permanent marker in the other, Michelle boxed up items she would need to leave for her temporary stay in Dallas; just long enough to woo her ex back into her arms.

Running the back of her hand across her forehead, Michelle was hot. Still in the midst of going through the infamous "change" she paced herself.

Writing "Lingerie for Keithe" on one of the last boxes, Michelle giggled and dropped her supplies on one box and sat on another. Pushing her brown sparkly headband to the middle of her head, Michelle fanned the extra warmth that February had brought with it.

"Maybe it's just me," she thought aloud about the heat that had surrounded her.

Twenty-four years ago Michelle had abruptly dropped everyone and everything she knew in Dallas and uprooted herself. She had left everyone without so much as an explanation; Michelle had just taken her heartbreak and left. Even so, her past had tracked her down in Houston. Thankful to God, Michelle was able to right the wrongs she had made in the midst of it all. She couldn't have asked for a better resolution by being reunited with Stoney.

Michelle had taken a leave from her post as one of Houston's hard-hitting civil court judges. With no thoughts of retiring anytime soon, although she saw tons of cases a week, she was excited about her time away.

"Enough of that." Michelle ended her assorting and packing for the day and stood to her feet, headed toward the kitchen. It was time for lunch.

Michelle really did wish she was able to communicate more effectively with Keithe on the subject of her moving. She didn't know if it was just her, but whatever had been bothering him, he wasn't letting on.

He took fewer and fewer of her calls. Even Stoney hadn't had an open line of communication with him lately. All Michelle could think was that the other woman she no doubt knew was in Keithe's life had something to do with his emotions. Whoever she was had Keithe's mind far away from her, which was something Michelle definitely wasn't too keen on.

Stepping into the kitchen, Michelle went right for the refrigerator. She chuckled when she reached her arm to retrieve the wheat bread from the cold contraption. Keithe used to make sure he bought his own loaf of bread when the grocery shopping was done. He could never figure why Michelle wanted to eat cold bread.

"Silly self," Michelle name called Keithe though he wasn't there. It was things like that that made Michelle miss Keithe so much.

With a smile on her face, she commenced to make a turkey and Swiss cheese sandwich. A sucker for everything pretty, Michelle added ranch dressing with avocado and one leaf of lettuce.

Putting the finishing touches on her midday lunch, Michelle got a hunch in her gut. Her womanly instinct rumbled something deep inside. In an instant, a feeling came over her; a wave of conviction for trying to stop Keithe from moving on plagued her mind.

"Hmm. Lord, I do miss Keithe." And just that quick she heard exactly what she was saying.

Michelle was not necessarily in love with Keithe. She missed him, which was the reasoning behind her going after him. Michelle missed companionship. She hadn't told Keithe because she didn't think it was really his business, but she too was back to being single.

The middle barstool was where Michelle took her seat. Placing her sandwich directly in front of her she prayed, "Dear God, thank you for this food, a portion of your manna from heaven. I pray you sanctify it for nourishment into my being." Usually ending her prayer with Amen, Michelle barely let a breath escape before she continued.

"Lord, I really am a changed woman. I love you with all of my heart. And I really, really don't want to do things that are not like you." Her gut quickly let her know if that were the case she would have sought the Lord first before deciding to relocate. Michelle blinked hard to get past God speaking to her. Instead of retracting her statement and asking God for His will to be done, Michelle ended her prayer.

"Thank you, Lord, for your son Jesus. Amen."

Without a doubt, Michelle had been in church long enough now to know God for herself. Her conscience let her know God should be consulted on every level and bypassing Him could be detrimental.

Michelle bit down into her sandwich. Thinking the crunch she heard was a pickle, when Michelle realized she hadn't put any on her sandwich she got worried.

As the pain shot up from her tooth, traveling up her jaw and to her head, Michelle knew her filling had fallen out.

Knowing God has a mysterious way of getting one's attention, Michelle knew her savior was speaking to her on a much deeper level than she cared to admit.

Chapter Nine

He was angry at Michelle for calling last minute, needing him to do something for her daughter. There it was, just like that, Keithe's real feelings surfaced.

Dressed for work and since he had agreed, Keithe only had plans to pick Stoney up, drop her off at her dad's home, since he was out of town, and head back into the office. Driving toward the Dallas–Fort Worth Airport, Keithe couldn't help but reminisce.

He remembered three years ago as if it were just yesterday: the realization that Stoney, who he'd initially met through Mike, was Michelle's daughter. A daughter she'd left in her mother's custody, then unremorsefully, losing contact with both.

Although the experience was out of a *Twilight Zone* episode Keithe was eventually grateful to be a part of the reunion, which grew to both being overjoyed with the ability to be back in the other's life. Inadvertently helping Stoney find the part of her that had been missing all of her life had been rewarding. But Michelle hadn't bothered, never mentioned, not so much of a breath, that she was indeed someone's mother. Nevertheless, when the time came to help her purge from her past, Keithe was right there for his wife to accept what God had done by allowing her a second chance.

Keithe had tried to put his feelings on the back burner so he could be there spiritually and emotionally for Michelle, who had lost all of her cool and dignity when reality invaded her world. And he did. He even gave of himself to Stoney, who had successfully used him to get closer to her mother. But the whole while, and even as the dust had settled, he hadn't been real with himself. He still had pain in his heart due to not being thought of in all the matters going on.

During that time, even now if he thought about it long enough, Keithe had been embarrassed. Humiliated was more like it. Even if no one thought him to be a fool, he was his worst critic. He'd given his best years, his twenties and thirties, to a woman he fell madly in love with, with her sharing the same sentiments. Or so he thought. Not being a dad was something he'd settled with when Michelle let him know early on in their marriage that parenting was not on her agenda. He was okay with that because he felt being an adopted brother in the Big Brother program in their community would suffice. And it had. At least until the day that Stoney and Michelle embraced one another in a mother/daughter hug.

"This is so wrong on so many levels." Keithe slammed his fist against his steering wheel's horn, making the sound blare underneath his knuckles. Adding a smirk and a friendly wave, Keithe felt like a moron as the guy in the vehicle in front of him thought him to be honking at him out of anger.

It wasn't their entire fault. It wasn't all Michelle's fault, and Keithe knew that. He didn't have to agree to go without being a father. He didn't have to just buy into the story that the scar on her bikini line was from a childhood accident. He could have protested or just been honest, letting his wife, fifteen years his senior, know he wanted to be a father. But he hadn't and now he was paying the price.

"By the time I meet someone and date them, get to know them and marry, sheesh, I'll be fifty myself." Keithe just didn't like the figures.

Taking the ramp that would take him to the Delta airline arrivals, Keithe slowed as he started looking for Stoney immediately. When he saw the Southern belle waving her hand excitedly, a smile etched its way onto Keithe's face. He honestly couldn't blame Stoney. She was just a daughter on a mission to find out who she was and where she'd come from.

When Keithe first met her, a fellow church member at Mike's church, Stoney was just a shy, lost young lady. She literally lived in the world alone, not knowing if blood relatives existed for her. Hooked on prescription drugs back then, Stoney had reduced herself to mere skin and bones due to all of the worry of not knowing what her life would evolve into. Through all of her own internal investigations, once she figured out Keithe could have possibly been married to her mother through trial and error, Stoney lost it, literally.

Stoney had been on a manhunt, stalking Keithe and eventually following him four hours from Dallas to the home he and Michelle had built in Houston. Breaking and entering into the house when Michelle was alone, Stoney's emotions and psyche got to be too much for her and she lost her cool, hurting herself and Michelle in the process.

But thankfully, today, Stoney got it all back together.

"Hey, Pops." Stoney bent down to speak through the window before she dragged her pink and green luggage toward his trunk.

With his car flashers on, Keithe released his seat belt and stepped out of the vehicle. Watching out for other cars as they passed, Keithe made his way toward the back of his Porsche. "Hey, Stone Cold." Keithe called out the nickname given to his stepdaughter from Mike.

With the look from his stepdaughter, Keithe quickly remembered Stoney no longer cared for Mike. Never knowing about Mike's lifestyle, Stoney felt betrayed when the truth about him being homosexual came out. At the moment, he couldn't blame her.

"I don't blame you," he said without following up.

Stoney let go of trying to handle her luggage and gave it over to Keithe. "Thanks, Pops."

Swearing she could hear Keithe growling, Stoney held up her manicured hands and backed her way to the driver's side of the car. Once again, it seemed she had over packed.

Sitting and fastening herself in, Stoney waited until her stepdad put the car in drive before she dug deeper. "What's really going on with you and your friend? It doesn't sound like you to be badmouthing Mike." Stoney could not have cared less, but figured it all tied into the way Keithe hadn't been corresponding with her and her mother. "Did he do something to you?"

With a check of his rearview mirror, Keithe thought of what to say. No doubt Stoney would go back and tell her mother all she thought she wanted and needed to know. "Oh. You know. Mike just being Mike," he said. "We just have that old best friend, grown man beef going on." Taking a quick glance over at Stoney, Keithe smirked and hoped it would be enough.

"Hmm. Maybe best friend beef, but grown man beef . . . that I doubt." Stoney crossed her arms on top of her seat belt. Dressed in a yellow cardigan set and brown khaki pants, Stoney crossed her feet at the ankles and wiggled her feet.

"I see you still haven't forgiven Mike?" Keithe was glad he could ease the subject from his own woes with Mike.

"You know I forgive because God honors that. But to forget is a whole other story. I just don't like liars and deceivers," Stoney said.

Keithe pursed his lips as he listened to the young woman who loved the Lord but quickly forgot about her own flaws. Which in turn made him think about his own flaws. "I see," was all Keithe cared to say. With so many different emotions going on in his own mind, Keithe pushed play on his CD player and listened as the music flowed from one inspirational song to the next.

There really was more he could elaborate on with Stoney as far as Mike being a liar and a deceiver, but he retracted his thought.

If his memory served him correctly, Stoney had known who he was before he could even fathom who she was. Yet and still, never did she let him in on the possibility of him being her stepfather. Stoney had simply befriended him, and asked him questions in hopes of him slipping up and telling her all she needed to know about Michelle. And he had.

Even with her harboring hurtful feelings from Mike's doings, Keithe knew Stoney loved the Lord and would eventually see the error of her ways. And to help the process, he would no doubt continue to pray and lift her up before the Lord.

Chapter Ten

Mike really didn't care one way or another just what Keithe thought of him. He knew for a fact his friend didn't understand his plight as a man fighting to understand his own pile of confusion. It was Mike who had to live with the decisions he made, the decisions he fought against or easily accepted. Either way, Mike figured it was his battle.

That was just it. Mike really didn't know if he had the power to choose or put down homosexuality. People told him he could, ministers preached to him that he could, but being honest with himself, he knew he couldn't. For one, because he'd tried over and again.

Sure he could date a woman and marry a woman for that matter. Even have kids with her. But that just wasn't the way the cards were lying for him. He knew if he chose that way it would only be a matter of time before he ventured off into another relationship with a man. Then another and another.

With his face appearing in full view in his bathroom mirror, Mike busied himself by putting his tweezers to work cleaning up wild eyebrows that his last thread job didn't catch. He made a mental note to let Barnabis know about the slacking next time.

For the majority of Mike's forty-three years, he'd struggled with the notion that he had been different. His desire to be in the company of men outweighed him seeking a virtuous woman as his wife.

He knew early on he wouldn't be looking for a "good thing." But as good as the Lord is, Mike still was able to obtain favor. Only because God is just good like that. God had forgiven him time and time again for not following the plan laid out for his life, Mike figured. There was no lying to himself. He believed the Word. He didn't get double-dipped philosophized, as others, when they would challenge that "Man wrote the Bible so how does one know God really thinks that way" approach. It was set in stone for him. He believed the Word.

He definitely agreed that God made Adam and Eve and not Adam and Steve, but yet and still, Mike couldn't kick the feelings he had for the Steves he'd come across.

Heating a fresh beaming white Laura Ashley face towel, Mike folded the cloth in half and laid it across his brows. Mike looked in the mirror and stared into his eyes. It was as if his eyes housed his heart. Though he was a happy man, he could see the heaviness of his heart through the misery his eyes held. From day to day happiness was his, but he still longed for joy. Internally he was miserable. It wasn't as though he didn't want to live a holy life. It was just that he couldn't. He didn't know how.

God's mercy was evident in keeping Mike from physical hurt, harm, and diseases that could easily be acquired from the carefree lifestyle he continued to partake in. So many of his friends who shared in his alternative lifestyle had been scarred by HIV/AIDS and others had died. Mike had been spared. With that alone, Mike knew there was a God.

At times when Mike honestly asked his Father in Heaven to keep him from his desires and flesh, He did. No doubt it had to be someone helping him hold his peace. But these days it had been a rare thing for Mike to ask for help. It wasn't as if he didn't like doing what he was doing.

He was a man fighting an internal battle of not wanting to be who he was though his actions showed different. Mike's internal man fought that which God had set in stone, in red, through his parables, in His Word. His want to be the heterosexual man God had created him to be fought with the homosexual man he had become.

Adding a moisturizer to his brown, smooth, and blemish-free skin with a released breath, Mike thought about the day he had planned.

"What in the world am I doing?" he asked, wishing God's voice would just shout at him boastfully in a thunderous voice, "Be who I made you to be." Like many times before, he wished God could shake some sense into him so he could testify how he once was.

He was running. Mike was running from himself, from his lifestyle, and most of all, from the shame he had brought upon the people who loved him and he loved most. His decision to do and be who he wanted to be had cost him the security of his church family as well as birth family.

Waiting for a moment to pass, Mike returned to a mug of lukewarm coffee resting on a coaster on his dining room table. Mike sat and drank the cool cup of coffee he'd been sipping since earlier in the morning. Elbows on the table, Mike sat in silence, looking out into his professionally combed backyard.

Before falling back victim to himself, the last few years Mike thought he had been winning his internal battle. His winning may not have been Charlie Sheen's "winning," but to him, being able to acquire beautiful, built black men had been trophy enough.

He had been able to hide and box up his active homosexual past. He had won the battle of giving in to his own desires because he'd been so busy maintaining his status as minister of music at his church home. Mike had mistaken working at the church for being next to godliness. So when temptation presented itself in the form of another male minister of music, there was no power in his loins to fight.

Shaking his head and thinking about all the time he'd spent wrapped up in choir rehearsals, choir annuals, and church services, Mike never surrendered all to the Lord. He just figured God had snapped His heavenly fingers and took the deep desires out. Now with everything that had gone on, being put on Front Street by church members who had figured the inappropriate relationship out, there were some things Mike needed to revisit.

It was in a blink he went from Brother Mike to a disgrace to his church, all because what looked like a duck couldn't quack like a duck. The worst part about it all was that instead of trying to dig deeper into what he needed to figure out for his life, and seek God for refuge, Mike had jumped the gun, trying to prove he could change and do whatever needed to be done to be the man people felt he should be. When he didn't seek God for the change, Mike fell, once again, back into sin.

Picking up his cell phone, Mike saw a missed call from Kenya. They had been in constant contact with one another since their January meeting, weeks earlier. Today they had a late lunch date, the third of its kind. Mike knew from the beginning that nothing would ever jump off for the two of them; however, the friendship they had started was promising. Because he still was at odds with his best friend, Mike was looking forward to see Keithe sweat just a little while longer.

Chapter Eleven

All Keithe wanted to do was drop Stoney off at her dad's and keep it moving, especially with so many cars parked in their driveway for a Monday afternoon. Whatever was going on, Keithe didn't want to be a part of it. He just didn't feel like being social today.

It had been a little while since Keithe last spoke with Bishop Ky Perry. Over the last three years, he had sporadically spoken with the bishop over the telephone, just holding casual conversation, especially since they had Stoney as a common denominator. The two were nowhere near being best friends, but cordial associates indeed since they both loved and cared for Stoney and her well-being.

Keithe had no ill feelings toward the pastor, whom he looked up to. Neither man could help they'd been drawn to Michelle; that is, the Michelle before Christ. Upon his initial move to the city, Keithe even debated joining Bishop's congregation. But because Keithe knew he would still befriend and be connected with Michelle and her possible visits, he thought it better to keep his distance. Keithe didn't want to bring any more drama to Bishop Perry's clan. He figured Michelle had done enough.

Before Keithe's marriage to Michelle, it had been apparent Michelle had had a former life that would be just the story an author needed to make the *New York*

Times Bestseller List, get a movie deal, and an Oscar nod not far behind.

In this midst of her life, pre-Keithe and during for that matter, Michelle had had several relationships. The short-lived union with Bishop Perry, who was not a minister at the time, was what brought forth Stoney. And even then, though he was the father, Michelle held the information at bay for twenty-one years.

Now that life was on the straight and narrow, Keithe hadn't dared to bring anyone any more pain and went on a search for a church of his own. He still couldn't believe he was in the middle of the nightmare. If he hadn't been married to Michelle he wouldn't have believed everything that had happened involving her.

"Looks like a lot of cars here. I hope everything is okay," Keithe said, referencing maybe someone passing away. He couldn't figure out what else could possibly be going on.

"Oh." Stoney shared one of her giggly laughs, seeing the worry on Keithe's face. "It's just Monday. The family chose years ago for Mondays to officially be family day. Because just about the whole family is in ministry," she explained, "they get together and catch up with one another. Plus Mercy and Grant are putting the finishing touches on their wedding plans in the next couple of months. Everyone is pitching in since April is only two months away."

Stoney's stepsister, Mercy, started out as a stranger, turned confidant, then best friend. They found out just how small the world was when Stoney realized the man who Mercy called Dad was indeed the Bishop Ky Perry, who was married to Mercy's mother, Kendra.

Getting out of her stepfather's car, Stoney hesitated when Keithe didn't move a muscle. It was as if his hands had been glued to the steering wheel.

"Pops." Stoney leaned down sideways on the outside of the car so that her eyes connected with his. "You can come in, ya know?"

"I thought you said your dad wouldn't be back until tonight." Keithe relaxed.

"Right, but you can at least say hi to everyone else . . ." Stoney said, standing back to her full stance once she heard the front door open. "Mercy!"

"Stoney!" Mercy squealed and ran for a hug. With her short strap purse falling off of her shoulder, Mercy slowed down for a quick second and lunged a department store bag she'd been holding at a silent Grant. Continuing her stride, Mercy yelled out, "Hey, girl," as the two embraced. "I'm so happy you could come up this weekend," Mercy exclaimed.

Giving a wave off to Grant, who was still standing in place, Stoney turned her attention once again to her stepsister and chatted it up a bit.

With his window already down, Keithe thought it proper to speak to the young man who wasn't more than fifteen feet from his vehicle. "Hey, dude. How's it going?" Keithe asked and then felt a déjà vu feeling come upon him.

With a short nod and a one-sided smirk, Grant said, "What's up?" and, just as quick, turned and walked toward his own car.

As if an epiphany had fallen upon him, Keithe saw the familiarity in Grant and heard it in his voice. He knew him. He didn't know where he knew him from, but he knew him nonetheless.

"Hey there, Mr. Keithe. How are you?" Mercy knelt down so she could expose her face to Keithe through the passenger side window.

"I'm good, Mercy. Congratulations on your upcoming nuptials. I will have to send my gift by Stoney," he offered.

"Well, thank you, sir." Mercy did a curtsey and grabbed at Stoney.

"Oh." Keithe hurriedly opened his door and headed to the back of his vehicle. Almost forgetting about Stoney's luggage in the back of his trunk, Keithe added pep to his step in order to retrieve the heavy travel bags for his stepdaughter. Closing his trunk, Keithe rolled the twenty-something-pound bag to the front of the house. On the way back to his car, Keithe stopped and gave both ladies quick hugs.

"See ya, Pops. Love ya." Stoney gravitated toward Mercy and the house as Keithe drove off.

"Where's Grant Jr.? Hey, Grant?" Stoney mouthed as she waved toward Grant sitting in his car, waiting for his fiancée to join him.

"Just a minute, Grant," Mercy threw his way while opening the door to the house. Almost running head-on into Kenya, who was on her way out, Mercy slowed her tracks.

"Oops," Kenya said. "I didn't see you all coming in," the older lady said to her nieces; one biological and the other through marriage. Although Kenya hadn't had the chance to bond with Stoney due to her travels in the ministry, she treated them just the same. Peeping around the two giggle boxes, Kenya squinted her eyes at the car that was making its way out of her sister and brother-in-law's circular driveway. Thinking he resembled her church peer, Kenya thought herself silly to think Keithe would have any business being at her family's house.

"Oh, was that your father? I'm sorry I missed him," Kenya said.

"Oh shoot," Stoney allowed to fly out of her mouth. "That's right; you've never met my parents. Well, now that you're permanently in town and so is my dad, I'll have to make sure you do so and soon."

"Sounds like a plan. Hey, but I'm headed out, ladies." Kenya pulled Stoney in for a hug.

"Yep. She has a hot date, Stoney," Mercy rubbed in as she walked off toward an awaiting Grant. "I'm sure she'll tell us about it later on." Mercy winked.

Stoney oh'd and aw'd.

"Don't be so sure about it." Kenya sashayed in the direction where her car was parked. Not wanting to keep Mike waiting, Kenya picked up her pace.

Chapter Twelve

Kenya left her Audi with the valet parking attendants at The Cheesecake Factory, across the street from North Park Mall. She wanted to make sure she was early rather than late. Something told her Mike was a precise person from their other lunch dates.

For February, the weather played fair with the sun-rays beaming a cool seventy-three degrees. Kenya wore a light-material cream sweater with a slight V-neck and glided toward the entrance in her dark-colored jeans tucked neatly in her Charles David chocolate-brown riding boots. Taking a deep breath, Kenya told herself, "Here goes nothing," as she walked toward an already-seated Mike. During their previous conversations and lunch dates, Kenya could tell that Mike didn't have any intentions of going any further with her than just friendship, but she wasn't about to allow him to make a decision that soon. She needed him . . . even if it was just for a little while.

"Hey, you," was the greeting Mike sent in Kenya's direction. Taking a step forward, Mike took Kenya's hand and leaned in and kissed her cheek. "I'm glad you could make it."

With a practiced smile, Kenya allowed Mike to pull out her chair. "Of course. Thank you for the invite." Kenya tried hard to accommodate Mike's Southern gentleman appeal knowing he must have had practice to pull off a manly charm."I didn't think I'd have a Valentine this year." Kenya saw how Mike's eyes bucked from his eye sockets.

She knew him. Well, she knew of him. Though there were plenty of Baptist churches in the Dallas–Fort Worth area, their paths had indeed crossed. Of course, it had been a one-sided awareness, knowing Mike wouldn't share the truth with her ; nonetheless, Kenya knew Mike definitely played with both sides of the heart: one for show and the other for pleasure.

"Breathe, Mike." Kenya laughed it off. "I'm just kidding around with you." She realized getting him to date her would be harder than she thought.

"Ha, ha, very funny." He did a fake eyebrow wipe.

"So how did your other auditions go?" Kenya asked, following up a telephone conversation that had been ongoing. "Have you heard anything yet?" Placing her purse on one of the two vacant seats, Kenya adjusted her bangle bracelets and pulled her cardigan back in place.

With his own lightweight canary-yellow designer sweater on, Mike reclaimed his seat and retrieved his napkin for lap placement. "Actually, I just got off the line with a church. I'm going in after I leave here to talk details." Mike was elated. Being without a stable minister of music gig for a while, Mike had been trying to find that next position. The gossip from his previous church usually preceded him on many auditions and had been the cause of him not having a stable job.

Giving an airy clap, Kenya sat tall and congratulated her new friend. It was hard for her to believe what she was actually doing. Just looking at Mike, one really couldn't tell he dabbled like he did. If anything, people would easily label him a metrosexual; but then some said that too played close to the goal line.

It was a fact that some Christians didn't usually like to even mention someone being homosexual. Especially if that someone could say the Lord's Prayer and send the whole church into unknown tongues. But there was a pinch of residue left in his mannerism that had set Kenya off. And that wasn't stereotyping Mike, as far as Kenya was concerned. It was just the truth. Nevertheless, she was moving forward; anything to keep her loved ones off her case and out of her past.

Kenya had concocted a plan to get herself off of her family and friends' to-do lists. And she surely wanted to get off of Deacon Morgan's radar. It wasn't like she didn't want the deacon asking her out. It was just that she knew she would give in. And if she gave in, there was no doubt she would fall in love with him. With that fear alone, Kenya just wouldn't forgive herself if she broke his heart. She had to first know if she could love a man without interruption.

With Mike, she knew it would be safe to build a world with him. He wouldn't ask for much and he wouldn't question her. Especially after she eventually gave him all of the details. She wouldn't have to worry about her past coming out, and if it did, Mike surely would be understanding.

Plus, it was too risky for her to allow someone to care more for her than she cared for him . . . at this moment. Especially when there was so much doubt about who she really was, or what she was for that matter.

She had tried to fast and pray, asking God to help her release her feeling. But she knew everything she had been asking was in vain. She would just have to go through the broken realm in order to be made whole. Not because God ordains that, but because she was a woman of the cloth and had treated her vows as nothing.

"Yeah. I'm pumped about it," Mike shared. "I have been floating around from church to church and I just don't like that," he admitted. "I'm used to having a foundation . . . having my peeps," he said with lots of energy just like every time he got when talking about playing the organ and directing choirs.

With her eyes glazed over, Kenya felt bad. She knew they were both sitting at the table lying to one another. She knew both of their secrets. And if she could help it, she hoped they'd be married before she or anyone else shared hers.

"Well, I'm all for you getting what your heart desires. You are very talented and it needs to be shared." Kenya spoke from the heart.

"Why thank you, sweet Kenya. Shall we order?" Mike lifted his menu and glanced over it.

"Don't mind if we do," Kenya agreed. "Oh and I wanted to invite you to dinner on Valentine's Day." Kenya didn't struggle to get it out. She figured since he wasn't going to play along at the pace she needed him to, she'd do all of the pursuing. "I'm just saying . . ." She saw fear in his eyes. "Since we're both single and I know you don't want to be sitting at home alone . . . Heck, I know I don't."

"Um. Sure," Mike agreed, knowing there would be some moving around of his Valentine's Day schedule he had already prepared with his latest male suitor. "Oh snap." Mike lifted the menu to his face and placed it right below his eyes.

Whipping her head around to see what had grabbed Mike's attention, Kenya looked over her left shoulder. "What is it?" she asked, turning back around just in time to see Mike put his right hand over his right eye like a blinder. "Who are you hiding from?" Kenya couldn't believe Mike was actually trying to hide from someone.

"Uh, Keithe's ex-wife," he whispered. "Michelle."

With eyebrows raised, Kenya decided to look over her shoulder once more: a double take. "Is she that bad?" she emphasized. "She's a beautiful woman and seems to be friendly." Kenya talked over her shoulder. "Are you two not friends?"

"No, it's not that. Actually, we are more cordial these last couple of years. More than we've been in all the years they had been married. It's just that . . ." Mike lowered the menu just a tad bit. "Since me and Keithe are really not on speaking terms"—he slid the menu back up—"I'm not up to finding out if she has an attitude with me also. That woman can be a beast."

"Oh?" Kenya questioned. "I didn't know you and Keithe were not talking." She straightened her body in the padded seat. "Is everything okay? Something I can help with?" All of a sudden Kenya felt bad. No, horrible. She knew without a doubt she had to be the reason for the spat the two best friends were having.

Shaking his head before he turned down her offer, Mike wished he hadn't expressed himself the way he had. Now he would have to try his best and retract the story. "Oh, no. It's nothing major." He put his blinder back up as he watched Michelle walking his way. "Just men stuff. You know? I'm sure it'll pass." Mike hurried his answer so that his voice wouldn't be heard once Michelle walked past their table.

The sound of someone approaching from behind came closer. The echoes of Michelle's designer heels were what Kenya keyed in on. Just that quick and with a scent of Chanel No. 5 lingering, Kenya watched as Michelle unknowingly passed by her and Mike.

"You're in the clear." Kenya reached over and rubbed Mike's forearm. Adding a laugh to her gesture, Kenya joked with Mike. "Remind me not to ever get on your bad side, dear."

"You won't," he insisted as he placed the menu on the table. "I wonder what she is doing down here anyway," Mike said, knowing Kenya wouldn't hold the answer. "I bet you anything she isn't down here for business. From what Keithe told me, she has been trying to get back with him. And hard."

That news alone put a singe of jealousy in Kenya's spirit. She didn't know why. Sure she had a slight crush on Keithe, but what right did she have to be jealous when she was sitting across from Keithe's best friend?

"Oh. Really? Well, she looks like the type to get whatever she wants." Kenya picked up her fresh glass of water with lemon.

"Oh, you best believe. Whatever Ms. Michelle Morgan wants . . . most of the time, Ms. Michelle Morgan gets."

"Unless he's not into getting got," Kenya said. "I'm sure his mind is on someone else by now. And plus, he did move away from her."

Raising his eyebrows, Mike sat, listening to what all Kenya had to say . . . and what she hadn't. It was apparent Kenya knew more about Keithe's crush on her than what she had let on.

Realizing she had shared too much, Kenya decided to gulp as much water as she could in order to not say anything further.

Mike had had a good time with Kenya. They chatted about the Christian peers they hadn't known they shared, the churches in their religion sector, and their own ministries. Mike had gotten comfortable with Kenya and wished he could really confide in her, but just couldn't risk it. There was no way he would allow another woman to fall for him the way he had allowed his ex, Vicky, to do. From where he was sitting, Kenya was really digging him as a prospect, but he knew he couldn't, wouldn't say the same.

Kenya opened up about how her gift to evangelize was set in her from birth and Mike painted a picture of himself being labeled "Baby Ray" on the piano at his father's church, which was his start to becoming a minister of music.

The two sat at The Cheesecake Factory for hours and shared their future endeavors and even made plans for future outings, starting with their Valentine's Day dinner. The pinky swears the two partook in made sure of it. Mike figured, *why not?* Kenya had turned out to be someone he could talk and laugh with. And there was always a midnight rendezvous he could have with his boy toy.

Plus, some of the name dropping Kenya had done had made Mike's arched eyebrows stand erect. By all means, he needed to find out just what circles Kenya had run with. And mainly because some of the women she had claimed to be super cool with were labeled "saved but suspect."

When a spark had lit in Mike, giving him a suspicious flare, it didn't take long for him to respond internally with a, "Naaaaaah."

"What was that?" Kenya had responded with a sip from a lemon and water–filled glass. Thinking she had missed his question, Kenya waited on Mike to expound on what he had said.

Not realizing his own mental debate had made its way into the atmosphere, Mike shook off the thought and category he'd placed Kenya in. Returning to the lunch set before him, Mike decided to put his best foot forward for the remainder of their date.

"Oh nothing. So what are some things you like to do in your free time?" Mike asked as he once again drifted off into his own world. When he looked at her, Mike could clearly see that Kenya was any man's dream. Any available, clear-minded, clean-hearted, saved, and straight man's dream. But, then again, he was digging her so maybe Kenya was just the total package. Period.

From her clear skin tone and glossed-over lips, beauty was only part of who she was. Kenya had shared with Mike how she excelled all through college. She'd received her master's in psychology and didn't stop there. Before she settled into any one career, Kenya had gone to theology school to learn even more of what God had already gifted her with: His way, His truth, and His light.

The only details missing from her biography were any remnants of any man.

Just learning all he could about the amazing woman who had been sitting across from him, Mike wished he could make a sound decision to want to be with someone like her. But since he was stuck not knowing how to get out of a world he'd kept one foot in, Mike would keep her at a distance. There was no way he would put another woman through what he'd put Vicky through.

He shook his head and wished he really could say he was the man for her, but he couldn't.

There was no doubt Kenya was digging him. That was cool but he wasn't going to allow her to get in over her head. She deserved the best.

Plus, there was something strange about Kenya almost throwing herself at him. Although he carried himself in a *GQ*, manly way, not many self-proclaimed Christian women approached him outside of being friends. Now, some self-proclaimed "Christian" men, on the other hand, approached him all the time. That alone was another story.

After his date with Kenya and now back at home and playing tunes on his grand piano set up in his formal living area, Mike really did have Kenya on his mind. He wondered just why she went for him when a good man like Keithe was sweating bullets just to be in her company. Whatever the case may have been, Mike made up in his mind to be who Kenya wanted him to be. But when it was all said and done, he hoped he could be just what she needed him to be.

Chapter Thirteen

"I cannot believe it. The wedding is in two months. I have so much to do. Thank you, sis, for coming down as much as you have. I know with your full schedule and all, there are more things you could be doing on the weekends instead of traveling to Dallas, helping me out." An emotional Mercy became teary as she talked to Stoney. Loving the bond between herself and Stoney, Mercy was unable to see through her watery eyes and had to take a break.

Hearing "sis" come from Mercy toward her warmed Stoney's heart just the same. With their chance meeting over three years ago while Mercy was a pharmacy assistant and Stoney a customer, it was with Mercy's help that Stoney was able to locate her biological mother.

"Ohhhh. Don't start all of that crying now, Mercy. Save it all for the wedding day." She walked over, bent down, and gave her sister a tight squeeze. "I'm just as excited as you, Mercy. And thank you again for allowing me to be your maid of honor." Stoney held the last syllable as she jokingly ran a goofy run back over to Mercy. Laying a big kiss on her sister's cheek, Stoney gave Mercy another gigantic hug.

"Girl, move with all the mushy stuff." Mercy kept gluing rhinestones on the keepsake boxes she was making for her bridesmaids, not bothering to push Stoney away at all. "You better move before you get burnt." Mercy aimed the glue gun at Stoney.

Stoney had lived in Dallas alone; actually in the world, period, by her lonesome. With just two friends in Dallas, Mike and Vicky, it wasn't until Mercy had lent herself to Stoney that the lost young girl Stoney was finally felt as if she belonged. And the same with Mercy.

Mercy had gotten pregnant with Grant Jr. and was at a place emotionally not knowing how to break the news to her mother, Kendra, and stepfather. The two young women were there for one another, with the end product leaving them being more than friends.

Through all of the hours together and research they participated in, it was found that Mercy's stepfather was Stoney's biological father. From that day of realization, nothing brought them closer than the ordeal they'd gone through.

Stoney had literally lost her cool, losing her mind in the midst of it all. So adamant about finding her mother, Stoney had kidnapped Mercy and followed Keithe on a four-hour drive back to Houston. Because of what she'd done, a guilty feeling had always lingered over Stoney. It had only been a few months ago that Stoney had finally ceased apologizing about all she had put a then-pregnant Mercy through.

While Stoney had so many hang-ups from being abandoned by her mother and left with a schizophrenic grandmother, there were so many made-up rules that confused the young Stoney. Even down to what she wore. Now new to expanding her wardrobe, wearing jeans or pants of any kind, Stoney pulled on and prodded her blue jean knickers she'd bought. Still getting used to wearing the latest fashions, Stoney made Mercy laugh with her constant pulling.

"What's wrong? Your pants riding high on you?" Mercy didn't try to hold in her laugh.

"Oh hush up now. I think I just got the wrong cut. I keep forgetting these hips aren't made just for anything to be put on them." Stoney stood and pulled some more.

Caught up in their clowning around they were doing, Grant Jr. made his way between the two sisters. "I want kisses, TT Stowy." He pulled on Stoney's shirt while he tried his best to get his two-year-old pronunciation intact.

"Aww, come here, Jr. Let Auntie smoother you with kisses too." She threw her love licks all over the toddler.

Racing him around the room in the air, Stoney made a pit landing back in the chair she started in. With Grant Jr. still in her lap, Stoney relaxed.

"This really is exciting. I mean, I'm so glad you and Grant stuck this out. You've proven it doesn't have to always end up just crazy," the twenty-four-year-old said. "You're a wonderful mother and great girlfriend. I mean, you are holding a lot of things down." Stoney referred to Mercy being a graduate student, working toward her doctorate as a pharmacist.

"Well, you know what the Word says: 'He will never put more on you than you can bear.' That's what I've kept in mind this whole time." Mercy took a mental break and leaned back in her upright chair.

Getting pregnant with her son at age twenty-one brought on a whole new outlook when it came to life. No thought to quitting school, Mercy could only credit her mother, stepfather, and her boyfriend, Grant, who stepped up to the plate and helped her keep her dream of completing school intact.

Able to live with minimal rent in the pool house in the back of her parent's home, Mercy was thankful to have her own small family stable. Blessed to finish out her studies in Houston, Mercy gave major kudos to Grant for taking care of their son for weeks at a time. Until she would come home for her mental break of college life, Grant would be the number-one caretaker in Grant Jr.'s life.

"I'm just thankful. I can't thank God enough for Grant being a stand-up guy. He takes good care of my baby," Mercy said, not forgetting to add that Grant took good care of her as well.

Laughing and with her eyes half bucked out her head, Stoney chanted, "Who dat is?"

"That's just my baby daddy," Mercy sang in a tiny voice, gave a hearty laugh, and then stopped. "Not! Bam!" She stuck her left hand in the air and waved it to show off the effects of her one-and-a-half-carat engagement ring. Both ladies started laughing. "Girl, let me hush 'fore I wake Grant up from his nap. My husband to be has to get his rest, you know."

"Um, huh?" Stoney gave off a cutesy smile.

Mercy loved her ring and tried to show it off whenever she could. She never mentioned the fact that she had been the one who had picked it out *and* bought it.

Sharing in a fun moment with Stoney, in the back of her mind Mercy couldn't stop thinking about Grant and how he'd been acting lately: standoffish, almost mute, and even, at times, disgusted. She didn't know what to think of Grant right about now. With the wedding just weeks away, there was no way she would share her doubts. There was no way she would call off the wedding of her dreams just because of a little shift in his attitude. Perhaps he was just getting cold feet. That was normal. No need to break things off. Besides she would not embarrass herself by doing so. Whatever it was, she just prayed he would soon get over it so they would be able to get on with their lives together.

When Stoney and Mercy heard a knock and then twist of the doorknob, they waited to see who would come through the door.

"Hey, Auntie Kenya," Mercy said. Standing to take a break, Mercy offered her arms to her young aunt who had been closer in age to her than she was to her mother.

"Hi, Ms. Kenya. Oops, I mean, Auntie Kenya," Stoney greeted the lady she admired. Kenya was exactly how Stoney envisioned herself: sold out to Christ and still beautiful on the inside as well as the outside.

With Kenya only being back in the city, permanently, for a little over year, Stoney still hadn't gotten the opportunity to get to know more about her. But that didn't stop them from having fun and loving on one another. With Kenya traveling in the US and beyond due to her evangelist duties, all the drama of Stoney stalking her biological parents she had missed out on. Stoney still hoped no one had filled Kenya in to a T. And if they had, she had hoped to prove herself a changed, healed young woman.

"Hey, girls. What y'all got going?" Kenya slapped her hands together and readied herself to help.

"Well, since you asked . . ." Mercy moved her material, scissors, and glue gun out of the way so that Kenya could have her seat. "You can take over gluing these rhinestones while I show Stoney how to wrap the bottom of these boutonnieres with this green two-sided tape."

Moving to her awaiting seat, Kenya was proud of her niece. Her only sister's baby, Kenya was very proud of her family.

"I'm so proud of you, Mimi." Kenya referenced Mercy with the nickname she gave her long ago. "Look at all this. You are really putting some serious work in, huh?" Kenya eased herself into Mercy's warm seat.

"She really is." Stoney leant her opinion. "She has everything down, even to the kind of glue she needs. Everything is marked off the list." They all laughed.

Knowing it was the truth, Mercy took pride in being truly involved in the planning and designing of her wedding.

"Are you nervous, niecey?" Kenya asked Mercy as she situated herself in her seat.

"Nervous for what?" Mercy answered as she walked toward her bedroom, checking on Grant, who had been taking a nap, wanting to make sure that their conversation hadn't bothered her husband-to-be. "Like the old folks say, if you love him and he loves you . . ." Mercy stopped short when she realized Grant Jr. was the only one in her bed watching television.

"Then what?" Stoney really wanted to know.

Confused, not realizing Grant had gotten up from his nap and left the house without letting her know, Mercy walked toward the living room and cut to the kitchen to check and see if his car was parked. "Then there is no need to worry." Mercy's voice trailed off as she looked out the kitchen window to see no car anywhere in sight.

Silently taking in the surroundings, Kenya believed just that. She believed that was all it took: for a man and woman to truly love one another. Yet and still, Kenya knew it would take more for her since she had crossed to the other side.

She was sure everyone was shaking their heads, not believing her niece, who was several years younger, was beating her to the altar. On one hand, Kenya couldn't care less what people thought. But on the other hand she couldn't help but to linger and wonder just what they were saying.

Yes, she wanted love. And yes, with the man of her dreams. But, just as luck would have it, right when she did finally ready herself for the next phase of her life, she had done things she couldn't believe she had done. She'd gotten in her own way. Or so she'd liked to think, which she was sure to be the truth.

There was some major cleaning of the heart and mind she'd have to do before she could let go and let God.

She had always come across lying men, no-return-ing-calls men, full-of-talk-but-no-walk men. If that's what Kenya had to put up with in order to begin a family, she thought, then she wouldn't. But then there was Keithe. Shaking him out of her thinking, Kenya wanted to hear more from Mercy, who had returned from the kitchen. "Sounds like that's enough to make it work. You shouldn't have to worry about your marriage," Kenya encouraged Mercy.

With a side smile, Mercy didn't want to let on her true feelings concerning her upcoming nuptials. "Yep. I guess you're right. Shouldn't have to worry at all," Mercy whispered as she sat back in her seat to finish her wedding decorations.

"Soooo." Stoney saw the look on her sister's face, but wanted to lighten up the mood. "Who has plans for V-Day? Auntie Kenya, any news on that new beau you won't share?"

"Yeah. You never told us about your date. How's it been going?" Mercy added, wanting to know details about Kenya's date from two days earlier.

Not really excited about dating Mike when it was all a façade, Kenya had to put on a front nonetheless. "Well, I guess I can share with y'all." She giggled. "Aaaaand, we are going out to dinner next week, on Valentine's Day," she shared.

"Ooooh, that has got to be something serious." Stoney's interest was sparked. "Guys just don't go out on special holiday dates with women they aren't interested in."

Yes, they do. Especially if they are gay, was what Kenya really wanted to say, but she opted not to. "Umm, huh?" she responded instead.

"Wow. Looks as though you two may just have a double wedding next year yourselves." Mercy cheered up.

"Whaaaat?" Kenya sang. "Do tell." She stopped gluing the rhinestones and waited to hear what Stoney had to say.

Blushing uncontrollably, Stoney was excited. "He's just a guy I've been friends with. We have the same major and have the majority of our classes at the same time. He asked me to dinner next week as well. Sooooo, we shall see." Stoney grinned.

Excited about Stoney's possibility, Kenya had to plaster a smile on her face that wouldn't give off how she actually felt. She never would have believed she would have become a liar and a deceiver, inflicting pain on herself. "Yep. You never know. A double wedding just may be in the works for us," Kenya said, knowing it couldn't be any further from the truth.

Chapter Fourteen

The weekend had passed, and spending the majority of her Sunday afternoon with Mercy and her wedding planning had put a damper on Kenya's spirit. She hadn't known she would be so affected by everything. She was feeling so ill about her own less-than-love affairs that she debated even stepping down from ministering her own niece's ceremony.

Kenya didn't know what she was doing. For one, she had up and done the forbidden with the forbidden. For someone who prided herself in allowing Jesus to guide her in every area in her life, her actions labeled her a hypocrite. Then she concocted some cockamamie story of being interested in Mike. Whatever Kenya thought she had planned was boiling in the pit of her stomach. It was so far gone and out of control that she felt it brewing and about to make her upchuck any moment. It was a front. For her at least she knew it was. She knew Mike wasn't really that into her or any woman. In fact, she could tell he had other intentions, maybe to just be her friend. But she needed more. She had gotten so far into her plan she just couldn't back away now.

"How long, God? How long will I have to suffer feeling like this?" Kenya wailed out as she walked and talked to God throughout her home. "I know you said you've forgiven me, but I can't get this off of me. I just can't."

She no longer knew what she was doing. On top of that, she no longer knew what she really felt. Or who she was for that matter. Kenya had gotten so far away from the real issue, which she believed was her doing everything just so Keithe would stay away from her. Kenya knew she had long ago deviated from the truth.

True, at first, she wanted someone in place to buy her some time, in order to get Keithe to move on. But in reality, it was her own pitiful and sinful lusts that she was trying to purge out of her system. It wasn't right, it was manipulative, but she didn't know what else to do.

The feelings of the indecent moments she'd shared in the dark, on the other side of the world, were still embedded in her being. She didn't like it, didn't agree with it, but couldn't shake it. Kenya hated not having control of how she should feel and who she should feel a certain way about. All she knew was to call on the name of Jesus.

"Lord, you have got to help me! Help me purge my past out of my heart, out of my loins. God, I hate feeling this way. You said by accepting you, I am a new creature. I've given myself back to you. Help me, Lord," she wept. "I . . . I've fall short, Lord. Too low to get back up," she honestly believed.

Not being able to shake the enemy off was what set Kenya in her bad decision making. She hated that she had resorted to such low antics, but when people had started talking, coming up with their own reasoning behind why she was still single, she didn't know what else to do.

Her pastor, one who said he wouldn't believe anything until it came from her, had pushed just about every single brother, minister, and now deacon he could into Kenya's direction. She knew he only did so to see if she would fall for the bait. In turn, her accepting the challenge would clear up some issues for him. In actuality, it just left her being overwhelmed.

In Kenya's mind, there was no doubt she would eventually marry the man God sent her way. Maybe. But first she had to do her part. She had to rid her thinking of being emotionally connected to the person who had introduced her to something she promised to never take part in until she was married. But she hadn't waited. And for that, there was a sinful connection, a soulful connection she had with her lover.

"*Lover*," Kenya said aloud. Just the thought of her having been a part of something she never thought she would made Kenya cringe.

There was nothing more that Kenya could do but cry. Being by herself only made it worse. With no strength to wait around until warm suds filled her Jacuzzi tub, Kenya opted for a shower, hoping her evils would wash themselves down the drain.

Even if it wasn't a Calgon moment, she felt better already. Being able to cry without ceasing, Kenya was ready to try again to move forward. Her emotions had switched from self-pity to being upset, angry with her suitor, a person nearly twenty years her senior.

Sitting on the side of her bed in her pajamas, Kenya stared at her cell phone in its resting place on her nightstand. In the past she had been able to fight against her wants to contact someone she had looked up to in the ministry, just to confront who she felt had taken advantage of her. Now, Kenya had a mind to call and put them on blast for allowing the devil to use them in order to tempt Kenya with success. The proposal itself had left Kenya confused, disgusted with herself, and wondering if she was indeed not as straight as she thought she had been.

When Kenya had shared her calling at the tender age of sixteen, her suitor had been her mentor, an older saint in the ministry. The pastor at her old church, Kenya believed, didn't have a clue, but blessed the mentorship. Kenya's mother, Herlene, a saved woman of God herself, counted it all joy that her daughter was chasing after God instead of boys, so she definitely didn't object to Kenya's flourishing relationship.

At first it was everything Kenya could have asked God for. She traveled to different churches with the seasoned evangelist who brought God's Word with evidence that He sat high and looked low. Whenever her mentor preached the Word of God, lives were changed, people were saved, and God got the glory.

Even on a personal note, they prayed together and talked about the goodness of the Lord. They even encouraged one another in their fasting. Although she had family, Kenya easily looked up to her mentor as family as well.

Back then, Kenya was so young and naive to even know the difference in someone waiting for their spouse and one who never wanted one at all. No one ever talked about this sort of thing. No, not in the church. Maybe it was because her mentor had never crossed any lines with her, but Kenya never had an inclination of her friend's true interest.

Over the years Kenya had learned from the seasoned evangelist, on several different occasions, to "keep her mind on Jesus at all times and to not even think about any man." That part was easy, as it seemed no men were ever allowed in the circle anyway. Her saved and godly-spoken-of mentor had been one of the many inspirations for Kenya believing that she could indeed wait for sex until her wedding night. Never noticing her mentor dating, rather spending all time after God's own heart, Kenya thought surely if they could go decades without giving in to the temptations that are sometimes brought about with dating, she could do the same.

The evangelist had never married and wasn't trying to be wed by anyone. Now that Kenya's eyes had been opened like Adam's and Eve's when they disobeyed God, Kenya could see all the signs.

It was all very evident now. Things which had seemed to appear one way had been a mirage. Kenya couldn't believe how she had been swindled, lied to, and disappointed all of those years before. What really threw her for a loop was how she'd allowed the truth to inch its way into her present life.

Unable to fight against the feeling of giving her former mentor a piece of her mind, Kenya picked up the phone to dial their number. Before she was able to press send, Kenya's phone vibrated underneath her fingertips.

"Oh, Lord," Kenya yelled out, jerking her neck when she saw the number on the screen. It was clear to her that God hadn't thought she was ready to make a call that probably would have broken her down even more.

Seeing Keithe's number on the screen, Kenya took in a shocked breath and debated answering. Whatever it was that he wanted she hoped it was church related.

"Hello," she heard Keithe say as she sat, just holding the line. Kenya was yet again amazed how God had made a way of escape from confrontation . . . or confirmation. It was the latter Kenya feared. "Hello?"

She took her ministry for real. Even if she were in the midst of driving on the wrong side of the road, Kenya knew God when he showed Himself.

"Hi," she finally let out. Scooting herself back against her king-sized down pillow, Kenya wrestled with allowing a personal tone in her voice, or keeping it strictly business.

"Hi, Keithe." Kenya really did feel something for the tall, dark, and handsome man. It no doubt had to be the God in him. Never having felt anything for any boy, or man for that matter, remotely what she felt for Keithe, Kenya couldn't decipher if it was enough to keep her from venturing back into the arms of the forbidden. Especially if she were to ever give the deacon a chance.

"Kenya. How are you? We haven't had time enough to chat lately. Well . . . outside of the group, that is."

It was a personal call.

"Oh, I'm sorry, Keithe. Just so busy running around doing so many things. Is there anything in particular going on?" Kenya fought to keep all things church related.

"Oh no. We're straight. I'm just talking about you and me." Keithe's sensual voice spoke volumes. "I've missed you." After hearing nothing but silence on the other end, he said, "Let me back up. I have missed our friendship. You seem distant ever since you and Mike have started dating."

"Um, huh," Kenya was finally able to release. "Is this what I owe the pleasure of your call to?" Kenya gave off a little giggle. She felt Keithe was about to get a little too honest for her. "Aren't you the brave one, Deacon Morgan?"

"Okay, okay. So I'm being the bold one tonight. Evangelist? I'm just going to be blunt. I like you. Care for you, whether you accept that or not. Mike's my boy. Like a brother to me . . . I just thought he came out of left field asking you out." Keithe was like Whitney Houston; he couldn't believe his own strength in being direct with

Kenya. "Maybe I should have put myself out there sooner to let you know how I felt. Maybe the rejection wouldn't have hurt so badly," Keithe said.

Kenya felt bad. At that very moment her heart warmed for Keithe. All of the avoiding she had done had only led right back to the very beginning of the whole flirting scenario. Now she no doubt knew she had been the reason why the two friends had stopped communicating.

"So what do you want, Deacon Morgan?" Kenya asked, though scared to hear the actual answer.

"Just a chance. That's it." Keithe, who had been inadvertently listening to Mother Gladstone's weird but precise way of putting things, was going in full force. "All I need is a chance for me to start all over. Evangelist Kenya . . . I'm Deacon Morgan."

Chapter Fifteen

"Mike." Keithe was routed to his childhood friend's voice mail. "Man, look. Whenever you can, I want to talk to you. I'm out of your business. But I do need to talk to you. Just call when you can. I'm out," he expressed through the phone. "Oh, and if it makes any sense, I just care about you both and don't want to see either of you hurt."

Keithe wanted to break the thick wall that had been built between them. Being in one another's lives since their childhood, Keithe didn't want bridges to be burnt with someone he considered a brother. It had been a week he'd been trying to get through to Mike. Ever since he'd spoken with Kenya, Keithe had tried to do the same with Mike.

Plus he wanted to find out what ol' dude's name was that Mike had been on a date with a while back. He seriously doubted it was the young man back at Stoney's dad's house he'd seen when he dropped her off over a month ago, especially since he was marrying Mercy, but still.

With no answer, Keithe went through the church doors and readied himself for Wednesday night's Bible Study.

"Yes'sah, Deacon Morgan," Mother Gladstone beckoned. "Would you like some water, a soder, uh, soder water . . . some tea," she so politely asked. "Or what about some honey?" The older missionary kindly flopped down on a bench outside the sanctuary doors with none of the beverages she named anywhere in sight. "Heeeeee," she squealed, laughing at herself, figuring she still had "it." "Ya early. Come on and sit with an old lady, son."

Shaking his head, Keithe wondered, if he did want a beverage, just who would get it since she decided to sit down before he gave his answer. Or maybe she never planned on getting him anything, anyway, he thought. He shrugged. Looking at the bench, Keithe did what he was told even though he couldn't figure if it would be her protruding hip he would be sitting on or the small space she'd left him on the bench. He took his chances.

"Um, you okay?" she asked, when it sounded like she was the one in pain.

"I'm fine," Keithe answered as he sat on a cushioned seat.

"Yeeees, good Lord you are. God is worthy to be praised." Pastor Peter's mother gave a wide smile with her 1980s gold teeth that lined her mouth, yet were holding on.

Keithe really didn't know if the praise was for him or the good Lord, but he wasn't about to ask.

"That's a fine job you and Evangelist Kenya are doing with them there divorce-arees, ya know." She tilted her head and tried to cross her ankles to no avail. "You one of them there divorce-arees too, Deacon?" Blunt was her middle name.

When he lifted his shoulder and nodded his head, Mother Gladstone shook her head in disgust. "A mess. Um. Back in the day when I was married to Vernon, Lee, and Woodrow, ain't nobody talk about divorce. That wasn't the going thang," she slurred while crunching her fingers in the air as quotations.

Thinking he ought to point out what she'd just said, Keithe just sat, trying to hold his tongue. He was afraid to respond out of fear of being reprimanded again. Or maybe, just maybe they had all died.

Missionary Gladstone was well known at the church as one of the elderly mothers who just didn't play. While the other mothers were as pleasant as they could be, Mother Gladstone was a tell-it-like-it-is saint.

"I see you still have the sweets for Sister Kenya, too?" She raised her bushy eyebrows, as if they would make her whisper. No luck.

"The what?" It took Keithe a minute to catch on.

"The sweets, the hots. Ya know, some kinda seasoning for that girl!" She was irritated. "Boy, you know what I'm talking 'bout." She smacked him on his shoulder.

"Oh! Oh, okay. Well, Mother. You know. Well . . ." Keithe wasn't comfortable in his seat or in the conversation, but he was ready to share the good news with her about him making a move. "Actually I spoke—"

As she raised her hand, Keithe didn't know if the older woman was going to backhand him or wanted him to cease talking. Looking directly at her nugget pearl and tarnished gold rings, Keithe held his breath and waited.

"I see you didn't take my advice. See, that's what's wrong with y'all young people these days." She flipped her hand over and wanted Keithe to help her up. "Help me up, son." Agitation rose up in Mother Gladstone. "Walk with me this way. I need to go get my cane 'fo' my son see me without it. I don't need him to stop taking care of his mother 'cause she hardheaded." She walked with a limp. "So you let your friend go after the lady you adore, huh? You know good and well that ain't gonna work. Right?" She stopped for a moment and dared him to object. "That's what I thought."

Placing himself on her right hand, Keithe offered his left hand to the woman who sure had her own unique way of giving out wisdom.

"See, son, it's not about sitting back and watching to see what's gonna happen. It's about doing what thus said the Lord. That's where a lot of y'all—yes, I said y'all—in the Christian realm get it wrong. We are God's prized possessions. He wants the best for us, but us's have to know it.

"A few years ago, a snake came through this church." She stopped and pointed downward. "Yes, right here. Showed up, yessir, and thought she was gonna take over. Thought she was gonna take the praise off the team. Take the beat off the drum. She thought she was gonna take the missus out of the mister. Yep, she thought she was gonna take my son from his wife. But what you gotta know is that serpents can only camouflage for so long. They ain't as quick as they think.

"You got to know that all that looks holy ain't holy." She looked to see if he took the hint. "All that looks like glitter ain't gold." Mother Gladstone waited to see if what she was saying was registering with the much-younger man. When she got tired of trying to add some intelligence to her spiel, Mother Gladstone decided not to hold her tongue any longer and just tell him like it was.

"Boy, you got to know that boy is gay and that girl is just using him to cover up some stuff. Just stupid," she said, throwing his hand away from her and walking away.

Left standing in the hallway, not moved by the fact that Mother Gladstone had recognized Mike being gay, Keithe couldn't believe her other revelation. If it were true, Keithe couldn't wait to figure out just what Kenya was hiding.

***

Mike had listened to the voice mail and figured it was typical of Keithe.

"That figures!" Mike said with a loud, drunken voice as he pushed seven on his phone's QWERTY pad.

It was one of Mike's pet peeves with Keithe: he never did *not* support him. But he could never just come out and support him, either.

From the very beginning of Mike figuring out his own change in his manhood as a teenager, Keithe simply shrugged his shoulders at his friend's findings and kept his beat. Even then Mike would have loved a dialogue with his best friend. Especially since his family gave him no time at all.

Mike's parents had long ago kicked him to the curb because of his choice in living a homosexual lifestyle. He was sure that even if he told him that he was bisexual, to make his lifestyle sound as if he wanted to give a woman a real chance, it wouldn't make a difference. They were so-called devout Christians and instead of just hating the sin, it seemed as if they actually hated him as well. Years ago he had even shown up at his father's church on a Sunday, just to attend worship. Before his tailor-made suit could hit the padded wood seat, one of the ushers had escorted Mike to the back of the church, to his father's office.

When he walked in his father had been wiping his reading glasses on his robe. He didn't even bother to look up as he heard his office door open.

"Whatcha doing here? Didn't I tell you not to show ya face 'til ya ready?" The good pastor looked through his spectacles he held in the air, in front of the lamp. "Are you ready?"

Mike had no idea he would be put on the spot when his every intention only had to do with hearing the

Word on first Sunday. "I was . . . I was. Um, I just wanted to come visit and see if we could talk," he managed to get out as he stood tall with one hand in his pocket.

"You mean, talking like when you called to tell your mother and me about you being gay?" The reverend threw his words at his first born. "Now you have the nerve to come face to face. Huh? After you done gone and tore your mama's heart apart?" Tears had trampled the wrinkles under the pastor's eyes. With a trembling lip he said, "Unless you've come to repent and to throw yourself at the mercy of the good Lord, it's best you go." He hadn't bother to finalize his sentence with "son," as he usually did.

When Mike took one step forward, wanting to embrace his father as he had all of his life, he was halted once he saw all of the anger that his father's face held. The fist by his father's side let him know that it was an anger that wouldn't die that day.

"I mean it. I can't preach God's Word and accept what you're doing," he cried openly.

"But I'm not asking you to, Dad. I'm asking you to be my dad. Like always. Nothing has changed." Mike hadn't wanted to leave without trying.

If it had not been for his desk in front of him, the slap he needed to land on his son's cheek would have done so. Mike knew it.

"Boy, don't you stand in my face, talking about nothing has changed. Listen here; you want to do all the gay pride stuff? Do it outside of the church, do it on your own time. But I will never accept it. Your sister got three babies by three different men." He pointed as if she were down the hall. "I don't accept that mess just like I don't accept your mess. It's tight, but it's right," he said through drying tearstains.

Mike knew, even after all of those years, his father's hatred toward his lifestyle had been the reason he had gone back and forth with who he was. He did try to detour his mannerisms, his likes, and his preferences in life. Mike knew when he declared at one point that he wanted to walk the straight and narrow, he only did so thinking his family would receive him once more. When he realized that road had become too hard to travel back down, it wasn't long before Mike reverted to what he said came natural for him.

It came natural to him, but it wasn't like he wanted it to. Mike knew if there was a choice given, he'd certainly choose to be straight. He wanted to be straight. He just didn't know how.

His reality was that he didn't get it himself nor did he have the answers. When people would ask him, he didn't know if he was born "that way" or if it was a learned act. He definitely knew it wasn't because of being molested as others had claimed linked them to the lifestyle. It wasn't that it couldn't happen. He just knew it wasn't the case with him.

And then when it came to being born gay, Mike knew deep within, if he believed in God's Word, the Bible, he knew God hadn't formed him in his mother's belly as a gay man. If anything, it had to be a spirit that latched itself to him.

All Mike knew was that he was drawn to the likes of men. It wasn't that he didn't like women, but he knew it was only for their beauty and their softness. Just the same, his likes for men were because of their handsomeness and hardness.

"Why . . ." Mike stopped short, not wanting to name the Lord as the recipient of his question. He knew he wasn't angry with God because he truly believed God loved him regardless. Mike just felt if he didn't bring up his lifestyle to God . . . if he didn't put it on the altar, he could remain doing what he did.

He sat at his kitchen table with his fifth mixed drink in his hand.

"I pay tithes . . . I get in the prayer line . . . I worship." He still didn't want to acknowledge God in his personal battle. "I just want to be happy as well." *Hiccup.*

Staring deep into his drink, Mike felt nothing. The more he wanted to clarify why he deserved to be happy, the more his tongue became heavy in his mouth.

"I claps my hands and stumps my feet." Mike gagged while tears ran down his face. "Why am I miserable?"

Being reared in the church, Mike couldn't even pinpoint when he'd made the jump to a lifestyle his father preached against Sunday after Sunday. He'd sat on the pews, he'd played the drums and sang in the choir. Whatever his parents needed of him, he was always willing and able.

There were sacrifices he too had to make as a child growing up with both parents in full-time ministry. He and his sister both. The majority of the time it was just the two of them, at home alone, figuring out a way to make life roll while their parents helped other families.

Sundays were mandatory days for them to be at church. In the summer, whenever the church doors were open, they were required to be there. But during the school year, things changed.

Because his father wanted better for his kids and believed in education, he allowed Mike and his sister to stay home during the week when church services were going on. They would barely see their father after they left for school in the morning. Sometimes not even before they'd rest their head at night. For that, Mike missed a lot of one-on-one time with his father.

There was always someone the good reverend would have to go pray for, a hospital visit that just couldn't wait. But in the same breath, there was always a fishing trip that had to get postponed, or a lesson on shaving or an afternoon rebuilding engines that was always skipped over. For that, a lot of Mike's time would be spent between his sister and mother.

"He didn't care! He didn't care!" Mike nearly jumped out of his seat, getting angry trying to figure out who to blame. "What was I s'posed to do?" He knew it was too late to go backward.

"How was I s'posed to know?" Mike gave in to his tears as he tumbled his glass over and laid his head face down in the mixed liquor.

It was too much. Mike couldn't put his finger on it. Who was he to truly blame? And if he knew, would he really want to blame them?

Chapter Sixteen

"Vicky! Oh my goodness," Stoney yelled as she saw her friend who had been a friend like no other. Running toward the forty-something woman who had been talking to a bridal consultant at the quaint establishment in the city, Stoney held her arms open wide.

Vicky squinted her eyes. "Are you kidding me? Stoney?" The two embraced. "Look at you, Stone Cold! Still got those hips, but, honey, you look fabulous," Vicky spoke with a high-pitched tone, not her own natural one. "What happened to your coffee-brown stockings?" They laughed.

"Hush, Vicky with a Y. You are so silly. Oooh, I miss you so." Stoney leaned in for another hug. "Look at you, girl!" Stoney squealed.

Vicky didn't look as if she had aged at all in the three years since they had laid eyes on one another. Her short bob had grown out to a long and flowing length. A silver sparkling headband pushed her hair off of her face and showed off her brown and clear skin. The smile that Stoney remembered remained.

Vicky had had three babies and all before the age of twenty-five. By looking at the ageless glow she held, she would have to be asked because no one would know she was a mother to teenagers.

"You remember Mercy." Stoney pointed to her sister on the other side of the store, who had already begun her appointment with her bridal consultant. "My sister? She's getting married in two months. Last minute fittings for us. Wait!" Stoney yelled and jumped back at the same time.

When she realized she had caused a scene when all eyes landed on her, Stoney threw a hand over her mouth.

"Stoney," Vicky laughed. "What is it?"

"Why are you in here, girl? Tell me. Tell me." Stoney waited. Even though Vicky was years older than her, there was such a bond between them that made up for the space in between.

The years that had separated them came only when Stoney uprooted from Dallas and moved to Houston to be closer to her mother, after their own reunion. But even their telephone relationship stopped after Vicky had given Mike another chance at her heart and he did with it as he pleased.

With Vicky and Mike attending the same church for years, even before Stoney joined, Vicky had dated Mike once before. During that time it was only through the grapevine she had found out about him having had a questionable lifestyle. Never confronting him about it, she just called off their dating and pushed her crush to the back burner.

Light years ahead and Mike gave the illusion of how he still had feelings for Vicky. He apologized for not being upfront about his life before and all but swore he had changed long ago and just hadn't shared it with her. Holding on to hope, Vicky had given him another chance. That chance left her depressed and pushing everyone out of her life, including Stoney.

"I'm getting married, Stoney!" The two squealed again and hugged out of reaction. "Oh, Stoney, he is so wonderful. Can you believe it? I'm getting married. A single woman with three—count 'em: one, two, three—chil'ren." Vicky hadn't lost her humor. They laughed.

"Hey now. You're a good catch, honey chil'. Don't front. You are an ophthalmologist . . . You did it, Vicky. You gave God all your worries, heartache, and pain."

"And He gave me another chance," Vicky said with tears in her eyes. "I wish he were here so you could meet him. You'd love Robert. He's goofy just like us, chil'." Vicky fished around in her purse and pulled out a picture of the two.

Taking the picture in her hand Stoney looked at it and then used it as a fan. "Hmmm sookie, sookie, now. He might be goofy, be he is a hot tamale, baby. You did well, Vicky."

"You know, what can I say?" Vicky turned her nose up nonchalantly and laughed. "Look, give me your address while I have you here. I want you to come to my wedding. No . . . I want you to come to everything." Vicky was already lost in her purse looking for a pen to write with when Mercy walked over and brushed up against her stepsister.

"Oh, Mercy." Stoney hadn't seen her walking up. "You scared me, girl. You remember my friend Vicky, don't you?"

"Of course." Mercy leaned in toward the taller and older woman. "Congratulations. You're getting married too?" Mercy smiled.

Beginning with a nod, Vicky couldn't hold back her smile. Every time she thought about Robert it was an automatic gesture. "Yes. After all the frogs I kissed . . . and we won't even talk about the last one." She handed a pad and pen to Stoney to write her info on. "I'm finally getting married." The two took a moment and admired one another's rings.

"He wouldn't even let me go to the jeweler with him. Wouldn't take any ideas nor would he let the kids in on it." Vicky snickered. "He knew they'd tell as soon as they could." She talked with her hand, so proud of her possession. "I taught them babies well," she told on herself and laughed.

Mercy stood there admiring Vicky's story. Still in love with her own ring as well, it was just the idea of her having to push for the wedding, push for the date, push for the ring.

Instead of second-guessing if that meant Grant was just not that into her, Mercy took it from the aspect of him not having funds except for the little bit from side jobs he did. She had told herself that it was the least she could do since Grant had had their son the majority of the time.

With a thoughtful look on her face, Mercy added a smile as she began to think of all the changes that would be made soon. With her being back in Dallas full time now, Grant could go back to school and find a full-time job. Even more than that, they would be able to expand on their family. With all the pain it caused her heart, Mercy decided to push all the negatives to the back of her thinking.

"Okay." Vicky took the paper back.

"Nice seeing you again, Vicky," Mercy said as she slowly turned to walk off, when she saw her consultant waiting for her.

"I'll be right there, Mercy," Stoney said, and turned her attention back to Vicky.

"Girl, but yeah. I'm so sorry I distanced myself away. But when Mike took me through all that drama, I didn't know what else to do. I mean I had lost my mind," Vicky explained. "It wasn't that I was desperate, but I believed that he loved me and wanted to marry me. But then the nut goes off one day and tells me he made a mistake. Again!"

Stoney stood with arms folded, thankful she finally was able to get Vicky's side of the story. She had been angry, hurt, and confused when she had heard through the grapevine what Mike had done . . . the life he'd chosen, over Vicky.

"I was so embarrassed that, girl," Vicky tried to whisper, "I pleaded with him to just go through with the wedding, and for us to just be together since everyone knew we were an item. I knew it wouldn't work, but, girl, I was devastated. The enemy even tried to get me to kill myself. I neglected my kids and everything. It wasn't until my cousin pushed me to see a counselor . . . Robert."

"God is good, Vicky." Stoney grabbed her friend by the hand.

"Girl, he is amazing. I don't hate Mike. I just hate what he takes himself and others through. He just needs to be real with himself. If he is gay, he just needs to accept that and stop—"

"Uh-uh." Stoney dropped her friend's hand in protest. She crossed her arms once again. "Uh-uh. Don't even say it. He can't accept what God doesn't allow. Girl, he needs to choose what God he serves and realize who made him. It's a spiritual warfare."

"I agree, but it does no one any good until he recognizes it for himself. I forgive him, Stoney." Vicky caught a direct glance into Stoney's eyes. "I'm sorry I just left you out there alone with your feelings. I should have tried harder to contact you after I healed." Vicky held her friend close. "You have to forgive him and love him right where he is, Stoney. Just look at the friend he was to you. You know you can't take that away from him?" Vicky asked with her eyes.

Stoney was softening. She didn't want to. For one, Mike had kept who he was away from her. Two: she didn't believe in same sex anything.

As if she were reading Stoney's mind, Vicky reminded Stoney of how Mike was there for her regardless. Even through the times when Stoney wanted and tried to take her own life.

"You have to forgive, Stoney," Vicky said as she squeezed her friend's hand and looked in her eyes through her own tears.

There was no promise Stoney was about to give to Vicky. Yes, Mike had been a friend. But within that friendship he only gave her what he wanted her to know about him. It would take God to heal her from the betrayal. Either way, Stoney knew she wasn't ready to ask for the help.

Chapter Seventeen

"Thank you for saying yes," Keithe said, wishing it were for different circumstances other than dinner.

Honestly feeling she would do herself a disservice if she hadn't agreed to meet him, Kenya was more than honored to dine with Deacon Morgan. Especially since it had nothing to do with the divorce group. Ever since their telephone conversation a week ago, her heart had softened from being afraid to let him in. Above anything she now wished she had given him a chance.

Maybe all along she needed Keithe to just be bold with his intentions toward her. With him sharing how he did indeed like her and want to get to know her better, Kenya was able to take in the realness of their awkward moments. Her womanly desire for a man had trumped her doubting herself. The hash tag she felt was plastered on her forehead, which read, "confused," seemed to be lifted with Keithe.

"I'm very flattered, Deacon Morgan." Kenya had finally let her guard down; her insecurities about Keithe liking her were finally being received by the single, saved, and, with her hair out of its ponytail holder, sassy woman.

"That just made my night." Keithe smiled from ear to ear and beckoned for the waiter. "We're ready to order."

Waiting for their food preparation, the two chatted over nothing in particular. There was minimal talk about church, which was Keithe's desire. He wanted to push Kenya to her limits with him. He wanted to know what it was about Mike and what it wasn't about him.

He was ready to lay it all on the line with Kenya. He just hoped she was ready. Especially with Mother Gladstone revealing that Kenya had secrets herself. In those secrets, Keithe hoped to find that her interests really weren't into Mike as it had appeared.

Once their entrees arrived and their waiter asked for the last time if the duo needed anything else, Keithe didn't hesitate. He offered Kenya to place her hand in his and prayed over their hearty meal.

"So now that I officially have you to myself . . ." Keithe smiled.

"Watch it, watch it, Deacon," Kenya oozed out and smiled as she took a sip of flavored tea.

Cutting into his steak, Keithe took a few bites and admired the view in front of him. Placing his knife to the side, Keithe was ready for more. The advice Mother Gladstone had been whispering to him behind the church corners started to get to him. He felt it was time to make a solid move.

Keithe had wanted to talk to Mike to see if they could smooth things over. He wanted his friend to know that nothing had changed about how he felt about Kenya, and just because he moved out of haste, it wasn't going to stop him from doing what his heart desired. When he hadn't heard back, Keithe did debate if he should proceed, but then he prayed about it and felt solace.

"I like you, Kenya. I asked you here tonight because I know that you knew," he emphasized, "that I liked you." He smirked. When he saw the smile vanish from her face, Keithe eased off his firmness.

"I'm sorry. I thought that was a given. I like you too," Kenya said. She no longer wanted to run just to avoid Keithe and his feelings for her.

"I can't tell," Keithe responded, leaving Kenya's mouth wide open. "Seriously. Is everything between us okay? It's like we went from partners to you avoiding me. Then the next thing I know, you and Mike are dating."

"He asked," Kenya flipped out of her mouth and continued eating, knowing she'd put a messy little bug in his ear.

With his eyebrows raised, Keithe said, "Okay. I move slow. I pray about things." He shrugged and picked up his knife once more. He wanted her to know in what order he walked. "Unfortunately that's all null and void now." Keithe took a bite of his medium-well steak. After a few chews, Keithe spoke on his real motive for their dinner. "So how's it going with you two, anyway?" He needed to pray.

"Shouldn't you know? Mike is your friend. I'm sure guys talk." Kenya wanted to test the waters to see if the two had patched things up.

Keithe figured it was time to come clean. "Kenya. Just like I told Mike, I really care for the both of you. Now . . . I don't know how much Mike has told you . . ." He was sure he hadn't told her much.

Kenya tensed. She never thought that far ahead. Sitting in front of the man who had a crush on her, who was talking about someone she was dating, Kenya held her breath.

"I don't know what he has told you, but Mike and I have been friends even before our teenage years." Keithe stammered, not really sure what confessing Mike's life would do for him. One thing he knew it could do was to save Kenya heartbreak and heartache. "And I just don't want you to get hurt . . . either of you to get hurt." He stressed the latter.

Not wanting to hear anything remotely close to what she figured would come out of Deacon Morgan's mouth, Kenya rushed the conversation once her defense mechanism hit an all-time high.

"Then whatever you are about to say, why don't you just keep it to yourself. Especially if it's about Mike." Kenya pushed her back into the cushion of the chair.

"Because I doubt he will let you know. That's why. And that's the truth," Keithe responded and sat back himself. "I know he should be the one to tell you that he—"

"Excuse me, but I'm not about to marry the man. I'm not sleeping with him and, lastly, I don't think it's any of your business. Who I date has nothing to do with you. I don't even know why you are doing this." Kenya's defense was skyrocketing. She was nervous and no longer cared if anyone around her noticed.

"Even if I care not to see you hurt, Kenya?" Keithe wanted to obey her wishes to the fullest.

"Yes, Keithe. I mean, did you think about Mike when you brought me here, ready to tell me about him being homosexual? Just how much do you care about Mike? What kind of friend are you to tell his business?" Kenya felt bittersweet about how she was treating Keithe. For him to go to great lengths, trying to protect her and Mike, he had actually been a great friend.

Keithe scrunched his eyebrows and opened his mouth to speak but Kenya wouldn't allow him to respond. If she had allowed him to interject, he would have told her he hadn't gotten to the point about Mike being homosexual.

"And now what? Now that you've spread Mike just a little bit thinner, now what? You don't know what it's like." She tried her best to whisper but felt her own personal emotions to gather. "All you so-called Christians are the same." Kenya pushed back her chair. "Have you even thought just maybe some people don't want to be gay? . . . No one wants to live a homosexual lifestyle. It's not easy. Believe it; it's not easy to sleep at night. Crying yourself to sleep every night doesn't cut it."

Keithe tried to catch her words she had slung at him at a fast speed. He couldn't tell what caused her to be so angry. But one thing was for sure: she knew more than he thought she knew.

"Kenya. I . . . I'm sorry if I've offended you. But, unless Mike told you he was homosexual . . ." He looked down at the table, embarrassed for her. "I haven't even said a word about . . ." He didn't want to say it. "How did you know?"

A blank look spread on Kenya's face. She grabbed her mouth with both of her hands and the color in her face went away.

"If you know that Mike is gay, why are you dating him?" Keithe wanted Kenya to fill in the blanks but knew it wouldn't happen.

Before he could say another word, Kenya removed herself from the table and disappeared. Left with two unfinished dinners, sitting in the middle of the restaurant, Keithe couldn't believe what had just happened.

Chapter Eighteen

Michelle slammed her Bible shut. She had been reading Corinthians, refreshing herself of her godly duties. She may not have spent the majority of her life believing and worshipping God, but as she often said, "I came to Jesus as soon as I could, just as I was."

She had been in Dallas for two weeks, rolling right in with the month of March, and still hadn't gotten the nerve to tell Keithe she had made his bachelor grounds her hunting grounds. Making Stoney swear to do the same, Michelle knew she'd have to come clean if she wanted Keithe back and that was that.

"What in the world?" She looked around her temporary dwelling that couldn't match her home back in Houston, even if she brought in the most experienced decorator Dallas housed. It was a top-of-the-line, four-bedroom condominium in the Highland Park area; however, it still wasn't as elegant as her home in Houston.

Michelle couldn't believe she had made such a drastic move. Was it the fear of being alone? "I did this, for real, for real?" she questioned herself, when she really honed in on why she uprooted herself from life as she knew it.

When she was in a short-lived relationship with the deacon at church, her desires, her want for Keithe had been moved to the back burner, if existent at all. It really wasn't until Deek, her ex-beau, delivered the news to Michelle over sushi that he was going back to his ex-wife. Or something like that.

Michelle had to admit, all she knew was that he had said something like, "My ex-wife . . . want me . . . I'm going, blah, blah, blah." *Why not,* sarcastically was what Michelle would have said had she been able to get it out of her seaweed-filled mouth. She opted rather to chew the remains, take a sip of water, and walk away gracefully from the table.

And that night while at home alone, not a single tear had dropped from her eyes. She simply reflected on all she had done in her lifetime. She had been a vengeful woman; out to hurt others before they'd hurt her. She just figured repercussions always made their rounds.

Now Michelle gloated on her being changed. She loved God for giving her the joy that her money never gave her. Money couldn't buy the joy of the Lord, that was for sure. She now realized joy, unspeakable joy, was there even when there was nothing to be happy about. Which was the emotional state she was currently in.

Sitting on the edge of her bed, gathering her black sheer Berkshire pantyhose at the toe, Michelle wasn't about to allow moving to another town pull her away from a God who allowed her to right her wrongs. Especially when it came to being able to proudly be a mom to Stoney.

In reality she had only been a mother for the past three years. Her C-section scar may have been in place for twenty-four years but that was the extent of being a mother. But with everything in her, Michelle now tried to show and tell Stoney just how much she loved and adored her. She knew without a doubt she would give her life for her daughter's if it ever came to that.

Yep. Michelle was amazed herself, but that was just how much she was thankful to God for allowing her another chance in being a mother. Even after twenty-one years.

For the better part of her luck, Michelle was excited about moving to the city just in the nick of time. Her church's National Women's Convention was being held in the city. Snapping her figure-shaping pantyhose in place, Michelle moved throughout her closet, looking for her best ensemble to suit her mood.

"You a mess, Kendra." Gracie slowed her pace so that her best friend could keep up. "You know good and well you need to drop a couple of inches in your heel. We are not in our thirties any longer." Gracie held on to her Bible tote, balancing herself with one hand on her hip. "As a matter of fact, we aren't in our forties either."

With a physical fitness background, both ladies could easily be mistaken for being in their late forties when indeed they were over that hump by ten years. With both knocking on sixty, they always gave their signature high-five to celebrate their fierceness.

Gracie, knowing her shoes were a tad bit too tight, walked a bit farther and came to a coffee shop located inside of the convention center. Not wanting to tattletale on herself about her own choice of footwear, Gracie put pep in her step hoping to find available seats.

Blowing out a breath through her neutral-colored, glossed lips, Gracie shook her head. "You knew those shoes were too tall, chil'."

"What? Oh hush. I didn't ever say I was gonna wear them all day," Kendra fought back. "Girl, this is so exciting. The Clark Sisters? Being able to meet them after the gospel musical will be too much, honey. Ouch."

Kendra enjoyed her time with her best friend, Gracie. Being full time in the ministry, a bishop's wife, and speaker herself, Kendra enjoyed time spent with her best girlfriend. "But for the time being, I need to rest these feet. Ohhhhh, girl."

Always a "thick sistah" even in her younger years, after Kendra contracted HIV in her thirties, her body form changed. Those who knew the two ladies knew that their physiques had traded places. Kendra was now the thinner of the two, though shapely, and Gracie wore the hippy title with no complaints from her husband, Marcus.

Though still shapely, Kendra made sure she watched her diet and still put in as much time at her home gym as she could. Being a socialite in the Christian community, it was imperative that Kendra always looked and felt her best, especially when trying to encourage others.

Kendra had battled depression when her first husband died. From there she fought her own war to live. When she refused to either eat right or take her medication, Kendra's body eased into a coma. Stuck in a dark world, with no way out, it took Kendra depending on her relationship with God to find her way back to life. On the other side, Kendra came through as pure gold, not knowing she was pregnant with her late husband's baby, Mercy, all the while.

Now, years later, with the great help of medication, Kendra's HIV was under control.

Gracie shook her head and puckered her lips. "You are too old to be that ghetto, Kendra." Gracie referred to her friend stopping midstride and taking her shoes off. "Don't stop here, chil'. Wait until we get up there to the table and chair." Gracie looked back at her friend and took the first step toward the coffee shop setup.

Patrons of the women's convention brought out big hats, fashioned heels, and all the Donna Vinci's that could fit in one room. Kendra stuck to her St. John's because she loved the preciseness of how it fit her size-ten figure. Gracie tried her best to purchase all the Donna Vinci's and the replicas she could.

"Look. That lady is leaving the table. There are two seats. . . ." Gracie couldn't believe what must have been luck for them to find a seat so soon. With all the dressed-up women walking around the convention with slippers on their feet, Gracie just knew it would be a battle. "Oh my . . ."

It hadn't been but three years since they'd last laid eyes on her, but still . . . *Why is she in our hometown?* was all Gracie could think.

Turning quickly, hoping she could get Kendra's attention before she saw the woman for herself, it was inevitable. The two women ran right into one another.

"Gracie! Oh, goodness. Honey, are you okay?" Kendra asked, pulling her church bag back onto her shoulder once she realized Gracie hadn't been the one she'd bumped into.

"Are you two okay? Look who's heeeeeere." Gracie slid the words out of the side of her mouth as she moved to face the woman who once dated both their husbands and eventually had a baby by Kendra's husband. It was Stoney's mother, Michelle.

Before Kendra could respond, Michelle had bounced back from the clash and gained her composure. Gathering her items from the floor and readjusting her purse strap, Michelle had gotten close enough to verbalize the trio seeing one another once again.

"Good morning, ladies." Michelle hadn't actually seen them coming. If she had, she would have opted to leave through the other entrance. "Don't worry, I'm leaving,"

Michelle acknowledged, hoping to leave peacefully. Even though their last encounter hadn't led any of them behind bars, Michelle was still embarrassed about several incidents she had brought the two women.

Kendra and Gracie parted, giving Michelle a small aisle of space to allow her through.

"Wait," was the first thing that rushed from Kendra's mouth. Not realizing her own outburst, she knew it had to be God ready to work through her. Her calling was just that: a ready, willing, and able vessel, no matter the circumstance.

With her own eyebrows raised, Gracie waited patiently to see what would come next. Because of the background the women had with one another, ranging back close to thirty years, Kendra stood in shock of what to do next. So in sync with her friend, her ace, her prayer partner, Kendra looked to Gracie for validation. Raising her eyebrows, the invisible nudge she received from Gracie as only she knew what it was, Kendra continued.

"Don't leave. Have coffee with us. Please?" Kendra managed to say to Michelle.

Growing older definitely brought along wisdom, if one allowed it. Kendra had gone through too many of life's ups and downs to keep things that belonged in the past to invade her life now. Heaven forbid, her future.

Turning to face the two women, Michelle squeezed her clutch under her arm and shifted her body on her left hip. With a weary look on her face, Michelle wanted to know the catch.

Giving herself a once-over in thought, Michelle could envision coffee on her white knit suit if the two ladies went to lay hands on her. And not in a holy way. With that thought Michelle was about to take a rain check until Gracie said, "No strings attached, Michelle. I mean, I know my husband's not going anywhere."

"And I know Bishop's not going anywhere." Kendra paused. "He's too old, for one." Kendra laughed to break the ice.

When all three laughed in unison, they moved toward the awaiting table, with Michelle wishing she could say the same about her husband . . . who she no longer had.

Before they knew it, hours had passed with them sitting in a God-ordained setting. Neither Kendra nor Gracie would have ever guessed Michelle had changed her stripes. From the story she'd shared with the ladies who used to be her nemeses, Michelle had stuck to the saved life once she and her husband divorced. The trio sat together showing that all things indeed happened for a reason. Kendra, never missing a beat, and shared with the ladies what her mother had once shared with her.

"God allows us to live long enough to straighten up, repent, and ask for forgiveness. He allows us to right our wrongs before we leave this earth."

"Yes, He does," Michelle agreed. "Thank you ladies for inviting me for coffee. This is still weird." Michelle chuckled, losing her nervousness.

"Only to unbelievers," Gracie added, grabbing Michelle's free hand. "This is something that only God could have ordained."

"Exactly." Kendra sealed the deal.

"And, ladies, if you two could please not bring up my obsession with my husband . . . my ex." Michelle playfully rolled her eyes at the two. "Especially to Stoney.

She thinks I'm a little off-kilter with the whole idea. But I prayed about it and I—"

"Did you really?" Kendra asked with deep questioning brows. "Did you ask God if you were truly making the right decision for you? I mean, Michelle, you are a beautiful woman, a judge, honey. And you just up and moved from your city to a man who left you?"

Michelle didn't take it personally. Stoney had always shared how blunt Kendra was. Why sugarcoat the truth?

"Of course." Michelle hunched her shoulders, knowing she hadn't wholeheartedly prayed to God about her actions.

"And what did He say? I'm saying, in His approval?" Gracie questioned with her chin resting on her hands.

Without answering, Michelle just pursed her lips together and nodded. She had felt so at peace with what Gracie had asked that she knew it was questioned out of sincerity of her heart. Not even aware of the tears that had built up in her ducts, when she blinked her tears made their home on her cheeks. "I just don't know how to do this." Michelle no longer tried to hold in her cry. "I've been manipulating people and my relationships all of my life. N . . . now, I have no one. I'm afraid of being alone . . . of dying alone."

The two ladies moved their chairs in closer to their new friend. "Don't do that to yourself, Michelle," Kendra insisted. "You are not alone. Just think about it. This very hour God had you sitting in this convention center . . . and He had me wearing these too little shoes." The three laughed through the tears.

"God has a way of doing things, of bringing people together. Even if you don't have Keithe . . . it may look crazy to some on the outside, but you do have us." Kendra was sincere.

"Ken's right. You have us. It doesn't matter if you're in Houston. That's nothing but a hop, skip, and a jump for us. And plus, we love to come down and shop," Gracie said.

As if her favorite subject had been announced, Michelle straightened up. "Oh, I can tell. 'Cause, honey, y'all are wearing them hats." Michelle gathered a napkin and wiped her tears away.

"Girl, you ain't seen nothing. I'm gonna take you to Ella's Boutique and let you meet my personal stylist. Mrs. Fannie keeps me stepping, baby!" They laughed. "Y'all need to get up off the mushy stuff. We have sat here too long and missed the preaching; let's not miss the midnight musical. Y'all have y'all tickets?" Gracie asked, never being able to rid her speech of her Southern drawl. Mainly because she never tried.

"And you know it," Michelle and Kendra shared.

Before allowing the women on either side of her to stand from their seats, Michelle grabbed their hands and prayed. "Lord. What can I say? You are remarkable. There was a time I didn't know who I was, and surely didn't know whose I was. But you are so merciful and loving. And you have been there all the time. I thank you for these two ladies and I pray that you bless our union. In whichever direction you would have us to go, Lord, I pray you forever stay in the midst. I'm blessed by you. I'm in awe of you and your loving kindness toward me. Dear God, I pray for your presence to forever remain in my heart and the hearts of these beautiful women. Amen."

"Amen," Gracie said as she raised her head.

"I couldn't have said it better, Missionary," Kendra joked around as all three ladies stood and gathered their belongings.

Chapter Nineteen

"There you two are." Mercy unfolded her feet she had had tucked under her body as she stood from the love seat. Walking toward Grant as he entered the house carrying a sleeping Grant Jr., Mercy was all smiles seeing her two favorite men. Grant Jr. was the cutest little dark-skinned baby with naturally curly hair covering his head. There was no doubt he looked just like his dad.

As Grant closed his eyes for more than just a blink, Mercy felt unnecessary heat rise between the two of them. It was if she was getting under her fiancé's skin for absolutely no reason at all.

"Anything wrong?" she questioned and offered to take the baby from her soon to be hubby. Their nuptials were just a month away, in April. Instead of April bringing showers, as the old wives' tale stated, Mercy was looking for April to ring in holy matrimony. But with the attitude Grant was slinging, the old wives' tale looked as though it would stand.

"I got him." Grant snatched away and walked quickly around Mercy, headed toward the second bedroom in the pool house, which was their son's room.

Deciding to wait until her fiancé returned to their living quarters, Mercy picked up the Sanyo remote and pointed it toward the television. Leaving the picture on but muting the sound, Mercy stood in her space and waited with arms folded. Mercy had had enough of playing the guessing game. She wanted answers and she wanted them now.

Two steps into the living space and Grant said, "Um, uh-uh," with scrunched eyebrows. Rolling the sleeves of his shirt up, Grant stood still until he mastered the task of the material lying three inches above his wrist. "Not tonight, Mercy. And what? You don't have any wedding stuff you need to do?" He took a step to the right but stopped short once she leaned on her left leg, letting him know she would follow his every step.

"Then when, Grant? You've been standoffish, not talking to me at all. I thought I was the one who was to have wedding jitters." Mercy flung her arms in his direction, wanting to strangle the young man she loved.

Waiting for something, anything Grant could offer, Mercy grabbed a strand of her natural and twisted hair. It was a nervous tick she'd picked up while in college. Mercy needed to know what was going on with Grant.

They'd met in high school where they started out as just friends. He made her laugh and didn't make her feel different because she wasn't afraid to let people know how much she loved God. She told him so herself. Grant had backed her 100 percent. Especially since he proclaimed the same. But now it seemed as though those times were few and far in between. There had been no laughs . . . and way too many tears.

He knew she was waiting. Still, nothing. Grant still stood with his arms crossed and no response. He was thinking. Grant knew he couldn't keep living the way he did. He no longer felt the way he had years ago toward Mercy. Things had changed, which was why he knew he had to talk to Mercy, sooner rather than later. But at the moment, he didn't have the nerve.

For once, he wasn't going to lie. Anyone from the outside looking in could tell that Grant did have jitters. But not about marriage. Just about marrying her.

His love for Mercy hadn't changed because she was the mother of his child. She was his first love. They'd even made their first major mistake together: premarital sex. But even through that, God had blessed them with a beautiful son.

Grant was an awesome father. To be all he could be for his child was a task he'd take on no matter what. Which was what he did while Mercy finished up her studies. That was what started it all . . . Mercy still able to live out her dream while he sat home, at her home, playing "Mr. Mom."

It wasn't until he saw the questionable tears in Mercy's eyes that Grant's heart began to melt. He felt his palms get sweaty and placed them in his blue jean pockets to soak up some of the wetness.

"Look, Mercy . . ." Walking closer to his baby's mother, Grant knew his attitude had come from things out of his control. He had been in the same predicament Mercy was now in: blind-sided by love. Unfortunately it just hadn't been with her.

When they'd gotten pregnant with Junior, it was an unwritten rule that Mercy *had* to finish school. Her parents would have it no other way. With him only working part time, not enrolled at school himself, her family saw fit for him to move into their quarters and raise the baby. No questions, only requests.

At first Grant didn't mind because he was still young, twenty-one, with no stable family support and no money. But as he got older, Grant realized he was going nowhere fast and sitting around waiting for Mercy's next move. Then he started going out more, making new friends in different crowds. Just like that, one thing had led to another.

He was now twenty-four, a grown man, experiencing different things that life had to offer. Grant even wanted to complete studies he had long ago left behind. But how could he? He was expected to be everything to Grant Jr. that Mercy could not be.

"I guess we really should just talk. Maybe you should sit down." He made the mistake and glanced at the television that had been muted.

"What is it?" Mercy saw the worried look on Grant's face and turned to stand by his side.

When the news channel panned a house fire on the other side of town, Grant squinted his eyes at the familiar surroundings the cameraman zoomed in on. When the camera set in on the street sign, he grabbed for the remote, shoving Mercy forward, almost knocking her off her feet.

"Grant!" Mercy was shocked and upset by his actions. Especially when she didn't know what was going on.

Grant glanced Mercy's way but only for a split second before he turned the sound up.

Standing in front of the television set, all it took was for Grant to hear the street name that all of the ruckus had been taking place on. When the reporter said the owner, who lived alone, had been rushed to the emergency room and had been in critical condition, Grant only went with what his heart was feeling at the time and it had nothing to do with Mercy. It took one swift move for him to get from in front of the television and out the front door.

With only a yell back to let Mercy know that it was one of his friends, Grant didn't bother kissing her cheek, nor looking back. If he had, he would have seen a confused, tearful, and heartbroken Mercy.

After one look at her engagement ring, Mercy walked back to the sofa, sat, and sobbed.

Chapter Twenty

"I guess this is a last good-bye, huh?" Mike held up a wine glass to his frequent visitor. "It's been nice, dude." That was it.

"Why would you say that? It doesn't have to be. Does it? I really don't want to leave . . . don't want to go through with it," Mike's young suitor said from his sitting position on the sofa. "I'm not gonna go through with it. I can't. I love you."

Mike thought he was about to drop his red wine all over his beige Berber carpet beneath his socked feet. Turning his back to the fireplace and facing his latest and greatest love, Mike held his breath.

"What did you say?" Mike asked.

"You know my situation," the youngster said. "But I don't want to go through with it."

"Yeah, but what does that have to do with me? Look." Mike set his drink down and forgot all about the good time he'd had only moments earlier. With the look on his young lover's face, Mike felt he was being a little too harsh.

He hadn't thought beyond their first encounter eight months earlier. To Mike it was all about just having fun, another fling. Enjoying his life the way he wanted to . . . answering to no one but God. And even then Mike was still having issues.

Feeling as if he was a little too rough Mike tried to change his tone. "Why would you switch up?" he asked.

"For me? I change like the wind and plus this life ain't easy."

Mike's latest tryst stood, upset that Mike's action was telling him more than he wanted to know. "You're saying that why? To get me out of your hair?" the young man asked.

"You're kidding me, right? No," Mike lied. He turned again and walked toward his enclosed patio. The only lighting that greeted Mike was the starts. Before he could turn to shut the sliding glass door, he stood face to face with someone he'd grown to admire. "We are men! Men don't love one another like this, man." Mike was infuriated with himself. He didn't even know what he was saying. Mike just knew he didn't wish this much confusion on anyone. Not even his enemies.

"Oh, so now you tell me? After all we've done . . ." The confused twenty-something tried to stare a hole in Mike through the dark. He was willing to stand the test of time with someone he felt he wanted to be with. "After you befriended me? After you shared with me who you really are?"

"Who am I?" Mike shot from his vocals. "Who am I, dude?" He pushed the young man, who could have easily been his own child's age had he done what his father wanted from him: marry and have babies. "One minute I worship God and everything He is . . ." Mike cried out. "Then the next minute I'm swearing against Him for not allowing me to know who I am. I don't know!" he yelled, crying out into the dark. "You don't want this." He slapped his own chest. "Because I don't even want it. I just don't know how to let it go." Mike's lip quivered as he lost his cool, falling into the closest lawn chair from the tears and the alcohol that had crowded his system.

The young man didn't know what to do. With Mike sharing his drunken, but true, feelings, he wanted further clarity. Yet and still, all the drama that was presenting itself still didn't detour him from what his heart felt, what his body felt. Walking over to an open chair right next to Mike, he sat in silence.

Mike said, "I . . . I'm just as confused as the next person, dude. If you can pull away from this . . ." He turned and looked into the young man's eyes. Sincerity ran across his face. "Do it. Some people are not going to share their innermost feelings about how they really feel about themselves . . . how they struggle . . . how they don't even hear God anymore." Mike closed his eyes and shook his head. "I get the stares, the whispers, and I try . . . I try to act as if it really doesn't matter. Like, I'm okay with being me, regardless. It's not the truth." He opened his eyes and looked back at the confused face looking back at him, only this time with a face full of tears. "I don't even want to be me, dude. Can you say you want to be you . . . the way you are?"

The young man just sat there, staring back at what could possibly be the older version of him one day. Would he be okay with what he'd done, how he'd disobeyed God's Word? Would his own children one day still want to be in his life? It was too much to think about. All he knew was that the present was what he wanted to focus on.

"I don't know. I know for now, you are who I want to be with." He turned his chair to the right in order to face Mike. "I can't . . ." He set a serious tone; he declared, "I won't allow you to just push me away that easily."

Fearing it was going to go in the direction he felt it would, Mike didn't know what else to do, but to just sit there. What else could he do? He had no doubt brought the drama on himself, yet again. Closing his eyes, Mike leaned his head back and prayed as he felt a tight hold and squeeze to his hand. The same squeeze Vicky had given him when he knew it would never work with her either.

Chapter Twenty-one

"I'm here!" Michelle yelled through the phone. "All moved in." She stood in the middle of one of her bedrooms, finally getting Stoney on the line. Knowing how important her daughter's studies were, Michelle didn't bother Stoney with the stress of her life. After initially letting her daughter know she had made her move, Michelle had been busy settling back into Dallas.

"Wow," was the only thing Stoney could say. She couldn't believe her mother was so lonely that she made a drastic decision: trailing her divorced husband to a different city.

Now living for the Lord, Michelle had outright left other men, married men and someone else's men, alone. All except her own. Or rather, her ex.

"I can't believe you did . . . that." So caught up in her midterm studies, it had finally hit Stoney. She wanted to be careful with her words but felt she wouldn't be doing her godly duty to help her mother if she played along.

"Stoney, you sound so blah. I told you I would." Michelle didn't hold as much fire about her decision as she once had. Conversations with Kendra and Gracie were making her see things differently. Yet and still she would at least give it a shot since she had made the full jump from Houston to Dallas. She had no choice but to make the best out of it.

"Yes. You did say you would. But I just can't believe you really did it." Stoney had taken a break from her research paper in order to talk with her mother. Swinging her glasses from her face, Stoney really wanted to be everything her mother needed since her mother went above and beyond to make up for all of their lost time.

"Ma, Pops divorced you. He moved from where you both had your beginning. Do you really think he will accept you with open arms? Wait . . . does he know? Have you even told him yet, because I've talked to him and—"

"And what?" Michelle straightened her stance.

"Uh. It's just, he hadn't mentioned you nor your moving there," Stoney responded.

Her shoulders slumped. Michelle was getting way too many negatives when it came to her quest to get Keithe back. During the impromptu girls' night out with Gracie and Kendra, the ladies had probed her with questions. It was as if God had put them up to asking questions that had been on her conscience. Now hearing she hadn't even been on Keithe's mind kicked her down another notch.

"No, he doesn't. Oh well, even if he doesn't, I'm here now. Anyway. When are you coming to town? Or do you plan to stay in Houston for spring break?"

Plans with her own new love interest had given her a reason to stay in Houston for a few days out of the week-long break. "I'm going to stay here for the beginning of the week. Since the wedding is getting closer, I'm coming down to close out some loose ends Mercy has. I want to help her out as much as I can."

Looking at the other line, which had clicked in, Michelle let out a groan and sent her ex-beau, Deek, to her voice mail. Not that she would listen to whatever

it was he had to say. But just so she could get his face
off of her display screen. He'd been calling repeatedly,
leaving messages; not one that Michelle had listened
to. As far as Michelle cared, he could just keep right
on calling. She was sure he wanted his key to his house
back. She'd ditched it so there was no need in calling
him back.

"Ugh. I wish that man would leave me alone. Hey,
Stoney. Dear, can you do me a favor? Can you please
call Deek and let him know I threw his key away, and
there is no need to call me ever again?"

"Mom?" Stoney questioned.

"Okay. Forget the last part, but please? Michelle
almost begged, knowing she wasn't strong enough to
hear anything that would come from the man she once
loved.

"Why not?" Stoney liked giving her mother a hard
time. "Sure, Mother." Stoney actually liked her mother's ex. She was just as saddened about the news of him
breaking it off with Michelle. Plus, she never got to say
her own good-bye. Giving him a call would give Stoney
the opportunity in doing so.

It was a given. The two women loved one another
very much. They crammed as much of twenty-plus
years as they could into the first year they were back
in one another's lives. They were happy. This was why
Stoney didn't want her mother to get her hopes up with
Keithe and fall into an unnecessary sadness.

"Mom." Stoney bit her lip, nervous but not backing
down. "I know you changed the subject but I wouldn't
be honoring you if I didn't speak my heart."

"I'm listening, Stoney." Michelle reluctantly listened.

Michelle had been slightly jealous of Stoney's relationship with God. To Michelle it seemed He left
His ear laid upon Stoney's lips when she prayed. The

connection Stoney had to God was an anointed one. Michelle did know that God loved her just the same but it was up to her to totally surrender and allow God to move completely into her heart.

"I love you," Stoney said.

Michelle giggled and said, "I know that, silly."

"Pops love you too. This is why I'm sure he felt the need to ask for a divorce."

"Devilment, Stoney!" Michelle teared up as she conjured up anything to say in order to stay away from releasing the curse word that was on the tip of her tongue. "God is not too keen on divorce."

"Nor is He too keen on adultery, battery, lying . . . but we all do it. You did it. To Pops," Stoney hated to say. "You know we are flesh. We are not perfect like God. We can try and Pops did. But, Mom, haven't you ever considered the fact that he just couldn't take any more? That there were no more emotions he could drain? Not even pain to hurt with? So instead of giving you the pain he felt, he let go."

Sniffles were heard on the other end. Michelle tried to wrap her head and her heart around the reality, but she couldn't. Keithe had told her that he forgave her. He still came around, and sometimes he still kissed her on the lips. Even a few months ago, she had persuaded him, seductively so, but she'd gotten him to spend the night. In her room . . . in her bed . . . under her sheets. So there had to be something there. Why else would he travel to Houston once a month? Sure, he came to see his parents, but . . . *Is that it?* Michelle silently questioned herself. "Fool," Michelle spoke aloud.

"Huh?" Stoney didn't understand.

"Oh nothing. Baby, let me let you go. I . . . I hear what you're saying. I really do. Just let me think. I need to clear these boxes that have been sitting here for far too long. I . . . I need to . . . Just let me call you back." She wanted to hang up, but Stoney wouldn't let her.

"Before you go and sulk, remember that Pops brought us together. It's deeper than what our natural eyes can see. 'Reason, season, or lifetime,'" Stoney recited. "You know the saying. If it had not been for God placing Pops in your life . . . in my life, we would have never connected." Stoney heard more sniffles on the other end and knew she was getting through to her mother. "As Christians we have to be careful how we plan our own way. You told me the story and only you know if it was God orchestrated, but you told me—"

"Okay, okay, Stoney. I get your point. I just want to talk to him. Really, really talk to him to see what the issues are."

You, is what Stoney wanted to shout through the phone but thought better than to add fuel to the fire. "Okay. Well. I hope you feel better. I will call you and let you know what Deek says."

"Thanks, dear," Michelle said before slamming her cordless phone into the receiver.

Chapter Twenty-two

"What's with the long face? You act as if you're not happy to see me, Kenya. Oops, I mean, Evangelist Kenya." Charlene used her relaxed tone with her counterpart. "Do I look that bad?" She gave herself a once-over. Dusting invisible particles from her thick blue jean dress, Charlene stood at Kenya's door waiting for an invite in.

Batting her eyes, not believing Charlene had the nerve to stand on her doorstep, all the anger Kenya wanted to throw the woman's way wouldn't leave her lips.

"Oh. Hi," Kenya shooed from her mouth and opened her front door wider to allow Charlene in. Unexpected as it was, Kenya thought she would have to fight her demons with Charlene somewhere else in the world . . . not in her very own city. Not in her very own home.

The two had been tag-team evangelists on their journey throughout the United States and beyond. Being the ones to render the sermons to the people, their own sins were brought into fruition by their giving the Word and not hearing the Word. On their year-long mission trip to Africa, it was always salvation the two women shared with the people. They preached on God's love, His healing, and His coming soon. Both preached about how a relationship with God is imperative in order to see the Father. However, hardly, if ever, did they preach about lust, sex, or the sins of the flesh.

Kenya got caught up, as people usually say when the time comes and guilt was felt. At least that was what Kenya felt. She had been feeling guilty about her actions even thought she hadn't seen it coming.

Being on the road for missions with her mentor, Evangelist Charlene Morrison, Kenya felt there was nothing she couldn't share with her. Even about her dating life. With no immediate Boaz in each of their lives, they had always been one another's dinner date, movie date, or any date for that matter, so there was no holding back when it came to talking about any and everything. In the end, Kenya realized she had been the one talking and Charlene had been the one listening . . . plotting and scheming a way to push up on Kenya.

"Gul, who's at the door?" Mother Gladstone asked as if it were her own home. Being left in the sunroom where Kenya was doing her hair, with plastic under her, around her, and on her, Mother mumbled about the curl rods being left in her hair too long. "Don't you forget me in here, now!" she yelled out once more. Retrieving her glasses from her pocket, Mother Gladstone tried her best to get her eyes to focus on Charlene through the glass pane.

With the booming voice coming from the back, Charlene yielded in her tracks from the unwanted hug she was about to lay on Kenya.

Usually not in agreement with how Mother Gladstone used her elderly powers, at the very moment, Kenya was so happy she was present. Initially not wanting to do the older lady's hair, Kenya was glad she had decided to do so after all.

"A friend, Mother," Kenya yelled over her shoulder. Looking back at Charlene, Kenya said, "I'm rolling her hair." She lowered her voice back to normal. "I didn't know you were in town. You have a revival?" Kenya kept a skeptical look on her face, nervously wondering how Charlene had found her.

Kenya thought she had left Charlene and that part of her life behind. The look on Charlene's face showed Kenya otherwise.

"No, girl. I missed you." Charlene didn't care to whisper. "I hadn't talked to you and I was worried about you." Charlene moved farther in the house, wondering if Kenya would ever shut the door.

"Oh. Well. I . . . I missed you too, sis." It was imperative to Kenya that she kept everything as if it were smooth sailing.

A tall, solid-built woman with the figure of a plus-sized model, Charlene closed the space between her and Kenya.

"You never called." Charlene inched closer, towering over someone she had grown feelings for. "Maybe you can give me a touchup since I'm here." Charlene grabbed her own hair, ready to see Kenya squirm. Looking beyond Kenya, Charlene glanced Mother Gladstone's way before the older woman had a chance to turn her head from staring.

"Look, Charlene, you have to go," Kenya snapped back, realizing she wasn't going to allow the enemy to steal all she had been fighting for.

She had prayed and cried, rolled on the floor and called on the name of Jesus. Confused by her own actions, Kenya had wanted to know if a part of her wanted the same lifestyle Charlene had chosen. Kenya had wanted the Lord to show her just who she was.

"Am I gay? Do I like women? Is that what is really in me?" she had asked over and over. She had stared in the mirror for hours, wanting to figure out just who she was.

Days, weeks, months had gone by with her fighting to realize just what she had done with another woman—with Charlene, and how it had affected her psyche. Not to mention her spiritual life. A moment of lust, no matter if it was a woman or man, was wrong. Kenya hadn't known why she had fallen into another woman's arms when men were throwing themselves at her all the time.

Parts of her knew that living a saved life was a daily walk with Jesus. She was never in denial that she didn't have feelings and that certain parts of her body didn't jump when a fine specimen of a man walked by her wearing some cologne that wrapped around her nostrils. But she was adamant about saving herself for her godly chosen husband.

Kenya just knew she was not going to give up her thirty-something years as a virgin to a man just because she couldn't control herself. But when Charlene had started talking sweet nothings in her ear, not being and staying prayed up for her own battles, Kenya talked herself into believing her virgin status would remain.

Just as Charlene was about to protest, Mother Gladstone called out to Kenya once more, all the while boring holes through Charlene from across the partitioned room.

"I'll leave. But . . . I came to town, just for you. I'll be here for a while. We'll definitely be in touch," Charlene announced as she turned and walked out of the door, but not before waving Mother Gladstone's way.

Attaching the lock as soon as she could, Kenya slammed her back against the door and tried to get her breathing on track.

Chapter Twenty-three

It didn't take the door to lock completely before Mother Gladstone started in on Kenya.

"If I do say so myself, that lady looked kind of butch to me."

"Mother Gladstone. Can you . . . uh, please . . ." Kenya shifted her hip and placed her elbow in the crease of her hip since she had hair products on the plastic gloves she had retrieved. "Plus people don't even call it that anymore."

"Humph. I'll stop when she stop wearing the block-heeled shoes. She ain't fooling nobody." Mother held her head strong against Kenya's pull of trying to make her turn forward. "And what is she doing barging up in here—up in here for?" She extended her pinky and pointer finger on both hands to get her point across.

With no choice but to laugh, Kenya almost spit saliva on Mother's head. The old woman was too funny for her own good.

"You remember, Charlene. Don't you, Mother? She is one of the other evangelists I was partnered with. Uh, uh. We traveled in ministry together." Kenya hoped her friendly tone had no evidence of the guilt that was eating her alive.

Finally turning her head forward, Mother criss-crossed her arms under her bosom, which also rested perfectly on her protruding stomach. "I hope that's *all* y'all did together. I dunno. She looks familiar though.

I wonder if that's Gertrude's daughter. Cecil and Gertrude had a daughter named Charlene. But that gal left home, *evangelizing* is what she said. She was evangalieing . . . Just as gay as a . . ." Hearing her own recollection, Mother realized that Charlene was one and the same.

Kenya squeezed her eyes as tight as she could, hoping Mother didn't take it any further than she thought she had to. But by the other tongues coming out of Mother's mouth, Kenya was sure she'd had a light bulb moment.

When Mother Gladstone turned her head as quick as a squirrel can run up a tree, the roller Kenya had halfway unrolled slipped off Mother's three inches of hair and landed on the floor.

"Mother!"

"Kenya! Dear Father in heaven no. Oh Lawd, Jesus. I told your dear mama, Herlene, I'd watch after y'all when she passed. And you go on and made me out to be a liar"

"Mother Gladstone. Now what are you talking about?" Kenya was nervous. Taking the plastic gloves off, Kenya let them fall to the floor as she scurried from Mother Gladstone's view. "Come on now. Let me wash this texturizer out your head before it breaks off your ends and stink up my whole house." Kenya started to the kitchen before Mother, avoiding her conversation as best as she could.

Shaking her head from side to side, Mother Gladstone used the arms of the chair to slowly and wobbly stand. "Kenya, you were gone with that woman over a year. A whole year. And the way she bust up in here like she was about to bust your head wide open to the white meat . . . That woman think she yo' man . . . don't she?" Mother finally stood to her full posture and asked the question, wanting the answer.

Kenya had left the room and was at the kitchen sink, warming up the water. Forgetting to secure Mother Gladstone with her cane, the distraught and teary-eyed mother of the church had to fend for herself.

"I told your mama I'd look after you, girl," she mumbled to Kenya who she could no longer see from around the wall. "That girl don' got hold to ya. You look all sunken in and thangs." Mother Gladstone yielded to tears, thinking she had made a revelation.

"I'm not on drugs, Mother." Kenya stood in the kitchen and yelled over the water to make sure her mother's dear friend had heard her.

"Ya sister was a skeezer, juggling oranges. God blessed her to recoup. You a squeezer, juggling apples. Lawd help me today!" Mother Gladstone moaned through her tears and lost her grip, slipping and falling on the plastic gloves Kenya hadn't bothered picking up.

"Mother!" Kenya yelled out, hearing the commotion and running back into the sunroom.

Lying on the hard floor, Mother Gladstone moaned through her aches and pains, having landed on her bad hip.

"Thank you for coming, Deacon Morgan. I couldn't get in contact with Pastor and couldn't think of who else to call." Kenya lay her head on Keithe's chest.

"No problem. Everything will be all right. He's already on his way. He's very close to his mother so he will be here as soon as possible. How's Mother Gladstone doing?" Keithe hadn't made it into the room due to nurse rotations checking up on the elderly patient.

Shaking her head in a fast motion, Kenya still held on to hope that it was all a bad dream. But it wasn't. "She has a concussion and a broken hip," Kenya said.

And all because of me, she wanted to add. If she hadn't gotten nervous about Mother finding out she and Charlene had indeed been more than tag-team evangelists, she never would have dropped the plastic gloves and left them there.

"Which way is she?" The two heard Pastor Peters scurrying down the hall toward his mother's hospital room.

"Right here, Pastor," Keithe directed and gave room for the pastor and his wife to enter into the room.

With tears in her eyes, Kenya thought it was only best to follow them into the room and give the details on what happened.

"I can take you home whenever you're ready," Keithe said, holding her by the wrist before she was able to get away. Knowing Kenya had ridden in the ambulance with Mother Gladstone, Keithe wanted to be available for her.

Shamefully, Kenya said, "I've already called Mike to come get me. Thank you, though," as she disappeared behind the heavy wood door.

A blow back to reality, Keithe had mistakenly taken Kenya's request for him to come be by her side as a sign that she wanted to involve him more in her life. Now it didn't look that way at all. He just didn't get her.

Right as he turned to head toward the elevators, Keithe bumped into a woman, tall and solid in demeanor, with a stern look on her face. Though it was the end of March and still a bit of a breeze was prevalent, Keithe thought it overdone for the lady's top button to be buttoned so high. It made his own neck itch. "Excuse me, ma'am." Keithe walked around her.

"No problem, sir. Maybe you can help me. I'm looking for Pastor Peter's mother? I had an appointment with him but the church said his mother had been involved in an accident. Is she in this room?" she asked, pointing in the direction Keithe had walked from.

With the woman presenting herself in a Christian manner, Keithe didn't believe there was any harm in sharing the information, but thought it strange that she'd come to the hospital. "Yes. They just arrived. You may want to give them some time. Evangelist Kenya will be out soon and she can probably give you an update."

"Did you say Kenya?" The woman turned and started her departure along with Keithe.

"Yes, ma'am. Did you want her? I can go in and get her . . ." He slowed down his walk, ready to turn back.

"No, no. No need. I will just catch the pastor another time. Thank you for the information." She took a quick left and departed down the stairwell instead of waiting for the elevator.

With the ding of the elevator, Keithe bumped into yet another body. With Mike on his cell phone, he didn't look up before he stepped into Keithe.

"Dude." Keithe gave him a nudge.

"My bad. Oh. Hey," he spoke to the caller on his line. "Let me call you back." Mike hit the end key without looking. Placing his cell phone into his blazer's pocket, Mike said, "What up, Keithe?" He was more than ready to let bygones be bygones.

"You got it," Keithe said. "I called you, man. What's up? Did you get my messages?"

Knowing he missed his friend more than he would let on, Mike decided to be frank. "Yeah. I did. Look, man. It ain't that serious. Kenya's cool." He shrugged his shoulders. "But . . . I'm not interested in her like that." Mike knew he had to be upfront and honest with himself first. "Now for her, as far as her intensions with me . . . I don't know what to tell you."

"I see. You got that Stevie Wonder 'Rocket Love' effect on her, huh? Dropping her, huh?"

"I got issues." Mike shook his head and gave a sad smile.

"Tell me about it." Keithe knew the feeling. "I'm right there with ya." The two dapped knuckles. "I told Kenya how I felt about her," Keithe said and eased his hands in his pockets. "Over dinner." He waited to see Mike's reaction.

Mike stretched his expression on his face and walked to the sitting area. "And how did that go?" he asked. Mike hadn't figured it all the way out, but had an inkling there was more to Kenya wanting to date him over Keithe.

Keithe hunched his shoulders. "In so many words, she digs me too. But it's something . . . I don't know what's up with her. I mean, she even got heated with me when I tried to bring you up."

Mike raised his eyebrows and shook his head at Keithe.

"What?" Keithe knew it was wrong. "Dude, she already knew . . . She told me."

"Word?" Mike wanted confirmation before concluding what he thought about Kenya all along.

"Word," Keithe confirmed.

Chapter Twenty-four

Mike knew it. He knew Kenya had crossed over into the dark side, even if she had finally seen the light and never wanted to return. Her actions, as far as pursuing him and the mention of being on missions trips with Evangelist Charlene . . . the Charlene everyone knew did who and what she wanted to do.

From their previous times together, and even before Kenya had brought Charlene into their conversations, Mike could tell how much Kenya enjoyed evangelizing in Africa. He could tell her heart was for God's people and sharing just who God is. It was when Mike would ask about the downtime in Africa that he could instantly see a darkness to what had only moments earlier been joy. That was when his own thoughts started to reel.

On the ride home from the hospital, Kenya couldn't stop dropping her bucket load of tears in her own lap. It was then that Mike decided to start asking questions, wondering if a weary Kenya would finally release the weight on her shoulders.

"She really is going to be okay, Kenya. She said so herself. Didn't you hear the doctors?" Mike offered, knowing good and well with all the tears Kenya were unloading, there had to be more to the story.

"Yeah. But . . . but . . . if it hadn't been for . . . then she would have . . . And now she has to . . ." Kenya couldn't get her words out. She just didn't know how to let it out that she had made a mess of herself.

Pulling up to a coffee shop, there was no way Mike was going to allow Kenya to make a public appearance with big red eyes and a runny nose; at least, not with him. "Sit here. I will be back." He got out of the car and trotted toward the double doors.

Mike was so sweet. Just like a best girlfriend sweet. He didn't mind listening to her whine and he urged her to share her drama and always lent his shoulder. Stopping for coffee was no surprise to Kenya.

"Here you go." Mike had walked to her side of the car. Handing her her skinny latte just the way she liked it, Mike raced back to his driver's seat.

He clicked the car keys backward and found the soft jazz station on his XM Radio. "Okay. Let me have it. What's the problem, Kenya? Let it out." Mike was ready for Kenya to be truthful. In turn, he was ready to be truthful about who he was. He wanted to give her the opportunity before he shared what he thought was up.

Having stopped her tear flow, Kenya was ready, truly ready to share her woes with someone. Not knowing what the outcome would be for herself, Kenya was tired of the plan she had concocted. She was embarrassed and just sad she had stooped to such lows.

"Well . . ." She hesitated. "You're not my type," Kenya said. When both realized what had come out of her mouth, the duo broke out into laughter.

"Oh, now you tell me!" Mike pretended to be heartbroken. "And you know you're not my type, right?" he questioned with his eyebrows raised.

With a head nod, Kenya let out a breath and shared the pain of what she'd done while in Africa.

"Just as I suspected," Mike said as he finally sat back and readjusted his seat. "I knew it had to be something like that."

"Really?" Kenya still sniffled while taking in her drink. Getting warm, she pressed the button to allow her window to roll halfway down. "Wow, and I thought I was really hiding something."

Mike laughed. "From who? Must be Keithe, because I know you didn't think I wouldn't pick up on it." He smirked. "Uh, radar."

"Keithe . . ." Kenya sighed as she allowed her admirer's name to ooze from her lips.

"Yep. My boy cuts for you bad." He closed his eyes to emphasize just how much he knew Keithe longed to get to know her better. "He told me how you two went out to dinner, too. You basically spilled the beans yourself about knowing I was gay."

"Oh, shoots. Do you think he knows about me?" Kenya wanted to know.

"Nahh. I doubt it. He didn't let on. He just said you had known all along about me and couldn't figure you out." Mike took a bite of the croissant he had gotten from the eatery. "Now tell me something. How you gonna cheat on me that quick . . . going out with Keithe and stuff? How you gonna do that, Anna Mae? Huh, huh? Eat the cake, Anna Mae." Mike played like he was going to stuff some of his croissant into Kenya's full mouth.

Opening the Lexus's door as quickly as she could, Kenya spat all of her latte content that had been in her mouth onto the pavement. "You, sir . . . are sick." Kenya laughed from her gut as she took a napkin and wiped her mouth.

"I know. I'm a hot mess . . . dot org, as Tamar Braxton says." He threw his brows up. "That's my favorite show." The two laughed. "But serious. Are you going to give Keithe a chance? He deserves it. I mean, this man has wanted to get to know you since he moved to town," Mike explained.

"What do you think I should do?" Kenya's mind was traveling at top speed.

"I think you should." Mike was adamant.

"Then I think I will."

Chapter Twenty-five

Being led by a waiter, Stoney greeted Keithe in mid stride. "Hey, Pops." She walked toward Keithe with open arms, hoping she was shielding Michelle behind her. No luck.

"Michelle." Keithe's eyes landed on his ex while hugging Stoney. "I didn't know you were in town, dear." Keithe knew Michelle's need for him to show his adoration for her, and just like always he gave her just what she wanted.

"Well . . ." Michelle started.

"Ah. Um. Pops. We didn't take too long getting here, did we? I hope you didn't wait very long," Stoney interjected, nervous as all get out.

"You know my watch is set to, um, women." He looked down at his TAG watch.

Michelle didn't like the comment and wrinkled her nose to show so. "I bet it is. Thank you, Keithe." They kissed as she sat in the seat he had rushed to pull out for her.

"You're quite welcome. So how are you two ladies? It's so good to see you two." Keithe didn't wait for them to answer. Being down in the dumps ever since Kenya had blown up at him at the restaurant and then done away with him at the hospital, Keithe had been working, churching, and longing. He'd had his first heartbreak since his divorce. It had him second guessing what he'd done by leaving the stability of his life. From the looks of it, Keithe figured he couldn't measure up to the woes of dating in today's world.

"I've moved to Dallas, Keithe," Michelle blurted out as she placed her Brahmin in the vacant seat by her. "Sorry." She looked at Stoney and shrugged. "I just wanted to tell you face to face, so don't think Stoney had anything to do with not telling you." Michelle was glad to get that piece of news out of the way. "Besides, I had been trying to tell you my plans for quite some time."

"Moved?" Keithe mumbled as he lost his smile. "Here? Dallas? Why?" he finally was able to ask. Which was the only short question he wanted answered.

"Because I'm ready for us to try again. I'm ready to get my 'R' back and be the Mrs. to your Mr." Michelle was ready to lay it all on the line. Whatever it was, she figured she could handle it, but if she didn't try, then she'd never know.

Stoney's silverware tumbled to the floor and when she went for it, she bumped her head on the table. Wishing she could stay under the table for the remainder of the afternoon, Stoney said a quaint and cute prayer, hoping her stepfather didn't blow the roof off of the restaurant.

"Michelle . . . What, now? Are you serious?" He bypassed all of his manners and placed his elbows on the table, hoping it would bring him into better earshot of Michelle.

Keithe knew Michelle was capable of doing a lot of things, but following him to another city just to get back with him? Especially when they were already divorced?

"You've got to be kidding me. Just how do you plan on doing that, Michelle, when you don't know if that is indeed something I want?" Keithe glanced over at

Stoney and felt sorry for her. Having been put in the middle of their disagreements had always made her nervous.

Michelle closed her eyes and thought of what to say. Up until now she had thought her plan wasn't as bad as how Keithe was now making it sound. "I just supposed that it was your moving here in the first place that didn't give us a chance to, you know, try to work it out," she came up with, knowing Keithe had more than tried to work it out, first with himself.

"I didn't want any more chances," Keithe let slip. Knowing there was a sting behind his words, Keithe lowered his head, knowing he had been pushed into a corner.

Stoney sat like a Ping-Pong ball in between the two. With their two-way conversation bouncing back and forth, Stoney's eyes traveled from Keithe to her mom and back again. She felt embarrassed for her mother. It was apparent that Michelle still hadn't gained the self-love she was sure was lacking in her mother. Stoney didn't want to overstep her boundaries, but knew that if she didn't intervene, Michelle could sink to an all-time low. She knew because she'd been there.

"You two. Let's just have dinner and maybe you all can try to talk about it later. Pops, I'm sorry. Mom should have told you about her moving down." She turned to look at her mother. "You should have. But we're here now and we just need to figure things out from here."

Just when Keithe was about to protest once more, the waiter walked to their table, ready to take their orders. There was no doubt it would be an awkward setting, but for Stoney's sake, Keithe knew he would try to put his anger and disappointment on the back burner.

Chapter Twenty-six

It was the first Sunday in April. And although the old adage said April brought showers, it couldn't be further from the truth. The weather was bright, crisp, and clear.

The divorce group members all assembled in their Sunday School meeting room and were in the midst of a heated, but Godly debate. Kenya stood at the front of the room, leading the women, and Keithe led the men. The two had talked, but only pertaining to the group. Kenya wanted nothing more than to express her feelings to Keithe but she wanted to move when God told her to move. She was still in prayer.

"And, furthermore, a Christian woman shouldn't want to be sized up as worldly women," one of the men offered.

"That's not what she's saying, brother. What the young lady is saying is just because we are saved and sold out to Christ, doesn't mean we want to be invisible to the Christian man. Why not get the compliments? Why not hold my hand if we are on a date?" a female divorcee offered.

"May as well ask for a kiss while you're at it. Lord knows what that will lead to," the man blurted out. A bit older than the others in the room, he wasn't backing down from courting the old-fashioned way.

With some laughter from the room, while others groaned and others gasped, Kenya jumped back into the mix. "So in this day and age, how many court? Truly date, and I'm talking about a monogamous couple." She held her hand high to show an example of what she was looking for. "*And* we're talking about without holding hands or kissing? Is it even possible? Anyone?" Kenya waited for someone in the thirty-person group to jump in.

"Well, I think being realistic is key, definitely." Keithe nodded toward the older gentleman who was speaking. "But I understand what my brother is saying. Don't forget the basis behind dating. It's to find out who God has synched you up with, in order to join in a union to fulfill God's vision. Because—"

"Because if you get in too deep, one thing leads to another and before you know it, you and your mate, your partner, are in the bed, bypassing that purpose," an angry voice rang out from the back.

Keithe swerved his head from side to side trying to see who added themselves to the discussion. Kenya didn't have to search for the voice. She knew who it was. Stiffened by the memories of her deception, Kenya just stood where she was.

"Who is that?" Keithe asked. "Please stand and share. Hi there." Keithe remembered her face from the hospital. "Thank you for joining us. Please continue."

"I'm just saying. I understand what the brother is saying." She patted the gentleman's arm, being that she was sitting behind him. "It's easy to fall for someone from the first time you hold hands, hug, and especially the kiss. You have to know what your intentions are. You don't want to go around hugging and kissing everyone who comes into your life.

"What if you think it's for a lifetime?" Charlene bore holes into Kenya as she was the woman who was speaking. "And what if it's only a season for them? Heaven forbid you allow the enemy to thrust you into someone's bed and do what God hates. Then your feelings are here, their feelings are there. Then what?" She finally removed her eyes from someone she had grown fond of, though for selfish reasons.

Keithe stood back and watched Kenya shrink into a shell. If no one else noticed, Keithe noticed the effect Charlene had on Kenya.

"Great . . . great insight, sister," Keithe said. "It gives us all something to ponder until next time. How do we date as Christians? Is flirting okay for Christians? Hugging, kissing? Let's talk about it next time. Let us all stand and, Brother Crow, if you'll pray for our dismissal, I'd appreciate it."

They all bowed their heads.

After the prayer it didn't take long before Charlene found her way to the front of the classroom. Keithe made sure he kept his ears open while busying himself with setting the chairs back in order.

"What are you doing here, Charlene?" Kenya stood with her arms folded across her chest.

"What do you mean? This is God's house. Isn't that what we preach? 'Get to God, at all cost?'" Being sarcastic was her way of getting under Kenya's skin.

"You know what I mean," Kenya tried again.

"You wouldn't answer my phone calls. You won't allow me to come over. So I should just read between the lines, huh?" Charlene didn't try lowering her voice.

"Can you hold it down?" Kenya lowered her voice and eyes. "I left that there, in Africa. It was a mistake. I thought you'd understand it by my not calling you or returning your calls."

"Are you kidding me?" Charlene inched closer. "You think it's something you can just pick up and put down. We spent way, way too much time together."

"Charlene, I will not discuss this here. I will not disgrace God's house with your or my mess. What? You want to testify about it? Is that why you're here? It's been almost a year."

Charlene said nothing but added a smirk to her lips. "Don't worry about it," Charlene comforted. "I'll be over your house after church and we'll talk then. I advise you to be there. And open the door." She turned and walked off.

Walking over to where Kenya had stood, Keithe was worried about her. "Hey. You okay? What was that all about?" Keithe asked.

"I . . . I . . . I can't . . ." Kenya walked past him, grabbed her purse off the podium, and ran out the door. It didn't matter how many times she heard Keithe call out her name, Kenya had to get out of sight.

Chapter Twenty-seven

"So, how the heck are you, Mike?" Keithe pulled up one of the sitting lawn chairs on Mike's covered patio. "You been well, my friend?" Keithe tried to break the ice.

"Nothing too new. Thanks for stopping by." Mike finally took a seat by his friend after pouring their drinks.

With a sip from a concoction of tea, lemon, lime, and orange Kool-Aid, Keithe really wanted to be the one to apologize first. "Thanks for letting me come over, dude. I really want to . . . Look, I'm sorry for getting into it with you. And to think . . . over a woman." Keithe raised his eyebrows, joked, and took another drink. He really didn't want to go backward since they had squashed the majority of their issues talking at the hospital that day.

"Ha-ha." Mike squinted his eyes and took a seat. "At least she's a good woman," he assured. "A very persistent, needy . . . Hmm, a little bit weird . . ." Mike twisted his hand in the air like Fred Sanford often did when declaring someone was "fruity." Keithe didn't catch on. Even with Kenya admitting to Mike about her personal life the day in the car when he'd picked her up from the hospital, Mike didn't feel it was his right to share the same with Keithe.

"But a very beautiful, intelligent woman to say the least," Mike added.

Taking a break to laugh at the additional description Mike had labeled Kenya, Keithe was glad things were back to normal for the both of them.

"Nevertheless . . . she was sweet on you." Keithe held his glass in the air for an impromptu toast.

"Oh, you funny." With the quickness Mike turned his chair to face Keithe. "I jumped the gun, man. Seriously. I was mad at you. You know. Wanted to get back 'atcha. That was the only reason I went along with going out with her." Mike was speed talking as if he were pleading with Keithe. "Cute as she is, I knew it was her from the jump you had been digging." Mike admitted about knowing it was Kenya that Keithe had had the hots for. "I mean, I seen why you had the sweetness for her. So when you ticked me off, I went for her. Stupid. I know."

Getting a good laugh out of Mike, Keithe knew his friend wouldn't be able to handle a woman like Kenya. Even if he were really into women.

"You did all that just because I told you that I'm worried about you, man?"

"Joker, when did you tell me you worried about me?" Mike sat back and picked up his own beverage again. He had to sit still and listen to this.

"Don't start." Keithe brought the cold drink to his lips.

"See, there you go." Mike pushed himself to the front of his seat. "You always do that. You like to tell me what I'm doing wrong. You go off on me, man, about my lifestyle—"

"'Cause, dude, what kind of lifestyle is that?" Keithe set his glass down on the high-quality granite, not getting why Mike did not understand where he was coming from. "That is not your life!"

"It is, though! It's the life I've been living since . . . forever. This has been my life. All by myself, forever,

Keithe." Mike got heated and stood. Putting some space between him and Keithe was best.

Shaking his head, Keithe wasn't about to allow Mike to make him feel bad. "Oh, no, dude. I've been there the whole way. I was there"—Keithe started counting with his fingers—"when you told your parents. When you got your first so-called heartbreak—"

"What was his name?" Mike tilted his head and squinted his eyes, wanting to see if he was going to make that lie last forever. He waited for Keithe to sweat. "See? There you go. You never, never took this as real. This is my life, Keithe. Yes, you were there . . . physically." Mike lowered his voice, not wanting to blow his steam. "Physically, you were there." Mike turned his back to Keithe. "But I bet you can't count on your fingers the times we've sat and talked about how I really feel about this . . . about me?

"Emotionally and mentally I was there alone." Mike looked over his left shoulder and into Keithe's confused eyes. "But that's all. You never asked what happened, what I was going through, what I really wanted out of life . . ."

With a lowered head, Keithe knew it was the truth. Keithe hadn't wanted all the details of who, where, why, when . . . and he definitely didn't want to know how. He just figured the less he knew the less he would be held accountable for. He never took in that Mike really didn't understand his own dealings.

"I just thought . . ." His words trailed off. He was sad that he just now realized how much he evaded being there totally for his friend when, in fact, Mike had forever been there for him and all of his heartache and pain.

"What? You just thought I was tripping? On drugs? Going through a phase? Whatever you thought, you didn't ask. You did just like my parents. You disowned what I was going through. The only difference was that you stayed physically." He looked back into the sky. "I didn't know anything myself. I didn't know if it was just a choice I was making, if I had been born this way. Whatever it was, whatever it is . . . I would love nothing more than to know, but I don't know how to let go."

Biting the inside of his jaw, Keithe couldn't believe he was having this conversation with *his* best friend. He knew for a fact he'd avoided this conversation for twenty-plus years and now he felt bad. He now realized while Mike had been his best friend, he in fact hadn't been the same to Mike.

Standing up with his fist balled inside of his pants pockets, Keithe asked, "But do you think you really want to?"

"What? Want to let go?" There was a pause. A blink. A shutter to his spine. "I look in the mirror and I see a fly dude. I see myself being this fly man, with a fly honey on my arm . . . and the next thing that comes to my mind is, just how long will I allow myself to be satisfied with her?"

"Like Vicky," Keithe reminded Mike, wishing he had listened and truly been there for Mike. If he had, another woman possibly wouldn't have had her heart broken.

"Just like Vicky." Mike shook his head, knowing Vicky was just the woman he was talking about. But over the years, there had been a Traci, Claudia, Melissa, Kharla, and the list went on. Even now, and almost, Kenya.

"The Holy Ghost is a keeper. A renewal to your spirit. If you seek to find Him . . ." Keithe stopped when he saw Mike waving his hand in the air.

"Now if I'd had someone speak all of that then . . . directly into me, maybe it would've worked. Not saying it can't now. But while all the preachers were preaching *around* me, including my daddy, first . . . what they should have done was to take me to shoot hoops and asked me what the deal was. The holy boldness they claimed to have would have asked me dead on . . . what my issues were, what I needed to talk about, and how could they help. Instead, they preached from the pulpit and hoped I got it." He shook his head. "I never did."

Nodding, Keithe understood. Preaching toward Mike wouldn't get them anywhere. What Mike needed was his friend to pray for him, pray with him when he asked, and continue loving him through it all.

Wrapping his arm around Mike's neck, landing him in a choke hold, Keithe placed a kiss on the top of his best friend's head. "I love you, man. Can you forgive me?"

"Already. I love you too."

Chapter Twenty-eight

She opened the door. Not because she wanted to, but because she more so had been threatened to. Kenya didn't want to know what the threat would turn into if she decided not to allow Charlene into her home.

Kenya knew the consequences just "trying" something would bring. Heck, she had preached about holiness or hell too many times to count. Closer than that, she had spoken about fornication, cast the lust demon out of folk, and lo and behold, there she was . . . walking the same plank. Now her one moment of "trying" something stood looking at her face to face.

"Look, we can make this easy or hard, however you want it to be." Charlene had walked into Kenya's house with authority and said, "I guess you call yourself ditching me . . . That's cool, but I just need to know some things."

There was fury in her eyes. Yes, Charlene had gotten wrapped up in the possibilities of maybe she and Kenya actually being able to grow something. It wouldn't be her first same-sex relationship, but she had hoped it would be her last. Especially with all the new laws and gays having the right to marry.

Charlene had even envisioned the two of them starting up a ministry together. But now, she knew that would never happen. What was a growing possibility to Charlene had only been a regretful fling to Kenya.

"Are you the one who told my business to the bishop?" she asked with a hard look into Kenya's eyes.

Confused by the question, Kenya had no idea what Charlene was talking about. But it was obvious Charlene's play days were up.

"I don't even know what you're talking about." Kenya slowly closed her door and stood with her arms crossed, not offering the woman to venture farther into her home and definitely not offering her a seat. Now it was obvious why Charlene had shown up at her doorstep. Her game had been squashed.

She had been in the Word since early Sunday School days. The books of the Bible, she knew them. Beating the tambourine like there was no tomorrow, Kenya conquered it. And she even cut a mean rug when the Holy Spirit hit. But it was a moment of weakness, away in another country that led Kenya to experience all she disagreed with. Now her moment of lust stood in her house, bossing her around.

Had she been prayed up like she knew she should have, it wouldn't have been as easy as it was for the enemy to cloud her thinking. But when offered the opportunity to go minister in another country, Kenya hadn't prayed if God was sending her or if she had just gone on her own accord. As a pastor once said, "There's a difference between being sent opposed to just went."

"Well, somebody did!" Charlene walked up on Kenya, close enough for her breath to be felt. "I don't know who did, but I'm going to find out!" Her eyes danced back and forth to either of Kenya's own.

Realizing her anger was overbearing, Charlene settled with, "You know they took my credentials?" She fell into Kenya's unsuspecting arms.

"Oh, my." Kenya was caught off-guard, yet couldn't care less who took what away from her. It wasn't that she counted herself better than Charlene, but from where she was standing, repenting and accepting God back into her life, Kenya was better off.

Is this why she just showed up? Kenya questioned herself. Maybe she had jumped to conclusions, she thought again. *All she needs is a friend, especially if she is going through losing her evangelism license through the church.*

"Charlene. I'm sorry. I truly had no idea." Kenya allowed herself to let down her guard. "No, it wasn't me." Kenya gave a one-arm hug to the older woman who had once been a mentor.

An opportunity of a lifetime was what Africa had been to her. Kenya thought about what a blessing it would be to be able to visit a continent she had only dreamed of visiting one day. When asked by Charlene if she would join the mission, she immediately said yes.

When one is given the gift to encourage, uplift, and pray over others, there is such a responsibility of being spiritually equipped for the task. Being a spiritual leader carries more weight than what meets the eye.

Being accountable over souls who were ready to call out to God was what Kenya was. Once she had landed in Africa, her sights were set on sight-seeing and photo opportunities rather than fasting and praying. Doing so caused her to just go through the motions at the nighttime revivals. She had acted in the spirit but not walked in it.

"I believe you, Kenya." Charlene lifted her head but kept her body close. "Now everyone knows about my personal life," Charlene said, sounding as if she was worried about it. "It makes me sick to think of how they will try to judge me now."

Kenya's eyes scrunched. She couldn't believe Charlene was actually worried about her reputation opposed to the actual sin.

"Maybe we can just sit on the sofa and you . . ." Charlene grabbed a lock of Kenya's hair and twirled it with her hands.

"No. Stop it." Kenya pushed the taller and more built woman off of her. "No, ma'am. Not here, not ever." Kenya meant business. She didn't want to but if she had to put up her dukes, then so be it.

Gaining her composure, Charlene played it smooth, ready to use reverse psychology on Kenya. "So it was you, then?"

"Nope. Not at all," Kenya shot back, adding her hard stance to her physique. "But it won't be none of that up in my house. Not up in here." She wanted to break it down to Charlene, who obviously thought Kenya couldn't take up for herself. Walking back toward her front door, Kenya realized some things and spoke her mind. "You come up in here, all wishy-washy with your motives. Is that how you've done it to people all of these years? Manipulate them, test and tempt them?"

Kenya wasn't backing down. She had allowed the enemy and Charlene's advances to wear on her in Africa, but Kenya had repented, fasted, and given her cares over to God. In her heart, she knew she had been forgiven. She may not have forgiven herself, but God had been too good to her. With this chance, there was no way Kenya was giving up or giving in.

"You will not come in my house and disrespect me." Kenya let her have it.

"Oh is that all? You don't want it to be in your house?" Satan was busy. "'Cause I have a room downtown. That ain't nothing." Charlene took a step and pointed as if Kenya could see where she was talking about.

At that very moment Kenya got the answer she had been waiting for. She may have been stunned by her own actions, but standing face to face with the lady who had thrown herself on her, Kenya wasn't falling into the notion of try it once, buy it the next time. It wasn't her. The moment that was had now passed.

"I'm not gay. I don't believe in it nor do I accept it. I love you as a person, Charlene, my sister in Christ. It's the sin I hate." Before Charlene could share with Kenya how ignorant she sounded, especially since they had shared beds, Kenya stepped toward her. "*I am not gay*. Like a sinner, a fornicator, a weak saint, I fell for the okie-doke. And yes, every time I think about that time and my soul burning in hell, I get sick to my stomach. But God is good." Kenya laughed in the spirit. "You know why? Because He has allowed me to have my mind, my body, and my spirit man back." Kenya danced as she moved toward the door.

"You can call me what you want, you can tell who you want, but even if you had been a man, I would be just as disgusted with the whole notion as I am now."

Charlene just stood and looked at Kenya. "Girl, go on and psyche yourself up all you want." She took her time walking toward the door. "You can try to believe it if you want to, but we will see. If not, then . . ." Charlene, with an evil spin, shrugged one shoulder. "We'll see how long I can keep all my lovers' names to myself. Like I said. If you are feeling froggy and you want to put me in the mix, then leap." With Charlene on the outside of her front door, walking as fast as she could, Kenya slammed it shut.

Kenya was sick. The farthest she could go was to her sofa. The empty pit she felt in her stomach grew with a vengeance every time she thought about her hasty decision to lie with another woman.

Just as the Bible stated in James, one sin when fully grown, birthed death. Though she fought a good fight, Kenya still had her moments that she felt she needed to crawl out of the grave with. And just like now she felt like her whole world was about to succumb to the way she felt.

If only she had been praying without ceasing, she wouldn't have gotten this deep in. But she hadn't and now she was here . . . at the verge of not knowing if Charlene would expose her or not.

The flirtation and all of the playing around Charlene had done with Kenya had been overlooked on her behalf. Instead of putting her mentor in check, Kenya had taken it as a joke, laughing it off, using her relaxed "girl, please" as a way to ward off the advances. One come-on led to another then another.

Not one to even occasionally partake in drinking of wine, Kenya thought about being in a beautiful country on a wonderful vacation; opposed to seeing God's glory on the other side of the world, and doing His work. Instead, Kenya became a little too relaxed in her surroundings and shared in drinking more wine than she could handle.

"I will keep my mind on thee." Kenya rocked as she sat on the sofa and recited a popular scripture.

When her intuition had told her to remove herself from Charlene's room one night, it had been too late. The wine had already taken effect, telling her that everything was okay. That was all Charlene needed to make her move.

First, by a one-way conversation of how Kenya had deprived herself long enough of a man's touch. And that God had been well pleased with her staying pure for as long as she had. The massage gesture didn't help Kenya fight against the wilds of the enemy.

Charlene played the mind games, the "what if" games with Kenya.

"If you weren't saved do you think you would have . . . ?" she had asked, giving different scenarios each time.

"I'm so stupid." Kenya shook her head. "Lord, I know you've forgiven me, but I need you to remove this dirty feeling from me."

Kenya had no doubt she would have felt the same had it been a man who she had lain with. But the thicket the enemy had made just for her angered her even the more. She was supposed to be stronger. She was a praise and worshipper. There was no way she was supposed to let the enemy play with her.

Kenya had continuously in her young adult life made a pact, a vow to the Lord that she would save herself for her husband on their wedding night. She meant it. And in all the times she'd testified about it and shared with young women to wait, the enemy heard her too.

In turn, Charlene, a woman who preached the Word, wound up being her Achilles heel. Kenya never thought to see it coming.

"Lord, help me to know that in due time you will help me to believe in the power you've given me, once again. I need you to show me that I will get past this."

Just like that, in her spirit Kenya heard, *And this too shall pass.*

"Even though I betrayed you?" she questioned.

I will never leave you, nor forsake you.

"Even when I turned away from you, Lord, and served another god; you could have killed me, Lord." Kenya lost herself in her pain. "I'm not worthy, Lord," she cried.

Come unto me.

Kenya realized that all she had to do was go to God in prayer. She knew simply, if she took one step, He'd take two. She knew without a doubt that His Word could not return to Him void.

Chapter Twenty-nine

"Come on in, gul." Mother Gladstone was sitting up in the bed; rather, tilted on her side. "I'm not gon' to bite you."

With a perched smile on her lips, Kenya walked through the doors of the hospital room with an armful of flowers, trying her best to cover her nervousness. Some days had passed since Charlene had barged back into her world and Kenya wanted to get her mind as far away from her as she could and could think of no better way to do so than to visit Mother Gladstone.

"I know you are not gonna bite me. Especially without having any teeth in your mouth," Kenya shot back.

Squealing like a baby pig, Mother placed her hand over her mouth so she could get a hearty laugh out. "You too much." She waved for Kenya to make her way farther in. "I didn't think you'd come back." Mother reached for the metal triangle above her bed in order to position herself comfortably. "Almost sent a TCB after ya."

Halfway to her seat, Kenya tilted her head and said, "Do you mean an APB, Mother?"

"Um, huh. That too. But look like them roots can use some good old TCB perm." She gave herself another holler.

"You know what?" Kenya rose from the seat she had just sat in and pretended to leave. "I think I'll just take my little nappy-headed tail on back to the house and take my flowers, too."

"Gul, you bet'sta get back here and put them poinsettias down," Mother still joked, loving the beautiful red roses Kenya had brought her. She quickly got her act together, definitely not wanting Kenya to leave anytime soon.

Placing a kiss on Mother Gladstone's cheek before she sat back down, Kenya was all smiles.

"I really am glad you are in good spirits, Mother. I've been beating myself up over and over." Kenya's brown eyes looked toward the door, hoping not to be disturbed as they were about to skate upon what happened at her home that day.

"I'm Okay. It hurts a mess of greens, but I'm fine. My bump going down too." Mother attempted to touch the back of her head.

Feeling overwhelmed, taking the blame for Mother having to have hip surgery, Kenya hoped this wouldn't start a spiral journey down for the active elder.

"You gotta keep in mind though. Chil', I was already limping 'cause of that old hip. God works in mysterious ways. Lord knows I had been putting off having the surgery and probably never would have. But I needed it." She bucked her eyes Kenya's way.

"Maybe, but I shouldn't have just thrown those gloves on the floor, trying to get away from . . ." Kenya knew she couldn't turn back. Plus she needed to talk to someone who could share some wisdom.

Yes, she had spilled the beans to Mike but there was really no spiritual guidance he could give her since he was struggling himself. Kenya just wanted to be pushed in the right direction.

Since Charlene had made herself known in and around the church, people had started to whisper even more. Kenya was sure Mother had heard about it all the way in the intensive care unit.

"I shouldn't have been in your business. Being all nosy. My son tells me all the time to keep my nose out of folks' business." Mother raised her eyebrows to see if Kenya would take the bait.

"Actually, you were just doing what mothers of the church are called to do. If *you* don't speak up about things, who will? It takes those personal relationships, one-on-one time to help others grow . . ." Kenya got it.

"Um, huh. Kenya? How in the world did you get caught up in such a mess? Honey, you been saved most of your life. I remember when you were a li'l ol' gul, singing in front of the church . . . praising the Lord."

Shaking her head, Kenya didn't know the answer herself. "I can't blame it on anyone but myself. The devil maybe; but I don't know. I thought I was stronger than that. Thought I had more power." It was a done deal. Mother Gladstone knew all Kenya had endured without Kenya having to repeat it.

"Oh you have the power; you just didn't tap into it. You let your flesh get in the way. And then as tall and strong as that . . . that woman look, ain't a wonder she didn't pin you down."

"She didn't." Kenya really didn't want to laugh but Mother Gladstone made it hard not to. "But she did allow the enemy to use her to pursue me. I'm sure I'm not the only one. I get so mad every time I think about it. I haven't even been with a man and here I am lying next to a woman. Actually thinking, no, acting like I had feelings for her." Kenya shook her head.

With her lips turned up, Mother said, "It wasn't an act. The enemy will play on your feelings and your emotions. He will tempt your heart. You just bought into it," Mother schooled her. "So how do you feel, chil'? Are you struggling with it? What's going on in your spirit?"

"I'm not going to say I'm confused, but I'm ashamed. I want to get married and have kids. I have the house and the dogs." Kenya was weak just thinking how she'd set herself back spiritually and emotionally.

"Be specific, daughter. Everybody can get married these days. And I wish they wouldn't call it marriage for everyone. God ordained marriage for man and woman. If same-sex partners want to get married, they need to think of their own name, shoots."

With no choice but to laugh, Kenya knew Mother had a good point. "You're right, Mother. I want to be married to a wonderful man of God. A big, strong, handsome, honest and reliable, dependable man at that; someone who can pray with me and for me. You know. Someone who will be happy to help with the kids. Help me in my ministry and grow in a ministry together."

Shaking her head frantically, from side to side, Mother wanted to knock some sense into Kenya. "Uh, um. You not gonna get all that, sugar. All those men dead. Gone. Buried. Probably dust by now. So what you need to pray is for God to send you one who is as close as possible to that made-up man in your head. If you stick with God's plan, He will get you as close as possible," she continued.

"Now He gonna put y'all some issues in the way, to see if you will depend on Him to help y'all through . . . so you all can grow together. But all that other stuff, uh um. Don't do that to yourself, baby."

They laughed.

"Something gonna be left out. Trust me," Mother added.

"But how can I get past what I've done? I turned my back on God and did what I wanted to do." Kenya was serious. The lump in her throat wouldn't allow her to finish.

"You did what everybody has done. Even someone who proclaims to have never did anything . . . oh but they have. We have all sinned and fallen short of the glory of God. You probably know the scripture better than me." Mother Gladstone shrugged her shoulders. "A sin is a sin. Shoot, I sinned all the time." Mother Gladstone eased her bed down from the sitting position. Looking at the ceiling she reminisced. "How else you think I got three boys in this world and they are all older than my anniversaries? Hmm."

Kenya's eyes bucked. She'd just assumed as everyone probably had; that her husband had died off years ago. It never dawned on her that Mother had actually been through some real issues in life.

"Gul. My sin just over three score years old and can't nobody see the remnants lest I tell it. Oh and I don't mind telling it. That's what's wrong with our chil'uns today. We need to be real with 'em.

"I had a price to pay for my sins. Wasn't all this help these days being a single mother. That makes it far too easy to keep having babies when they don't have to take full responsibility for 'em. But look how God has blessed me in spite of *my* mess, Kenya.

"All three of my boys are in the ministry. And you know my youngest boy's daddy *still* be trying to get with a sista. I'm too old to go out like a sucka. You know old folk go to hell too." She tilted her head toward Kenya.

"Yep. I know." Kenya shook her head.

"So, Kenya, if you truly want to be married and for God to give you the true desires of your heart, why on His green earth are you fooling around with Mick?" Mother butchered Mike's name.

"Who?" Kenya extended her neck, trying to figure out who Mother had coupled her with. "Are you talking about Mike?"

"Um, huh." She lay back on her pillow, mumbling an upset thought.

Figuring she'd laid all else on the line, Kenya felt obligated to get the rest off of her chest. She was thankful for the older woman. It wasn't that she couldn't confide in her sister Kendra or Gracie, but she truly didn't want to disappoint them as she had disappointed herself.

"It was all a front. I knew he wasn't really into me and it . . . it kept other men at bay until I had figured myself out."

"Oh so you already knew he was batting for the other team?" Mother rose up off of her right shoulder to get a look at Kenya. "You lucky I don't have my cane near me. I tell you what; I'd bop you a good'un right on the top of your head. What is wrong with you, Kenya?"

"I don't know, Mother." They treaded into the heap of mess Kenya had gotten herself into. "I was so confused by all I'd gone through with Charlene. I thought my whole life was changing. Thought I was gay. Thought I'd figured something out about myself. But then when I went into a fasting and prayer session, I knew better. I had just gotten caught up. I sinned."

"What all that mean? Chil', we already gon' over all that." Mother was getting tired.

"Well, when men started flirting with me . . . Christian men, I felt dirty and ashamed. There was no way, I figured, I could share with them what I'd gone through. So it was best for me to stay by myself."

Pushing the up button on the bed's remote, Mother had to sit up for this one. "Keithe? While you going all around the fruit tree, everybody knows Keithe has the

hots for you," she squealed, bypassing the mulberry bush.
"Yo' mama must've dropped you on your head . . . twice."

Laughing along with Mother even though she was
the butt of the joke, Kenya said, "Why twice, Mother?"

"'Cause that man has a fine profile view when he is
coming and going and you don't seem to notice. You
lucky I didn't have no girls. I would have put all of 'em
in his face. Jerlene, Perlene, and Candy. That's what I
was gonna name 'em."

Shaking her head, Kenya didn't know what to do
with Mother Gladstone. "I don't know what to do about
that. I could never tell that to him. It don't matter now
anyway." Kenya shrugged. "He thinks I've chosen his
best friend over him." Kenya ducked when Mother
picked up the remote and acted as if she'd throw it her
way.

"I ought to." Mother stopped short of losing her religion. "Ooowee, you lucky."

"What? I have too much going on. Keithe is a good
man and I just wouldn't want to drag him into my
mess."

"Yeah, he a good man, but he gon' get on my bad
list."

"Why would you say that? He hasn't done anything
wrong." Kenya stood and walked toward the attached
bathroom. Locking the door behind her she kept talking. "It was all on me, not him."

"Naw. I'm talking about because he was suppose
to been back an hour ago with my plate." The toilet
flushed. The faucet turned on.

"What?" Kenya yelled out, looking around for something to dry her hands. "You didn't tell me he had been
here . . . today. I gotta go." She burst through the bathroom door, back into the room.

Sitting all the way up, Mother was about to get a good laugh once she saw Kenya's face. Keithe had just walked through the door.

"Here you go . . . Mother Gladstone." Keithe saw Kenya standing with the strap of her purse on her shoulder. Kenya saw him standing with the darkest of jeans on, hugging every muscle in his lower torso.

"God, you are worthy," Mother Gladstone said as she looked in the same direction as Kenya.

Keithe and Kenya hadn't officially talked since being at the hospital. And ever since the last divorce group meeting when Charlene barged in, Keithe had been holding down the classes himself.

"Hi," he said.

"Hi," Kenya replied.

He couldn't help but to see how beautiful she looked, even in a jogging suit and her signature ponytail lying on her shoulder. Keithe still hadn't been able to pull Kenya to the side and squash all they had birthed the night over dinner.

"Boy, what took you so long?" Mother interrupted their stare down. "Did you have to go make the soul food yourself?"

"Soul food? Mother should you—"

"Gul, don't start with me. I had a broke hip, not a broke stomach. I'm about to tear them feet up."

"You didn't . . . ?" Kenya asked Keithe. "Pig feet?"

"I did," he said and nodded.

"He had to," Mother said with her eyes closed. "But you were leaving anyway so it shouldn't bother you. Bring it on, son." Mother held out her hand.

"You are too much. I gotta get going anyway." Kenya walked over and laid a kiss on Mother's forehead. "I have to go help my sister with the rest of the wedding gift bags. You know if I don't she'll be calling you and complaining about me." Kenya eyed Mother Gladstone.

"A wedding, huh?" Keithe said. "Guess this is the season for weddings." He thought about how busy Stoney had been helping Mercy prepare for her big day.

Nodding, Kenya said, "Yep. I'm officiating my niece's wedding and of course wanted to volunteer my time as well."

"Oh, okay. Speaking of weddings, I need to buy someone a gift myself. Thanks for the reminder. Maybe I can pick your brain on what I should get for a young couple?" Keithe figured throwing in a flirtation moment wouldn't hurt.

"Maybe." Kenya walked closer, toward the door. "I can possibly give you some ideas," Kenya agreed. "Just depends on the couple."

"Sounds like a good plan to me," Keithe said with raised eyebrows.

Just as he was about to give more in-depth detail of Mercy and her beau, Mother Gladstone said, "You two are pitiful," as she shook her head.

"What?" the two spoke simultaneously. Knowing without a doubt what Mother Gladstone was referring to, the two stood speechless as the older woman situated herself and the tray in front of her.

Rolling her eyes, Kenya opened the door and was about to make her exit before Keithe stopped her by putting his hand on her shoulder.

"Don't forget. Maybe we can still get together soon and talk. About whatever you want."

Looking over at Mother Gladstone, Kenya nodded and said, "I'd like that."

"Be safe," he said.

"Always. You too."

***

"Look here, when you go to those restaurants, don't let them give you all these hooves with the nails. You ask for the ones that are clipped off, too," the elderly lady spoke on how she liked her pig feet prepared. "They know what they be doing . . . just giving you what they want to give you. Sit down," Mother ordered, upset over Keithe just ordering and not knowing what he was ordering. "You just let her go, huh?" Mother Gladstone went back and forth between her pig feet, greens, black-eyed peas, cornbread, and peach cobbler.

"I don't think she's really interested in me like that. So why bother?"

"Keithe Wonderboy could sing a tune to that lady liking you." She spit pig feet bones in her hands and placed them on the plate.

With his nose turned up and a frown on his mouth, Keithe said, "Well that is my name."

Rolling her eyes, Mother said, "Y'all trying me today, huh? It's a shame. No respect for your elders." She spit more bones from her mouth.

Keithe wanted to go more into what he suspected with Kenya, but didn't want to start rumors. Plus he really wanted to talk to Mike, especially after Charlene had hemmed Kenya up at the church and brought her to tears.

"Look, God has shown me some things with Kenya and its come to pass. He's also shown me you. That's your wife." She crunched on gristle. "Don't play dumb, boy. You know that friend of yours ain't no bit more stuttin' Kenya no more than them there bunny girls stuttin' Hugh Havenot."

"Hefner," Keithe tried to correct her.

"Naw. Havenot. 'Cause old as he is, he have not a grain of salt thinking them young girls want to fool around with his old wrinkled-up self. That man betta get it right with Jehovah. And I ain't talking about that boy calling himself 'HOV,' either," she said. "Ooooh, they all make me sick. Jesus is coming back soon, you know," she spoke randomly.

Laughing at the church's comedienne extraordinaire, Keithe wanted to even the playing field.

"Yep. We all need to get it together."

"See there. I wasn't talking 'bout everyone else. Was I? That's what's wrong with y'all young'uns. Ain't used to being called out. Can't take no responsibility for yourself. Anyway." Mother grabbed a wet napkin and wiped her hands. "Be boastful, move in God, and be there when Kenya is ready to share who she is. Mick will understand. I'm sure he already does."

"Yes, ma'am." Keithe listened, sure she was talking about Mike. "If you say so. I'm prepared."

Chapter Thirty

Keithe had finally had time to sit and think. He still couldn't believe Michelle had taken the liberty to move to his neck of the woods. What was worse? He couldn't believe he was considering taking her back.

Ever since Kenya had blown up on him over dinner, ignored him, and stayed as far away as possible as she could, Keithe had major doubts with how he was feeling about Kenya. The boldness Mother Gladstone had urged of him was gone. He'd overstepped his boundaries, he was sure, as far as Kenya was concerned.

He couldn't help it; there were little idiosyncrasies that had him questioning different aspects about Kenya. Seriously, why had she become so upset that night at dinner? Keithe had no idea. All he had asked was if she knew Mike was gay, *why* was she deliberately dating him. *She* was the one who had said she dated with a purpose only. And the only real purpose any woman would date Mike was to learn the perfection of arched eyebrows and blended hairlines.

"I'm just saying," he spoke aloud.

"Earth to Keithe?" Michelle had snapped.

He hated when she did that, snapped at him, beckoning him to do whatever it was she wanted him to do. Michelle made him look as though he was her son, rather than husband—ex-husband. He'd forgotten that soon.

"Sorry. I guess I drifted off," he said.

"No bother. You look cute and innocent when you do so." Michelle gave him her famous smile. "Thank you for dinner."

Opening the menu, Keithe still had no idea what he was doing. "No problem." He remembered how much he loved her compliments.

He felt so broken. Like he couldn't win for losing. Being that dating wasn't what he thought it would be, Keithe figured he had made the wrong decision divorcing Michelle. Obviously so if she was the woman now sitting across from him.

All he could think about was, *If someone loves you more than you love them* . . . Maybe it was true for their relationship.

Their daily conversations had warmed his heart, no doubt. Keithe figured not having Kenya in his direct presence made him vulnerable to all Michelle had promised. Whatever the case, it was working.

Michelle had taken the thoughtfulness, or so she thought, and spilled her heart about her life AK: After Keithe. It was way too obvious how she left out Deek and their year or so relationship. She obviously wanted him to focus on "them."

"I know you think I must be crazy," Michelle leaned in and whispered to Keithe. Her eyes showed just how excited she was to be in his presence. Alone. "Don't you? Tell me how you feel."

Looking over the menu, Keithe raised his eyebrow, deciding to not voice his opinion on the open-ended question.

Michelle continued, "I've tried to move on, Keithe. But when I think of how we would sit in the bed, review our cases together, go for lunch . . . and even how we would have our own impromptu Bible lesson at home, it hit me hard. I miss my friend, Keithe." Michelle reached over the table and held her hand open.

Reluctantly but pleasantly, Keithe obliged and gave his hand to Michelle.

He knew she was waiting. Waiting for him to say, "ditto," or maybe even, "I miss you too." But he couldn't. He felt if he opened the gates there would be no turning back.

First he had just listened to Michelle share with him how she missed her "friend." That was him. Michelle probably couldn't see it, but he did. It wasn't Keithe necessarily who Michelle was missing. Rather, it was companionship. She was used to having someone in her world, a man, constantly around. Keithe figured it would be up to him to help her see her error.

"I'm just glad you are allowing us a chance . . . to at least see where it can go from here, Keithe."

"I would never deliberately ignore you. We are better than that, Michelle." He shifted in his seat. "I do care for you." He readied himself. "And coming here tonight, I contemplated on my feelings for you. But I had to be true to myself." He paused. "I *do* love you. But *still* I'm not in love with you.

"It would be so unfair to you, Michelle, when . . ." He was afraid to throw Kenya's name in the mix. "When my heart is with someone else right now."

Michelle loosened her grasp.

"I don't really know how l feel about you moving here. But I'm here for you. As a matter of fact, the lady my heart is with is actually not that into me," he shared.

Unfolding her napkin, Michelle laid the piece of cloth on her lap. "Um, serves you right," she mumbled.

"What did you say?" Keithe had heard her loud and clear.

"I said I'm sorry to hear that." It was hard for Michelle to look him in the eyes. She must have looked like the biggest fool to him, she thought.

"What is it about me?" she questioned. Not really wanting to know . . . if it would hurt her. The older she got, the more her emotions were in charge. At least in her personal relationships.

Finally giving in to her emotions, Michelle bypassed mannerisms and placed her elbows on the table. "Am I some psycho? I mean, men leave me. No one stays. No one has fought for me . . . wanted me like . . ." Michelle cut her eyes toward a table with a couple engrossed in a deep, loving conversation. With the two sitting on the same side of the booth, Michelle choked back tears.

"I fought for you, Michelle. I prayed for you. Loved you like I have never loved another." He reached out for her hand. Holding her hand, which still bore the wedding ring he had picked out for her all by himself, Keithe let his head flop. "You are a God-given gift. Then you gifted me by showing me how great God is. You allowed Him to transform you into this magnificent woman who just wants to line up with His Word. I get that."

"Then what?" Michelle still wanted to know.

"I was fighting an internal battle to stay married . . . temptation to stray. If I had sinned I didn't want to hurt you in the process."

This was a first for Michelle. She never knew Keithe had fought to be faithful to her, instead of cheating on her. Unlike she had done to him for years, he had decided they part ways.

The tears stopped. Her love for him deepened all the more and she silently scolded herself for messing up all those years before.

"You truly are a good man," Michelle said through loving tears.

"I can only take that compliment if you accept some of the responsibility of molding me this way," Keithe urged.

"Agreed." Michelle smiled.

He held up his glass for a toast. "Forever, love?"

"Forever, love," Michelle agreed.

Chapter Thirty-one

"So how have you been doing, baby sister?" Kendra asked Kenya as the pair took a break. Two weeks until Mercy's big day, the two sisters spent the majority of the day finalizing the wedding plans.

"I'm doing . . ." Kenya let out a breath. "Well, I guess . . ." A beat passed. "I'm so tired of trying to keep things together." She bawled.

Sitting on her sister's living room sofa, staring at the flat screen, Kenya couldn't tell if she was coming or going.

"Whoa. Want to talk about it?" Kendra, nearly twenty years older than her younger sister, sat beside her and pulled Kenya into her arms.

Having taken over the role of mother for her sister, ever since their mother had passed away a few short years earlier, Kendra wanted to be what and who Kenya needed her to be. And for now, that was a listener.

"There is just so much, Ken. I don't even know where to start." She didn't want to look her sister in the eyes. Either way, she knew it would only be a matter of time before she had to get her heartache off of her chest.

"Start with telling me . . ." Kendra hesitated but couldn't take pretending as if she didn't know the rumors that had been going around about with her sister. "Tell me if it's true."

Kenya's eyes widened.

Kendra was a bishop's wife and if there was anything she heard throughout the church, it was gossip.

It didn't matter if the two didn't attend the same church. With conferences, conventions, and members of one church knowing other members at other churches, people talked. The only person Kendra was waiting for to tell her if the information was true or false was Kenya.

"Come on, Kenya." Kendra moved in closer to her sister and pulled her closer in her arms.

That was all it took for Kenya to release more of her tears. Lately it seemed all she did was cry. She was tired of it and the only way to get it out of her system was to come clean.

She nodded, displaying instead of telling Kendra it was in fact the truth. Not even caring how her sister knew, Kenya was somewhat relieved. Embarrassed, but relieved.

"I'm not gay, Kendra," Kenya released in almost a whisper.

"Well what are you?" Kendra threw a bit of an attitude, wondering how a woman could be with another woman and not call herself gay.

Having thought they were close, as sisters ought to be, Kendra thought if ever Kenya had some life-altering news to share, she would be the first to find out.

Getting up from the sofa, Kenya then decided to lay everything out for her sister. "Look. The reason why I didn't want to tell you is because I didn't want to disappoint you," she said.

"Me?" Kenara pointed to herself. "Baby girl, I'm the last one you need to worry about." Kendra sat with her back against the cushions. "It's the Lord you made a vow to, not me." She crossed her arms, knowing she indeed was upset with her sister.

Walking back and forth in front of the sofa, Kenya got angry every time she thought about the predicament Charlene had put her in. "Charlene came on to me. Kept making passes at me. Just wouldn't stop," Kenya said.

"Um, huh." Kendra raised her eyebrows and just listened.

"She just kept pressing me, bothering me . . . wouldn't talk about nothing else but how she liked my skin, my perfume . . ."

"Um," Kendra released.

Kenya finally sat back down. "Then she just touched me and kissed me." Kenya wanted sympathy.

"Kenya, look." Kendra pulled her leg onto the cushion. "I'm the last one who can judge or say you are or are not going to hell. All I'm saying is, deal with it. If you are homosexual, I'm going to love you, honey, regardless." Kendra didn't see why Kenya was pushing all of the blame on Charlene.

"Huh?" It was Kenya's turn to act like she wasn't in the know.

"Did she rape you, Kenya? Force you to have sex with her? I keep hearing you say Charlene did this, said this . . . but what did you do, baby girl?"

"I'm not gay, Ken!" Kenya jumped back against the cushions and grabbed her chest. "What are you saying?"

Knowing she would have to add a little tough love to her sister, Kendra didn't cut any corners.

"Look, Kenya. Okay, you say you're not gay . . . let's leave that right there." She moved an invisible NOT GAY sign to the invisible table. "Now let's deal with you participating in a lustful act. You were willing and able . . . you did it. Let's stay right here." She clasped her hands together. "Take ownership of what you also allowed to happen. Only being true to God about your faults is what's going to release the burden. Only with a sincere heart will God know if your repentance prayer is for real."

Kenya just looked and knew Kendra was telling the truth. No, she wasn't gay, but yes, she participated in a lustful act . . . whether she was enticed or went willingly.

"Honey, there are so many lustful demons in the church; women befriending the first lady while on the side being all up in the pastor's face. Oh, not with me!" She saw the worry in her sister's eyes. "They know I don't play. Then you have people wanting positions because it will get them closer to the opposite sex in order to make them a part of their lives. And no, ma'am, I don't have to tell you about homosexuality in the church.

"But you can't look at it as a gay issue. You have to look at it as a human race issue. People want love. Something is missing and God is the only one who can fill voids. That's when the flesh rears its ugly head.

"I'm sure you have a void. Not married and some of these ol' busted ministers running up in your face, trying to get in your skirt; it's hard to trust anybody, honey.

"Now, I'm not for"—Kendra made quotes in the air—"gay marriages, if that's what y'all want to call it." Kendra went off on a rant herself. "Mama would sho'nuff roll over in her grave, but—"

Kenya interrupted. "Kendra! Oh my goodness. You sure you ain't kin to Mother Gladstone? Geez."

Kendra rolled her eyes. "I'm old, Kenya, dear . . . but not that old." Kendra fanned herself. "I gotta go check on Mother Gladstone before she sends the po-pos out for me." Kendra went off on another story.

"I'm not gay, Kendra." Kenya sat back down and rested. "I just made a mistake and if it had been a man, it probably would have turned out the same way."

"Well, spare me the details." Kendra got up and walked to her purse. Removing her medicine bag, Kendra took her daily HIV medication. Long ago had the symptoms of the disease left her system. People questioned why she still took the medicine if that were the case. She would simply tell them God made the medicine and the doctors and so she was just following His orders.

"I'm grateful you recognize your faults." She popped the pills in her mouth and swallowed without water. "Moving forward is the only way."

Kendra had so much sympathy for people because God had sympathy for her. Over thirty years prior, Kendra was too hot to handle and too cold to hold. She did what she wanted and who she wanted. Lied and cheated and even stole her best friend, Gracie's, ex-fiancé.

She hurt so many people along the way, some wanting to kill her for just being a deceitful, hateful, scornful, and jealous woman. But God . . .

When many would have cast their friends to the side, Gracie was the only saving grace Kendra could count on. Even after Kendra passed HIV to Gracie's ex, Dillian, and later married him, Gracie was there. After he passed away, Gracie was there. During her own bout with HIV and wanting to give up on life, Gracie was still there for her. So now when it was Kenya's time to go through trials and tribulations, she would pay God's love forward.

"I may have my own opinion on things, Kenya-boo." Kendra loved her sister and treated her more as a daughter than sister. "But doesn't make them right. The only thing for certain is God's Word. I believe what you say. I know how the enemy can come in and do all kinds of things to your psyche.

"Doesn't mean you won't have to go through." Kendra rubbed her sister's back. "Looks like you have already been going through. But get ready because them church folk, once they hear it, they gonna act as if they ain't never spit in the grass or peed in a bucket."

"Huh?" Kenya looked bewildered with her sister's last statement. "You have *got* to be some kin to Mother Gladstone." Kenya wiped her eyes and shook her head.

"I'm that bad, huh?" Kendra questioned.

"Very! Leave the old clichés to the ones that have been around forever. You're not there yet." The two burst out laughing and hugged.

Chapter Thirty-two

It only took Pastor Peters a second to sit behind his desk. Charlene was glad. She held her mouth in an O shape, because, *Oh,* baby, was she about to tell it like it "T-I-Is." Charlene was ready to lay it on heavy.

Her own world had already crumbled. The jurisdictional evangelist, over the entire evangelist's unit under their church as a whole, had heard one too many stories about what Charlene actually did on her mission trips. Not only that, but the leader had passed all the information to their bishop. Needless to say, Charlene was demoted in her leadership role. It had been apparent that the laying on of hands was just the tip of the iceberg.

The word had gotten out. Obviously Charlene took opportunities in becoming the best of friends with her ministry team members: the women. But it was more than a friendship she had wanted from them.

"Ms. Charlene, it's been a great while since I've seen you last." Pastor Peters addressed her, not as evangelist, nor sister, but with her government name. "And so you wanted to see me. Quite eagerly I see. You've rescheduled back to back for some weeks." He looked through his schedule book.

All Charlene knew was she wasn't about to go down alone. Not everyone had to be talked into anything. Some went willingly. And those names, Charlene were dropping like hot potatoes.

Hearing his greeting, Charlene tilted her head, not believing the nerve of Pastor Peters disrespecting her.

"I apologize for those previous cancellations. My mother had an accident and then things coming up with the ministry. You know how it is. But how can I help you?"

His demeanor made her mad and helped her keep in her sympathy for his mother instead of showing remorse for the old bat. It may not have been right, but at this point, Charlene couldn't care less.

"Yes, I wanted to speak with you . . . personally." She eyed his secretary sitting beside her. "Privately."

Charlene's track record of coming up with "good ideas" for the church had come to a halt. It wasn't until she had put in another "God told me to" idea to their bishop about the need to go minister to the people that others had come to the defense of the ministry itself.

Apparently women had started speaking out against her. They had shared with one another how Charlene had approached them, sexually. Once they started exchanging stories about the fifty-something woman, their Holy Ghost wouldn't allow it to go on.

"It's fine." Pastor Peters nodded for his secretary to remove herself from his office. He knew without a doubt the meeting wouldn't take long. And from what he'd learned, even if Charlene were to come with accusations, he wasn't ready to buy in to it.

"I have an idea why you are here. I have the memo." He held up a faxed letter. Their bishop had interoffice mailed a letter stating her dismissal. "So I believe I'm ahead of you," he went on.

"No problem." Charlene shifted in her seat. "But why I'm here . . ." She was ready to share. They may not have been lies about her sexuality, her preference of being with women, but Charlene didn't think it had anything to do with her right to spread God's Word. She had led hundreds if not thousands to Christ. She had given God's commandments over His people.

People had been healed and delivered from spirits. No one could tell her God's power didn't live in her. She knew for herself that it did.

"I just want you to know that Kenya isn't too far behind me. If the church is cleaning house, then I believe you should know that—"

Pastor Peters leaned in toward Charlene. "Not here. You won't be able to take anyone from this church, under this evangelist team, down with you." He peered into her eyes, wanting to make sure she understood just where he was coming from without saying names.

"Your doings have been going on since we were kids, Charlene. So they finally caught up with you. Good riddance." He shrugged and he relaxed in his chair. "God don't play. But you aren't issuing no names out up in here." He pointed downward on his desk. "Charlene, anything that anyone has done in your presence no doubt was something brought on by you. So, if this wasn't what you wanted to talk about, then I'm all ears. But if you think I'm gonna listen to you rant, you have another think coming."

"We are all adults," she countered. "Every single person who goes out to missions, we are adults. I can't *make* anybody do anything they don't want to do." She sat up. "And furthermore, who are you and Bishop and whoever else to tell me I don't have power?"

"But see, that's where you are wrong, Charlene. I've heard you bring forth the Word. I've seen folk get saved and filled right at the altar under your ministry. But let's just put a name to this. If you are living a woman-to-woman relationship or acts, God is not pleased with it. I'm not saying it, Charlene. The Word is . . ." He lifted his Bible that sat on his desk. "God can use whomever he chooses to bring forth His Word. You remember the donkey, don't you?" He hoped he'd pull more out of the symbolism than just the donkey being the donkey.

"It's the sin that God hates. It's not you. It's not you the ministry is coming down on, it's the sin. From cover to cover we have to tell it like it is. We have to believe it for ourselves before we can spread it.

"God loves you; your sin is no greater than my own. I was a whoremonger. I was a young minister, my dad died and I took over the church, and I tried to sleep with every new face that came through the church's doors." Pastor Peters didn't mind sharing since he had preached about it so many times.

Charlene sat, her wall breaking down by the second. Hearing her own story being repeated through his own, Charlene was cornered with her sins.

"Did I preach the Word and what it said against fornication? Of course I did, but God got tired of me and gave me a way out. He allowed me to be caught. Brought me to my knees." Pastor Peters dropped his head as he recounted over thirty years ago. "I lost my position, my credentials. I lost the trust and support of God's people. I was crumbled. But I did it to myself." He pointed to his chest.

Tears were evident in Charlene's eyes. The heavy load of being who she was and doing what she did was too much. All of her defense mechanisms she had planned to throw at Pastor Peters were being torn down.

Charlene didn't want to give in, but while the pastor spoke, she was able to focus on her sin. Pastor Peters handed her a Kleenex as he continued.

"My sin was no different than yours. It took for me to see what I was doing. What I was *really* doing. How I had sinned against God and His people. God didn't make his women to be used and abused. Romans says it best what He meant for his people. It's us, flesh, who often get it wrong.

"After it was all said and done, God didn't let me die in my sin. God forgave me. And eventually, so did His people." He held up his hands to symbolize being able to pastor once again.

"I . . . It feels like this . . . this is who I'm supposed to be," Charlene muttered. "How can I stop something that seems as though I was born to be?"

He shared, "By prayer, fasting, and letting yourself truly have a talk with Jesus. Put down your title and make your true request made known to the Father. People often say they want to be real with themselves. But how often are we real with our Father? Do you believe all of God's Word?"

"What do you mean? Of course," she said through tears.

"Do you believe Jesus died on the cross for your sins?"

"Yes."

"Do you want to be cleansed of your sins?" Pastor Peters reached out his hands for Charlene. "Do you *want* to stop the lifestyle you're living? Are you tired of it? Do you believe God made man for woman and woman for man?"

Her head nod preceding her words, Charlene knew she wasn't outright happy with herself. She had fought the battle for years, by herself, trying to figure out why she couldn't allow herself to be the woman who God had ordained her to be. She saw now it was because it was true: even those in authority need to confess and get and receive prayer for their own struggles. Charlene had been trying to fight the enemy herself. She knew now she couldn't do it on her own.

"I do," she cried out. "I do believe God's Word. I do believe God made no mistake in me. I believe that God can cleanse me. I know He can. I know!" Charlene released her hands from the pastor as her hands went in the air to worship the Lord.

"Please forgive me, Father. I know your son Jesus died on the cross for my sins. Please forgive me . . . Help me, Lord. Help me." She brought her hands to her chest and repeatedly hit her heart. "Help me! Renew me, Jesus. Thank you, Lord. Thank you. Renew my mind. Purify me all over again, Lord."

"Lord do it for her, Jesus." Pastor Peters had come from around his desk and laid hands on Charlene's head.

"Lord, you knew about this divine appointment on this day, this hour. Lord, you are the knower of all things. You knew this day was coming, dear God. Only you knew. Our dear sister Charlene is here, in need of you to come into her heart once more, God. She is here, Lord Jesus, to pour out her heart and soul to you.

"We rebuke the enemy, we rebuke those desires. We cast them to the pits of hell to never be seen or heard of again. We believe in your Word. We call all temptation, all lusts, and all self-led spirits under subjection to your Word and cast them out. Purge, Lord." Pastor Peters wasn't letting up on the prayers that would restore and bless Charlene's soul.

Chapter Thirty-three

"Heeey, now. Glad I didn't miss the meeting," Mother Gladstone said. "Move on back now." Mother forced Charlene to walk backward, back into the office.

Beep, beep; she hit the horn on her scooter. "Gul, you moving too slow." Mother Gladstone zoomed around a stunned and wordless Charlene in her prescribed motorized wheelchair.

"Y'all ain't all the way finished, is ya?" She knew the answer to it. "I'll only be just a minute."

Pulling forward, then backward, trying to make a space for herself in her son's office, Mother Gladstone finally turned the key off.

"Baby, you gots to be ready when you gets one of these here. Sit down, sit down. Go'n and sit back down, baby," she said, realizing that Charlene was still standing.

Charlene obliged.

"You too." She threw a hand at her son without looking his way.

Pastor Peters did the honors. He didn't try to protest or talk his mother out of her . . . whatever it was she was up to. He knew her peculiar way of ministering to the women was her wisdom given to them the best way she knew how.

"I know the pastor and wife usually do the dual counseling, but under the circumstances, I understand my daughter-in-law is at home with the flu. Is that right, Pastor? Bless her heart." She showed what she really thought about everything on her face: lips turned under and rolling her eyes.

"So I'm here for any womanly"—Mother looked over her glasses—"questions or womanly"—she looked again—"advice." Mother sat with her hands in their usual spot: on the top of her stomach, underneath her breasts. "Do tell what all you all counseled about."

Pastor Peters filled his mother in on how he led Charlene back to Christ. How she had released all the pain in her heart.

"So how you feeling now?" Mother asked Charlene.

"Like he said, Mother, I just poured myself into my ministry from the very beginning. You know how hard it was for women to be accepted as anything more than being by a man's side in the ministry. It was heaven forbidden if she called herself preaching. It was like a competition." Charlene had nothing to lose and was willing to share all she had been battling.

Charlene's eyes were two times the size they normally were. All she could think was how now in her mid-fifties she'd be alone. But surprisingly, it was all well with her spirit.

"Okay. Well, that's quite good to hear. But I would like to know, are you repenting to God for bringing others along for the ride, or just because you sinned against His Word?"

Pastor Peters looked between the two women.

"Every day I'm regretful of what I've done. I have nightmares that remind me of me being lukewarm." Charlene stopped as the tears gathered. "My aunt used to watch me while my parents would go to the church and pray early in the morning, and at night when service would run long, she'd take us home for them. They were so into the ministry sometimes I couldn't tell if they knew I was there or not." She wiped her face with a used Kleenex. "Back then you couldn't stay home alone and you sho'nuff couldn't tell your parents who you wanted keeping you.

"I promised when I got older I would not put church before my kids. Having someone watch my kids who couldn't care less about them was out of the question. Then I just decided I wasn't gonna have any all together."

"Why would you decide that?" Mother asked.

"Until I was thirteen years old, she molested me. My aunt molested me every single time I had to go home with her. Every time!" she yelled and threw her hands to her face.

Pastor Peters jumped and walked around his desk once more.

"Charlene, I'm so sorry." He laid his hands on her shoulders. Mother grabbed at Charlene's hands.

"You don't have nothing to be ashamed of. The devil has tried to destroy your life, sweet angel," Mother Gladstone said.

"He has destroyed it! I'm no angel! You see, I turned around and did the same thing . . . only this time I got so-called willing participants. I'm no better!"

Squeezing Charlene's hands tight, Mother's glassed-over, cataract-filled eyes filled with tears. "In all my life, a sin has been a sin, regardless of what is done. You were a child with no one to protect you—"

"But they were supposed to. My daddy preached and prayed for so many people but never listened to me. I tried . . ."

Shaking her head, Mother wasn't going to allow Charlene to lose herself on what her parents didn't do. "They did what they knew to do at the time. Now was it right to not listen to you? No. But if no one taught them, they didn't know."

Charlene knew this to be true. The older she had gotten the more she shared with her parents about being molested. And it was true. They had only done what they knew to do at the time. The heartache and break she had witnessed on her parent's faces so many years ago reminded her they were just as pained as she was.

"Have you forgiven your parents?" Pastor Peters asked.

It took Charlene only seconds to nod.

"And have you forgiven your aunt?" he asked.

"She died," Charlene said between huffs. Having never shared her being raped with anyone besides her family, she didn't realize how long ago her aunt had died. "She died when I was twenty. Beat to death when her boyfriend found out she was gay. That's when everything in my life went even further downhill.

"When I heard people saying she was gay because all the things she did with other women, I figured I was gay. How could I not be?" She looked between Mother and Pastor Peters.

"Because you were a victim, Charlene." Having grown up in the church together, Pastor Peters thought back on their youthful days and how Charlene was always secluded and standoffish. He wished he would have known something then.

"But thank God you don't have to remain," he said.

"Honey, you can put down that curse and never pick it back up," Mother said.

"I know. . . ." she answered with her eyes closed.

"But you have to want to, Charlene. Yes'm, you have to want to. You can't know it's wrong and delibrly—" Mother Gladstone said.

"Deliberately," Pastor said.

"Deliberately." Mother chopped up the sound while squinting her eyes toward her son. Then she mouthed, "I'ma bust you in your eyes." Never missing a beat she continued. "You can't keep doing what you're doing. Or you will keep dying a slow death. A death that's going to place you in hell," she said.

"I know. And everything within me, the freedom I feel now, I'm only looking toward the hill," Charlene said.

"Because, honey, that's the only place your help is going to come from," Mother Gladstone agreed.

Chapter Thirty-four

There was beautiful music playing over the loud speakers and a lot of chatter was taking place in the sanctuary. While the wedding planner was in full swing with manning the decorations, the coordinator smoothed out all of her loose ends. She eyed her watch but didn't have a care in the world since she was being paid by the hour.

Mercy had left Grant outside, making a call to only God knows who. Kendra and Gracie ran around making sure everyone was in their places.

Kenya was on her way but had called and said she was stuck in traffic. Mercy already knew Kenya would be bringing her date. She'd called ahead of time to make sure it was okay if he came, and to inform Mercy that he would be meeting her at the church. They'd planned for a late-night hang out session afterward and it would be easier for them to take one car.

This was the last rehearsal before her big day, which was less than twenty-four hours away, and Mercy was excited about everything coming to an end. All of the jitters Grant was having had lent themselves to her, and not necessarily in a good way.

Since the night the news broadcast had displayed a house fire and Grant ran out of the house, there had been even more silence between the two. That night it had taken him until the wee hours of the morning to return home stating that it wasn't his friend's home that caught fire, but a next-door neighbor's. Who the friend was and even a name never escaped Grant's lips.

Mercy had been extra nervous and knew without a doubt she should have called off the wedding. But to her, she'd be letting down her family, herself, but most of all . . . her son.

Because Bishop had been in her life, Mercy never had to go without having a father figure around. Her biological father had died of a massive heart attack while she was in her mother's womb. All Mercy could think was that there was no way she could subject her son to a broken home before it even had a chance to officially grow. As far as Mercy was concerned, the less people knew about the inside of their marriage, the better. Whatever it was that Grant was going through was hurting Mercy deeply, but she was not a quitter.

"Here you go." Stoney handed Mercy the gag gift–styled bouquet filled with different colors of tissue paper, ribbons, and glitter.

"Cute. Real cute." Mercy didn't break a smile. "Oh no, ma'am," she said when she saw what Stoney had for her next.

Giggling uncontrollably, Stoney placed the paper plate, ridged hat on her sister's head. "Girl, stop. Enjoy every moment M and M. Go ahead and play along . . . geez."

"With that? You could have done better than that, Stoney. Who did this, Grant Jr.? You are wrong for that." She broke out in laughter for the first time since she had stepped foot inside of the church. "It's okay. Your day is coming, honey," Mercy guaranteed.

"I'm sure, but your day is now." Stoney smiled. With a surprised look on her face, Stoney waved at the door when she saw her mom make her way through the sanctuary doors. Then she realized where they were and became nervous.

Stoney's eyes grew big. She had known of all of the ruckus that had gone on between her mother and father back in the day. Not to mention her stepmother, Kendra, and Mrs. Gracie and the battles between them. From all her mother had filled her in on, Stoney was getting more nervous by the minute.

With Michelle looking around the room for her, Stoney turned just in time to see Kendra's eyes lie on Michelle.

Without a thought, but knowing she had to put some pep in her step, Stoney doubled up her walking as she made her way to her mother. All she knew was that she had to get to Michelle before Kendra did. Halfway there, Stoney called out, "Mom!"

"Michelle!" Kendra called out simultaneously.

When Kendra's arms opened as she continued her stride toward Michelle, Stoney didn't know what to think. She hoped for the best, but wondered if Kendra would actually throw a blow at her mother in the church.

Slowing her pace, Stoney came to an almost halt and keyed in on what was happening. She blinked. She couldn't believe what she was seeing. Totally stopping in her tracks, Stoney put her hands on her hips.

"I am so happy you could make it. Thank you for offering to help, Michelle." Kendra held on to Michelle's hand after their embrace.

Shrugging, Michelle retorted with, "You're welcome. I figured, why not. It's not like I have a life," Michelle said as she flopped her hand to her side.

"I must be dreaming," Stoney mumbled to herself and eased closer to the two.

What Stoney hadn't known was that the Michelle and Kendra had been talking cordially. Since their chance meeting, in an odd kind of way, Kendra had become a confidant, a mentor to Michelle. In turn, Kendra knew why Michelle had had extra time in her schedule. With things not working out with Keithe as she had hoped for, the two women decided to close the gap they'd had between them in all the years. All that Kendra knew was if Gracie could forgive her for her wrong, surely she could do the same for Michelle.

"When did all of this happen?" Stoney made her way in the middle of the two. "Really?" Stoney looked into Michelle's eyes and wondered why she hadn't brought her up to date with her new friends.

"Where shall we start?" Michelle finally laid eyes on Stoney. "Hey, honey. I was looking for you." She veered off from the question in Stoney's eyes. Michelle was just ready to go with the flow.

"And so you found me." Stoney was still shocked, giving her mother sass. "Isn't this a pleasant surprise?" Her eyes watered. "You two amaze me on so many levels. I want to be just like you two one day." The three of them participated in a group hug.

Mercy appeared just as the three pulled apart. "Enough of this mushy stuff. Hi, Ms. Michelle." Mercy leaned in for a hug. She had spent time with Michelle and Stoney as she visited her stepsister in Houston over the years.

"We have things to do, ladies. Chop, chop." Mercy clapped her hands.

Kendra and Michelle made their departure. They headed toward another room that housed flowers, greenery, and accessories, ready to help out the decorator as much as possible.

"I'm here!" Kenya was out of breath. She wanted to make sure she wasn't late for rehearsal.

Her only role was to show up and officiate; however, she wanted to make sure she went over the specifics so that neither Mercy nor Grant would be caught off-guard with the questions, prayers, and especially the recital of the vows. Kenya wanted to make sure the flow of the ceremony was all it could be and more.

Placing her purse on the first pew she saw available, Kenya moved down the aisle where Stoney and Mercy were standing and asked, "Are all of your bridesmaids here?"

"Check," Mercy said and did an invisible check mark in the air.

"Oh she checked us all right. We are here." Stoney looked around and waved toward the other brides-maids, who had gathered into the sanctuary. Walking off, Stoney went to gather the few who had scattered off in various directions. "Hey, ladies, let's get in our places."

Nudging her aunt with her hip, Mercy was nosey. "Soooooo, where is your dude? I thought he was meet-ing you here?"

"Uh. Girl. We calmed that down." Kenya rolled her eyes. "Actually he is just cool and he's no bit more in-terested in me than I am him. But you know what? He has turned out to be a great friend."

"Word?" Mercy questioned with her hands on her hips. Her mind jumbled in thought but wouldn't dare start with the questions. Nope. Not when it was her day.

"Word," Kenya replied. They both laughed. "It's a long story, niecey. I really wasn't interested in him. I was only kicking it with him to avoid his friend because I had to work out some issues of my own. If you learn

anything from me, just don't try to figure anything out
yourself. Just let God do it."

With wrinkled eyebrows, Mercy just listened. Then
nodding in an agreement, Mercy asked, "Was his
friend that horrible?"

"Not at all. Actually his friend was just . . . right there."
Kenya couldn't believe it when she saw Keithe walk
through the doors. "What is Keithe doing here?" she wondered aloud.

Mercy held on to the fake bouquet Stoney had handed
her. She was looking back and forth between Kenya
and Keithe, who had made his entrance deeper into the
sanctuary.

"Mr. Keithe? You like Mr. Keithe?" Mercy said more
to herself than her Aunt Kenya, who had already taken
off up the aisle.

"Who likes who?" Stoney asked as she walked up and
stood by her sister. "Oh, there's Pops. It's about time
he got here," Stoney said and walked off with Kenya on
her heels.

"Hey there, Deacon Morgan. What are you doing
here?" Kenya asked with a questionable look on her
face, having walked over to the man who she no doubt
had a crush on.

"Hey." Stoney walked up to hug her stepfather, burying
herself underneath Keithe's arms. Shying away, Kenya
was embarrassed to think Keithe was Stoney's boyfriend.
Had she known that, there was no way she would have
walked to greet him.

"Oh. Auntie. Kenya. I'm sorry. Have you met—"
Stoney tried to introduce the two.

"I'm sorry, I wasn't trying to interrupt . . . I thought . . ."
Kenya turned and started walking away, not knowing what
she was trying to say.

"Huh?" Stoney was confused. "No, you're okay. I was going to ask if you met my pops?" Stoney took the bag from Keithe and kissed him on the cheek. "You are so awesome. I thought I had gotten it from your condo last night when I left." She continued talking as she looked in the bag to make sure the content she needed was accounted for.

"We've met," Keithe chuckled and shared with Stoney as he held on to her. With a reassuring look on his face, Keithe could tell what Kenya thought about him and Stoney. "We attend the same church."

Loosening his hold on Stoney, Keithe moved in close to Kenya. With a hug he said, "Stoney's my stepdaughter." He wanted Kenya to relax.

"Get out!" Kenya let her thoughts escape.

"Wait . . . wait a minute." Stoney stopped her rummaging and stood back. Reeling in the conversations that she, Mercy, and Kenya had had about men, Stoney wondered if her pops had indeed been that very same crush. With her eyes widened, Stoney pulled in her lips and didn't want to blow Ms. Kenya's cover.

"Okay. Well. Thanks, Pops. I'll leave you two alone. I mean, um. Yeah. Um. I will call you later." She leaned in for another tight squeeze and a peck on the check.

"I don't know if I will be at your place or Mom's . . ." Just that quick Stoney remembered that her mother was in the vicinity. Knowing her mother was pressing her way to get over Keithe, Stoney figured it wouldn't be a good thing if Michelle saw just who Keithe had the hots for. "Oh, shoots." Stoney knew if Michelle saw Keithe and Kenya in one another's face, there would be trouble. "Pops, I need to talk to you for a minute," Stoney spoke in haste and moved in once again to take Keithe off of Kenya's hands. "'Scuse us, Ms. Kenya. We will be right back."

Kenya shrugged her shoulders, thinking nothing of the exchange, and excused herself from the sanctuary and went down the hall to the ladies' room.

Grabbing Keithe by his hand, Stoney raced her stepfather out through the sanctuary doors and toward the foyer. Looking both ways, down either hall, Kenya needed to make sure the coast was clear.

"Mom's here," Stoney tried her best to whisper. "And from the way you and Ms. Kenya are making goo-goo eyes at one another, I think you better split."

With his hands deep inside of his pants pockets, Keithe said, "Stoney, stop being so paranoid." When Stoney gave him the "oh, okay, you must've forgot" look, Keithe became a little testy.

"Look, me and your mother already had our talk. We are divorced, Stoney. I love you and your mother very much, but—" Keithe was cut off as Michelle and Kendra walked up to them down the hallway on their way in to the sanctuary.

"Hey, Keithe. What are you doing here?" Michelle walked up to her handsome ex-husband and gave him a tight squeeze.

"Hey, you," he greeted her. "Just bringing Stoney her items she'd left over at my place. *And*"—he looked at Stoney and knew she didn't want him to share what he was about to—"I'm trying to school our daughter on the understanding we have." He used his pointer finger to point back and forth between the two of them. "How are you doing, Kendra?" Keithe asked, not wanting to be rude as he saw her standing politely with her arms folded.

"Say it ain't so. What's going on, Stoney?" Michelle asked, rubbing her daughter's back, knowing Stoney worried about her too much.

"Oh, nothing. I just want to make sure you both are happy . . . and when it's time for you to move on, that there are no hurt feelings left." Stoney was sincere in her approach to the truth.

"But we are friends and will always be as such, Stoney." Michelle added Keithe to make it a trio hug.

Looking directly at Keithe, Michelle wanted to make sure the sincerity of her words was heard.

"I'm so sorry for all of this inconvenience, Keithe. I can't believe I did all of this, just to try to get back with you. And I'm just as sorry, Stoney, for putting you in the middle. But I'm doing better." Michelle looked over at Kendra and reached for her new friend's hand and gave it a squeeze.

"God is good," Kendra said.

"All the time," the three Morgans chimed in.

Just as Kendra was about to share how blessed she, too, was to be able to mend ties with them, there was a ruckus heard coming from the sanctuary. As she headed in that direction, the others were hot on her heels.

Chapter Thirty-five

"Huh? Who is this, Grant?" Mercy inched closer. With Grant Jr. running into the arms of a man she didn't know, Mercy stood with tons of questions.

Mercy couldn't deny that the man she had been staring at didn't look familiar, because he did. It was just that Mercy couldn't put her finger on where she had seen him before. "I'll wait." She shifted on her right hip.

The whole incident wouldn't have thrown her off-course, but soon after her baby took off running, her fiancé did a fast walk in the same direction. When she looked over to someone, anyone to see if they too had gotten a jolt to their stomach, when Mercy saw that her bridesmaids held questionable looks on their faces, one with suspicion and disgust, Mercy couldn't leave it alone.

"Who?" she asked again and again. "Grant, surely you can talk. Who is he?" Mercy threw her voice, mixing it with sarcasm. Giving Grant plenty of time to open his mouth and share the truth with her, Mercy tapped her foot.

When Grant couldn't open his mouth to tell the truth, Mercy took it upon herself to get the identity of the stranger.

Reaching out for Grant Jr., Mercy said, "Who are you, sir? Because obviously my fiancé doesn't seem to be able to talk at the moment. I mean, my baby knows who you are . . . and if you are an extension of the fam-

ily, then I need to welcome you." She shifted Grant Jr.
on her hip. "Don't you think?"

"Uncle Mike, Uncle Mike," Grant Jr. repeated. Making it clear to Mercy that he was no stranger to her son.
In turn she knew he couldn't have been a stranger to
her fiancé.

"Oh." Mercy swung around, getting more agitated by
the minute. "So it's clear. You're Mike. Everybody say
hi to Mike." With her nose flaring, Mercy was on edge.
She had this feeling she just couldn't shake, and it was
rotting in the pit of her belly.

The smile that Mike had kept toward Grant Jr. the
whole while quickly faded away. Shaking his head back
and forth, Mike couldn't believe he had just walked in
on the wedding rehearsal of his lover. Wanting to say
something . . . anything . . . he couldn't. Feeling like he
was in the midst of a movie, Mike froze and waited for
Grant to break the ice, to lie, or make up some story in
order for him to be able to leave the premises in one
piece. When Mike saw Keithe, Michelle, and Stoney
walk up, he knew it wouldn't happen.

Having overheard the one-sided exchange as they
walked into the sanctuary, Stoney couldn't hold her
peace. "What is he doing here?" Stoney said, confused
as she glared at Mike. It didn't take long for Stoney to
take over the question asking for her sister. "What are
you doing here, Mike? Did you need something? Are
you here for someone?"

Hearing her sister ask back-to-back questions jolted
Mercy's memory. It was Mike . . . the Mike. The one
whose stories of betrayal Stoney had shared. Automatic tears found their way through as Mercy's sus-
picions became a reality right in front of her. She was
no fool. All the late-night creeping and phone calls
all came back to her. Not to mention when Grant had

run out of the house at the mention of another man in distress. She just stood thinking, wondering if the man standing in the church's sanctuary had indeed been the one Grant ran to rescue.

Mercy knew in her spirit that there had been more to Grant and his secret life. Her woman's intuition told her so. She just never figured it would be a man on the other end.

One of the bridesmaids came to take Grant Jr. from Mercy's arms at the sight of Mercy not being able to hold her composure. Kendra praying a prayer even before she reached her daughter, Mercy was barely able to stand.

Through bated breaths and crowded tears, Mercy yelled, "Somebody is going to start talking! Somebody is going to tell me what is going on . . . and now." Mercy had had enough.

"Calm down, Mercy." Stoney cried with her sister, realizing what was taking place. She felt the pain as if it were her own.

When Kenya had asked Mike to meet her there, Mike hadn't thought about whose church or whose wedding was taking place. Being that he never allowed Grant to speak about his own personal life, Mike hadn't thought that far ahead. Kenya went to another church so how, Mike thought, had they connected?

He knew when he'd met Grant he had told him he was a father and engaged to his child's mother. And at the moment, Mike thought back to when Grant tried to tell him he couldn't go along with something. If Mike hadn't been drunk off of his stoop, all emotional, he was sure he would have remembered before now. *This is what Grant was talking about.*

"I'm Mike." He blew out a breath and put his hands in his pocket. Looking around the sanctuary, all eyes were on him. Then his eyes finally landed on Stoney. "I . . . I didn't know," he tried to explain to her. If there was anyone he felt he needed to come clean with, it was her. She had once been near and dear to him.

As soon as Mike saw fury in Stoney's eyes, her mouth flew open. He closed both his eyes and mouth.

"How dare you walk up in here and ruin people's lives? What did you do this time, Mike?" Stoney peered at Grant with the same daring eyes.

Right when Mike was sure she was about to let him have it once more he heard, "You made it."

Mike opened his watered eyes. Kenya leaned in to give him a hug. "I see you've met everyone." Kenya had walked back into the sanctuary from her visit to the ladies' room. She still held a smile not realizing what had transpired. Even with the tension so thick, Kenya had not allowed herself to see all the tears.

"This is my niece, Mercy, and her fiancé, Grant. This here"—Kenya pinched his cheeks—"is Grant Jr. With his cute little self." As Kenya finally pulled her eyes off of Junior and placed them on Mercy when no hellos or how do you dos were exchanged, Kenya sensed something was wrong.

With Kendra and Stoney holding Mercy on either side, Kenya became worried.

Her niece, was all Mike could get his mind to reel in.

"This . . . this is your friend, Aunt Kenya?" Mercy huffed, shifting her weight from her mother, back to Stoney, tears now pouring from her eyes. "Junior seems to know him. Grant seems to know him . . . but nobody will tell me how. My son is calling this man Uncle Mike and I don't know why!" Mercy became irate once more.

At the very moment Mercy was mad at everyone, especially herself. Mercy had been making herself believe that the little secrets Grant had been keeping were nothing much. The Internet sites, receipts from clubs she'd looked up to find out were swingers club, had just been a phase he was going through, she had told herself. But she knew she had only been lying to herself.

Grant's mannerisms had changed. He'd also been pressuring her to have sex, bypassing the vow they'd made together two and a half years earlier: their vow to wait until marriage to have a sexual relationship.

"I'm in love with Mike, Mercy," Grant let out, with a matter-of-fact tone in his voice. When he closed his eyes, Grant never saw the punch Mercy threw.

"Mercy!" Stoney called out, grabbing at her sister once more.

Not once opting to hit her back, Grant shed tears as he backed away and defended himself with words. "I'm gay, Mercy. I can't do anything about it. Ain't that right, Kenya?" Grant decided to ride on the gossip that had been spread about Kenya. Grant rubbed his face and allowed spite to build in his heart. "Heck, we might as well make this a coming out party. Come on, Kenya, share your testimony, 'Hi, I'm Kenya, and I'm gay also.'" Grant rolled his eyes and blew a breath through his lips. It didn't faze him.

Kenya didn't know what to do but move out of the way. Everything was moving too fast for her.

Just hearing the announcement alone sent Mercy into another tailspin. "Oh no! Oh H to the—"

"Mercy, what is going on? Watch your language in God's house!" Bishop said, confused about the scene he had walked in on.

"Daddy, they brought hell up in the church. Tell my daddy, Grant." Mercy walked up on Grant once again and pushed him in the chest. "Tell him who you are, what you've done!"

By the time Bishop had made it farther into the sanctuary toward his daughter, Grant had moved to stand in front of Mike, as if Mercy was going to go after him next.

"Don't, Mercy," Stoney cried and held on to her sister.

Grant Jr. had scurried from one of the bridesmaids and held on to his mother's skirt until his grandma picked him up.

Leaning down to bring her grandson to her hip, Kendra came eye to eye with Grant and his next move. When she looked down and saw Grant reach for Mike's hand she said, "Grant, no."

"No, what, Mrs. Kendra. Bishop? I've done everything you all wanted me to do." Grant looked back at Mike, who was trying to release himself from the scene. "Don't go," Grant said as he caught sight of Mike tipping backward. "I have to do what I want to do. What I feel." He looked forward at Mercy and her family. "I've kept my baby, darn near raised him alone, while Mercy got to get all educated. It wasn't an option for me, huh?"

"Grant, that is not true," Bishop said. "We just made the decision that Mercy would finish her schooling then you—"

"That's the problem. I'm always the *then*. Well, y'all can have it." He felt Mike let go.

"No . . . no. This is wrong. Stop," Mike shouted and fought off Grant's attempt for him to stay. "This is . . . It's not right." Mike looked at Mercy, who was crying uncontrollably.

"Son, I think it's best for you to head on out of here, too." Bishop took two steps toward Grant and knew if he'd take another, he'd be *at* the altar on his own Sunday repentance instead of insisting that others come.

When Mike saw pain in Kenya's eyes, he felt a pang in his heart. It wasn't until he laid eyes on Stoney as he walked backward that he realized how many women he'd hurt. Maybe inadvertently, but, nonetheless, they were hurt.

Right as he turned to make a departure, Mike bumped into Keithe, who grabbed his friend around the shoulders. Looking past Mike and into the small crowd that had accumulated, Keithe didn't want to think what he was assuming was the truth.

"Mike . . . man." He closed his eyes and shook his head. "Are you okay? Where are you going?"

Shaking his own head nonstop, Mike couldn't answer Keithe. He couldn't even look up from the heaviness his heart and his mind felt.

"Go home, Mike. I'll be by later, okay? Just go straight home. Answer the phone when I call," Keithe said.

Standing next to Keithe the whole while, Michelle grabbed for Mike and took him in her arms. It hadn't been a secret that Mike had never been Michelle's favorite person, but through God's love she saw a hurting soul and wanted to comfort him just as Kendra and Gracie had done with her. It was then that Mike released tears he'd been holding in. Yet and still, he knew if he stayed a moment longer more turmoil would brew.

With his hand on Mike's back, Keithe looked across the way to where Kenya had been standing. When he saw her run up the aisle and out of the sanctuary leaving tears behind, Keithe knew he had no choice but to follow her.

Chapter Thirty-six

Everything around her was going black. The dizziness crept to her eyelids but not before Kenya's view of the flowers, the tulle, the runner, and everyone in an uproar landed in her memory. If no one else got it, she did. As she tried to squeeze her eyes shut, trying her best to block out what was really going on, tears formed to no avail.

Apparently while Kenya thought she was the only one with drama, she probably had lesser. Just seeing tears on her loved ones faces had brought on an immediate heartbreak.

Kenya had stood and watched as the drama unfolded right before her very eyes. Things were so heated coming from Mercy, which she knew was pain and resentment, that Kenya wished she had on her Air Maxes instead of her slingbacks for the speed she needed to make her exit easier.

Kenya didn't have to read in between the lines. She didn't mean to break down as she had, but it was too much for her to take in, Mike being involved with her niece's fiancé. All the guilt she had been trying to control of her own faults and her own actions attacked her all at once. The only thing Kenya could do was to run from it all.

With her hands still surrounding her face, Kenya looked both ways down the hall, trying to figure which way to escape to. When she heard her name being

called, Kenya looked back and saw Keithe coming after
her.

"Kenya, don't," he said as she ran down a connected
hall. If she kept running, eventually she'd be in her sister's office, away from all the hurt and pain that she felt
she'd somehow caused.

She couldn't believe how things had panned out. She
couldn't help but feel everything was somehow connected back to her.

"Grant and Mike," she whispered through tears, questioning herself. "Dear, Lord," she panted as she walked
around in circles in the office.

Kenya had created this ridiculous game and played it
herself. She knew Mike had had a questionable lifestyle
but needed him to cover her own. In the midst of it all,
he had his own relationship with Grant. No doubt she
would be exposed. All she could think was how God
had forgiven her. But how could He let something like
this happen?

She didn't know how, but something told her all of
the secrets were about to come out, especially hers.
And it was all going down in a roomful of people she
loved.

"Oh, Jesus!" Kenya thought about what Mercy must
be feeling. Anxiety running through her body, Kenya
went to leave the office, wanting to head back to Mercy.
Before she could cross the threshold, she slid right into
Keithe's chest. "I . . . I gotta go check on Mercy. Dear
Lord, she must be devastated." Kenya burst into tears.
Then she thought about her own hidden mistake being
brought forward.

When Keithe grabbed and held her tight, Kenya
broke down in his arms.

"I got you, Kenya. Don't worry. Bishop has Mercy." He
wanted her to focus on her own ongoing pain. "What's

going on with you? I thought you knew Mike had a questionable lifestyle." He reverted to their dinner. When no answer came he said, "I mean, this is some wild stuff, if it's what I think it is . . . But what's done in the dark will always come to the light and—" She didn't let him finish.

"But with Grant? He's just a boy. And Mercy. Poor Mercy. How could they?" Kenya looked up into Keithe's eyes. It was obvious Keithe hadn't heard Grant spill the beans on her own sins. Had he?

Holding her head between his hands, Keithe wanted so badly to claim her as his own. If he could've, he'd kiss her forehead and let her know he'd protect her.

"We all sin, Kenya . . ."

"I know that!" she shot at him. "We all have our own crosses to bear. If I hadn't been playing games with Mike, he wouldn't even be here. There would've been no reason for him to come by. What have I done?" She brought her hand to her forehead.

"You have nothing to do with what Grant and Mike have going on." He wanted to soothe Kenya's heartache. Realizing she admitted to playing games, Keithe questioned her. "Games?" Keithe said. "What games were you playing?"

With disgust, hating that she had opened a can of worms, Kenya knew she had to share what she'd done. Her heart had been leaning more and more toward giving Keithe a chance; rather, hoping Keithe gave her a chance. Now she wasn't so sure. That was one of the reasons she wanted to meet up with Mike in the first place. She needed Mike's help with assuring Keithe that she was interested in him, always had been.

"Keithe, there is something I have to tell you." Kenya removed her body from Keithe but held his hand. Leading him to the two chairs in front of the desk, Kenya

didn't bother to wipe her tears. "From the very beginning, I thought you liked me. I wasn't sure, but the more
you made it known I couldn't deny it. I was scared." She
looked down.

"Can I ask why?" Keithe didn't want to leave a stone
unturned.

"Because I liked you also. But it was me. I'm ashamed
to admit it, but I was holding on to some things I had . . .
some things I had done." She blew out a breath.

"Like?" He held her hand.

A sick feeling settled in the pit of her stomach. Kenya
knew she couldn't back down, forever leaving Keithe
wondering. Especially if she wanted to see if the two of
them could actually form a real relationship.

"I knew Mike was gay. I'd seen him around, heard
things. So the day he came into the classroom, I felt
it would be my chance to use him . . . in order to keep
you away," she wanted to clear up. "It sounds bad but
I didn't want to hurt you." Kenya told the truth. "I had
done things to confuse myself. I didn't want to bring
you in the middle of it. Not until I knew . . ."

"Knew what? What did you do, Kenya?" Keithe half
smirked and threw out a nervous laugh. "What?"

With a hard squeeze to both of his hands, Kenya
took in a breath and then shared, "Until I knew for
sure if I myself was gay. You see, when I went away on
missions . . ."

Keithe's head was spinning. Hearing what Grant
had shouted in the sanctuary, Keithe thought he had
mistaken his words. He had wanted so badly to believe
he had heard wrong. But now with Kenya rehashing
her past, he figured he'd only heard what he wanted to
hear.

"I thought I had feelings for her. I thought this was
something I had been harboring," Kenya was sharing.

He had heard her right. Kenya had been in the act, er, practicing, uh, participating . . . He didn't know what to call it besides fornicating with a woman.

Keithe was angry. There was no way he could handle this. As much as he loved Mike, he hated his sin. The mere thought of two men together made him so angry. He'd heard when a man gets that angry about gay men, he must be harboring feelings himself. Keithe knew without a doubt this couldn't be further from the truth. He definitely knew it now because his heart grasped the same hate for Kenya's situation.

Kenya felt Keithe's hand loosen its grip. She stopped mid-sentence and knew right then and there . . . it was too much for him. She sat staring into the eyes looking back at her. What else could she say? There was nothing left to say but she tried anyway. "I searched my heart. I asked the Lord to search my heart." Kenya was embarrassed. When she heard the Lord speak, *Be transparent*, she had to continue. "It was a moment. The first and last moment at that. I was weak and when the opportunity came I didn't even fight it. Didn't even look for a way of escape. I wasn't walking in the spirit. Wasn't fasted up, wasn't prayed up . . . just there.

"At first I was confused, thinking I had discovered I was gay. But I now know if it were a man, I would have done the same thing. I was walking in flesh." Kenya was weak from coming clean, along with the day's events.

"Charlene?" Keithe simply asked as he lounged back in the upright chair. *So that is what Mother Gladstone was trying to tell me,* he thought.

An easy nod came from Kenya.

"I want to feel some kind of way right now. I don't know what," he thought out loud. "So you knew all along . . . You knew Mike was gay?" He watched Kenya's head acknowledging she knew. "What about him and Grant?" Keithe asked.

"Not at all." Kenya still felt like a traitor even though she had no clue. "I hope Mercy believes me. I was willing to lie to the end just to keep my embarrassment out of the limelight. But now, with this happening, I don't care. This may not mean much, but, Keithe, I truly admire you. Always have from the very beginning. I just didn't know how to get over what I'd done. I thought I didn't know anything about me anymore." She touched her chest. "Thought all my walking with Jesus was in vain. But God saw fit to give me a chance to really pour my heart to Him," Kenya shared.

"And?" Keithe questioned. Just that quick he felt Kenya's confession. He felt her sincerity in allowing herself to be transparent in front of him.

"And . . . all this has been a lot. I can't promise I can emotionally be there like I would need to be in a relationship, at least not right at the moment. But I'd love if we could be friends." Kenya looked at the door, knowing it was time to return to the others. She had to face what she'd done.

"I'd like that, Kenya." He grabbed for her soft and sweaty hand. "I'm just a call away."

Not questioning if she needed or wanted him to pray strength on her, Keithe took it upon himself to cover her in prayer.

Chapter Thirty-seven

"How could you?" Stoney had followed Mike through the sanctuary and out the glass doors. "Vicky's life wasn't enough to try to ruin? You needed more notches under your belt?" she hollered in between her cries. "I trusted you." Stoney recounted how she once looked up to Mike as a brother.

Trying his best to walk away without recourse, Mike remembered he had parked on the other side of the church. Stopping in his tracks, Mike put one hand in his pocket and another on the bridge of his nose.

The two had once been friends; no, more like sister and brother. Mike had helped her through the unknowns in her life.

Meeting him at her church, Stoney was young and naive to know Mike's true struggles. For him, never sharing who he was, she felt betrayed when the truth finally came out. Her friend Vicky had to be the one to tell her. That was, after she had fallen in love with him and hoped to spend the rest of her life with him. Just that easy Mike had loved her, betrayed her, and dumped her.

"Answer me. How could you do this to my sister?"

To her surprise, Mike turned with tears in his eyes. "How do you figure I knew Grant was your sister's fiancé?" Mike talked through a stopped-up nose. "You think it's easy living this way? I'm gay, Stoney. I'm out!" he yelled, and threw his hand high. "I'm out. You happy? But do you think it's easy? And to love God as much as I do . . ." He pulled his hands to his heart and closed the gap between them. "Do you seriously think it's easy for me?" He turned and continued to walk away.

"Yes, it is. It is *just* that easy, Mike," she snapped. "You have a choice in how you are living. You have a choice in giving up that life and living right."

"A choice? So you are saying I have a choice and I chose to be gay? No. What I choose is to act on it or not, and even then it's not my choice," he shouted angrily. Too many times people had told him how to act, when to act, and the places to act. "So you mean to tell me, when you were hooked on prescription drugs, you chose to do that? Or Vicky chose to keep having kids back to back with different men? Or that your mother had a choice and in her right mind chose not to raise you? . . ." He no longer cared if he hurt her feelings. "I didn't think so! Whether it was something born in me or spiritual warfare, I fight daily. I don't choose this. If I could snap, blink, or stomp it out of me I would."

Stoney stood silent. She listened to him. He, adding her own situation and her emotions to the scenarios, caught her off-guard.

"I'm not some malicious, cold-hearted jerk who goes around breaking up families. Yes . . . I was wrong for doing that to Vicky. But it doesn't mean I don't love her."

"You didn't tell me. You never shared with me who you were." Stoney cried for their past.

"This is me, kid." Mike walked closer. "This is Mike. I'm gay, homosexual, lover of the same sex. Whatever you want to call it, it will not change who I am."

"But, is that who you want to be?" Stoney calmed down once she thought about Mike not being able to *make* Grant do anything. It was apparent: if Grant was gay it was by his own account.

Mike nodded. "I'm okay with who God made me to be."

Stoney shook her head.

"My God, Stoney. The God I read about in the Bible is my God too. How could I love Him if He wasn't?"

"The Word says you can't have two Gods. You can't serve two, Mike."

Mike closed his eyes and swallowed. "I don't feel that way. All I know is I'm not serving some made-up gay God. I'm not reading in between the lines. I know what the Word says. And I believe it. I'm fighting it . . . I am. But I'm still a believer. Even if it looks like I'm losing."

There was nothing else to say. A sorry couldn't heal the past and answering questions all day couldn't negate the fact the Mike was gay and Stoney still loved him like a brother.

Only a heartfelt cry could seal them. It was an unspoken fact that Stoney would stick by her sister. But that wouldn't keep her from praying for Mike. Sincerely.

Three years had passed and although Stoney had Mercy, Mike couldn't be replaced. He knew her like only a blood brother would.

The two embraced through guilt, sincerity, and pain. But most of all, forgiveness.

Chapter Thirty-eight

All the signs were there. Heck, they were divorced for crying out loud. So what did Michelle expect? Though she held up good in front of Keithe and Stoney, it was still so very new to Michelle that she just may end up alone for the rest of her life.

She had moved in haste. The fact of the matter was that she had moved in self, flesh. Michelle hadn't listened when she consulted God, for if she had, her mind and body would still be in Houston instead of in the midst of the uproar, sitting on a pew at Stoney's father's church.

She tried not to badger herself too bad. Though she was saved, Michelle was still on the surface level of praying and listening. She hadn't bothered to get deeper into God's Word for herself. If she had, she would have heard Him reply with a *no* to her moving from Houston. Looking around at all the commotion and tears, Michelle knew that would change in her life. Prayer and listening to God's answer was something she would have to be patient with.

Yes, God hated divorce, but what was done was done. There was no way He wanted her to continue to hurt herself emotionally.

Her cracked tooth, and even Kendra and Gracie's impromptu girl talk, had been God's way of telling Michelle to cover her heart. Her heart was deceitful and she followed it all the way from Houston and made her way into Dallas, though temporarily.

She had done well until she saw Keithe literally run out the church after that Kenya woman. Michelle wanted to die from the heartbreak she felt just seeing Keithe fight for something he truly had wanted. That something that wasn't her. Michelle thought, *if that was a sign from God, I surely got it.* Sooner rather than later she would wrap up her living arrangements in Dallas and leave, heading back to Houston.

A hand on her shoulder was the only thing able to bring her out of the thoughts she was drowning in. Her eyes, flooded with tears, were too heavy for her to look up.

"Mom? Are you going to be all right?" Stoney asked with Grant Jr. propped on her hip. Still struggling with her own pain about how things had ended for her sister, Stoney couldn't bypass checking on her mother, who had sat in one spot for what seemed like forever in her own tears.

With her lip tucked, Michelle moved her head in a practiced motion, too afraid of hearing her voice and the cracking she was sure it would do.

"Are you ready to go? Do you just want to leave your car here and we can come back for it?" Stoney worried about her mother. "I'm going to take Junior and—"

Shaking her head, not wanting Stoney to take away from the baby's needs in order to tend to her, Michelle cleared her throat. Before she was able to give her plans, Michelle blinked as she saw a familiar face coming through the sanctuary doors. It was Deek.

"I will take care of her, Stoney." Deek gave Stoney a salute as he made his way closer to where they were sitting.

Realizing that it wasn't just her imagination, but indeed Deek, Michelle pulled herself up from a slouched position by holding on to the pew in front of her. A slow turn to her right, Michelle paused before she looked up into Deek's eyes. Her heart jumped.

Without strength to stand to her feet, Michelle's neck lost its stretch and she bowed in a flood of tears.

The day Stoney had called Deek to inform him that her mother didn't have his key was the day he poured out his heart to the young woman.

"I don't want my key, Stoney. That's not why I've been calling her," he proudly expressed.

"You don't?" Stoney wanted to understand.

"No, I don't. I've been calling because I love and miss your mother." Deek was honest. "My wife. My ex-wife . . ." he over-emphasized. "I have to admit, she pulled that mess about missing me and wanting to get back with me. Apologizing for running me off and cheating. And yes, I fell for it." He lowered his voice, ashamed. "But it didn't take long for me to open my eyes." He wanted to spare Stoney the details, but definitely wanted an opportunity to share it with Michelle.

"I've been calling your mother, leaving her messages. I even stopped by the house. She won't open the door or anything." He was testy.

"She moved," Stoney began to share with him. Feeling that Deek honestly loved her mother and only wanted the best for her, she gave him the details of her mother's move to Dallas.

Not sharing her address, Stoney had told him how he would be able to corner her in public. No time like the present.

"'Chelle." Deek tilted her chin with his hand. "I love you." He spared no time. "I don't care what brought you here to Dallas." He no doubt could figure it out if he tried hard enough. "All I want to know is if you're going back home . . . with me? I love you, Michelle."

It didn't take Michelle but one minute to stand up and fall into Deek's arms, realizing their breaking up was what had set sadness in her heart.

"I love you too," Michelle responded and released her transformed emotions into tears of happiness.

"But I have to know." Deek pushed the love of his life away in order to look into her eyes. "Can what happened in Dallas stay in Dallas?"

"Yes . . . I never should have—"

Deek held up his hand, needing her to stop the ranting she was about to start.

Placing his hand inside of his blazer pocket, Stoney gasped a breath of air and switched Grant Jr. to her other hip. A fresh set of tears found room to shine.

Michelle turned to Stoney to see what the gasping was about. Trailing her daughter's eyes to the box in Deek's right hand, Michelle brought her own hand to cover her own intake of air.

"Deek . . ." Michelle started.

"I want to apologize for not explaining myself better. I should have told you that I needed closure with my ex-wife. But that never meant I wanted to let you go. I need you in my life. I love you and want to spend the rest of my days with you."

Not allowing his old college-turf knee to bother him for the moment, Deek got down on one knee, with the help of his wife-to-be, and asked for her hand in marriage.

"Michelle. Will you marry me, honey?"

Michelle never looked at the ring. She was only amazed at how God had allowed her what she had always wanted: a man to want her. A man to proclaim his love for her and a man to pursue her. Deek was that man.

In all of her dating, Michelle had always been the aggressor. She had been the one to hint around at marriage and even propose to a few men. She had been the one to remind her beaus of anniversary dates, birthdates, and special dates. It was never what she wanted for herself.

She wanted a man's man. One who knew what and who he wanted. One who took charge of the relationship and allowed Michelle to be the woman she wanted and needed to be. Michelle had all that and then some in Deek. And there was no way she was letting him go.

"Yes. Yes! Of course I will marry you," Michelle happily agreed, knowing it was Deek all along she wanted. Her fear of losing him was what pushed her to fight with what had been familiar to her. She would always love Keithe, but she knew he had been placed in her life for a season and a reason. He deserved more. And so did she.

Chapter Thirty-nine

After all the commotion at the church, Keithe drove Kenya home. He didn't want to push the issue but he needed to show her that he cared for her . . . no matter what. It took the majority of the night, but Keithe stayed and sat attentive as he listened to Kenya's woes.

Even though he was still stunned, devastated, and taken aback by her admission of not only fornicating, but doing so with a woman, Keithe didn't waiver from his plan to have Kenya in his life as long as she'd have him.

Having dedicated this time and night to Kenya, it had hit Keithe like a ton of bricks: the conversation he was freely having with Kenya was the same conversation he had deviated from numerous times when Mike wanted . . . no, needed to talk to someone. Keithe had been unwilling to lend himself. But because of his admiration for her, Keithe stayed to help Kenya through.

Embarrassment and guilt spread through him at rapid speed. The mere thought made him feel as though he had rejected Mike all over again.

It wasn't until the wee hours of the morning that Keithe made it to Mike's place. He was drained, tired, and needed a shower, but his responsibility of being a friend, a true friend, drove him to his best friend's place.

Before he even got out of the car to ring the doorbell, Keithe called Mike on his cell phone to make him aware of his arrival. Mike answered on the first ring.

"Hello," Mike answered.

"Open the door, man." Keithe sounded groggy; no different from Mike.

All Keithe could think about was how confused a person would have to be with the struggle of not knowing what the physical man wanted to do while the spiritual man wanted to do another.

He felt so stupid. It wasn't until Kenya explained to Keithe, broke down how her flesh, at the moment, fought her spiritual life and won. She didn't have to go into how she really did have a relationship with God and that she would have never thought to do such . . . just like he was sure Mike had initially fought the same battle. Only he didn't have anyone to talk to about it.

"Dang." Keithe parked his Porsche and hit the steering wheel. Over thirty years had gone by without Keithe even questioning Mike why or how, or asking him what he needed from him. He'd just felt it was something Mike wanted and chose to do.

But the present was here. Keithe didn't want to dwell on the reasons of how right or how wrong it was for Mike to do what he did. His beliefs were his beliefs. The reason for this visit had everything to do with Keithe being the support system, prayer partner he should have been from jump.

When Keithe turned his key back and took it out of the ignition, he looked through the passenger window and saw his friend's front door open. Right after, someone walked out. As he focused on Grant leaving his best friend's home, Keithe thrust himself back against his driver's seat.

"What? What now?" he said to himself. Wondering why Mike was still holding on, he sat there and even pondered starting up his vehicle and coming back another time. But Keithe had to remember to remove himself and his personal feelings from the situation. Plus, he'd beaten himself up enough for going above and beyond for Kenya and giving nothing to Mike. Keithe had to both man up and be the friend Mike had been to him all the years before. Either that or walk out of his life all together.

He didn't know if it was difficult because Mike was a man and Kenya was a woman: a woman he was deeply interested in. Whatever the case, Keithe realized he loved them both. He owed Mike his understanding just the same.

After Grant had pulled away in his car, Keithe hesitated in getting out. By the time he shut his car's door, Mike was already at the edge of his yard to greet him.

"Hey," Mike said in the dark.

Keithe nodded, then decided to say, "Hey," as well. Just in case Mike hadn't seen his gesture.

"He didn't have anywhere to go." Mike knew what was on Keithe's mind as they both walked back toward the front door. "It's not like I hadn't told him. I told him awhile back that it was over."

Waiting for Keithe to make his way through the front door, Mike continued. "Keithe, I had no clue who he was tied to. Had he *ever* mentioned Mercy's name, Bishop Perry, anybody, I would have known. But I wouldn't even allow him to share with me who he was. Didn't care." Mike went to the kitchen to put some coffee on.

"So he's staying here with you, now? I mean, he jilted Mercy; surely he can't go back there," Keithe mentioned.

Mike took in a breath. "Right. No, he can't stay here. But . . . I did just call him in a room for a week at the Marriott." He shrugged his shoulders while drying his hands on the kitchen towel. "I guess I'm partly to

blame, so I have to help the young man get on his feet."
He questioned Keithe with his eyes.

"Hey." Keithe threw up his hands in defense. "I'm just listening."

With a twisted lip, Mike nodded. "You didn't have to come over, you know."

"Yes . . . yes, I did. Look, I owe you . . . an apology." Keithe scooted to the edge of the leather sofa he had relaxed on. "There is so much time I have allowed to just go by . . . with me having the same mind frame . . . not giving you me." He placed his palms on his chest. "You know . . . in a friendship way."

"Oh, 'cause I was about to say, 'I knew it . . . I knew you were my *brother* for real.'" Mike held up his dap fist for Keithe.

"Uh. No, bro. You on your own with that one." He tossed a throw pillow at Mike's head. "But I'm for real."

Mike yawned and already knew what brought this on.

"Oh. Oh! Kenya told you about her little trick or treat, huh?" He watched Keithe roll his eyes and nod his head.

"Right."

"So now you come over with your 'woe is me, I didn't really know, I'm sorry, It was me . . . not you . . .' programmed conversation." Mike wanted to go on.

"Look," Keithe cut him off. "I'm not going to allow you to play this down. And no, I wasn't going to go there, but I'm not going to sit up here and say I believe it's okay. That's not why I'm here. I'm here because never, not once . . . unless I can't recall, did I sit and allow you to tell me who, why, what, when. I didn't allow you to share the details of how you knew your life had changed from straight to gay. I didn't let you vent when your parents pushed you to the curb. I just assumed like they did, I guess, that you had just chosen to wild out."

"You for real, aint'cha?" Mike scooted from sitting on the arm of his sofa to the cushion.

"Fo'sho, Mike. I'm not gonna lie to you though. I guess it did take Kenya to break it down to me how she lost her battle. At first, I didn't think it was wilding out what you were doing." He shook his head.

Pumping his fist in his open palm Mike was relieved but angry. He had suppressed his need for anybody to care for him all the years prior. Now that Keithe was confiding and apologizing, it brought emotions out of Mike.

"What? You thought I wanted to try it out just to be trying it out? But you were supposed to know me. You should have known I was struggling with this," Mike shared.

"Maybe I should have. But in all fairness, Mike, I was young and you know that wasn't the 'in' thing to do. You know this." Keithe wanted Mike to understand his point of view as well.

Nodding, Mike agreed, "You're right."

"So where do you go from here?" Keithe did believe in miracles. He believed that God sat high and looked low. There was no doubt God watched and waited for His people to say the simple words of surrender. But sitting on Mike's sofa in Mike's home, Keithe wasn't holding his breath to Mike's surrendering.

"You know, Keithe, I can only take it one day at a time. For some years I was able to hold back what I felt on the inside. Then something just switched in me . . . like I wanted to be a family man . . . have a wife and kids. That's when I went after Vicky. That lasted only a minute because I was still lonely, feeling like I had no one to care for me. That was because I wasn't being who I know I am: a gay man."

Keithe's eyes saddened. He was happy he had cleared up the friend part of their issue, but internally, Keithe knew God would have to handle the rest.

"I'm not saying God is pleased with what I do . . . but I know He loves me. And if you ask me if I would accept a miracle transformation from above, of course—" Keithe cut him off.

"Be careful what you ask for." Keithe knew prayer changed things, and sometimes in a blink of an eye.

"Then be careful what you pray for," Mike returned. "I just need a friend. A real friend, Keithe. Someone who loves me regardless."

"And you know I do," Keithe said.

"*Now* I know you do," Mike answered with peace in his heart.

Chapter Forty

Everything was paid for: the tulips, the lilies, the roses, the ribbons, the tulle, and the rest of the decorations. Even the honeymoon had been paid for, but they weren't bothered with that. They had their own honeymoon idea in mind.

Michelle thought it was only something that could happen in one of those juicy fiction books. She didn't care. She'd be the character any day if it meant being paired with Deek.

"I can hardly stand it," Michelle shared with Stoney who had helped her get ready. "I never had a wedding." She became misty eyed. "I guess I never felt worthy." She could no longer hold in her emotions.

"Mom, you are more than deserving." Stoney comforted her mother by rubbing her shoulder. "You can't keep holding on to that. Look at me." Stoney bent down and placed her face in her mother's view. "If God has allowed me to start with a clean slate with you, there is no devil in hell that can change otherwise. It's over. It's been over." She nuzzled her nose on her mother's, not wanting to mess up her mother's lipstick with a peck.

"You're right, Stoney. My baby." Michelle couldn't help but think about the second chance to live through Him. "You are my angel."

"I am, aren't I?" Stoney asked with a giggle.

Yesterday the same church had been in an uproar due to a relationship coming to an abrupt end. Even after all was said and done and Deek had proposed, getting married was the furthest from Michelle's mind. At least so soon.

It was Kendra who came to Michelle with the ideal of nuptials being exchanged. With all monies invested there was no doubt a wedding needed to take place. Whether it happened or not, Mercy gave her blessing. Michelle couldn't say no.

That was another miracle Michelle had to give God props on. Women who she had once hated and hated her had turned around and treated her with a cordial, godly friendship. At almost sixty, Michelle finally concluded with herself she only had hated them because she'd secretly envied them and their ability to be blessed with good men in their lives. It wasn't until Michelle consummated her relationship with God that she realized that the spirit Kendra and Gracie possessed was because they didn't strive for fulfillment with men, but rather with God. Michelle finally got the memo.

There was no time like the present to live a fulfilled life and Michelle was looking forward to marrying and spending the rest of her life with Deek. With her family present and now, finally friends and extended family, Michelle realized she really didn't know a better way to start. Love was present and that's what mattered most.

"Ma? You ready?" Stoney ran in place for a second, excited about her mother finding love. Rather, love finally finding her. And from a man who actually pursued *her*; Deek was that someone who wanted and needed her in his life.

"You know I am, Stoney." Michelle puckered her lips regardless of her lipstick and kissed her daughter.

"Okay. Let me go make sure Pops is ready." Stoney had been ready to stand by her sister Mercy's side at the altar. Things were now different. Due to life's curveballs, Stoney was now ready to take on the responsibility of being her mother's maid of honor.

Walking to the entrance door of the sanctuary, Stoney high-fived Keithe and said, "She's ready."

Throwing up her thumbs to the organist, Stoney cued the music. Pointing a finger-gun to her daddy, she let Bishop know he could get ready to officiate the wedding.

Standing on the opposite side of Keithe, under the threshold, when Michelle had come out of hiding, the two became misty eyed.

With a dazzling, off-the-rack wedding dress Stoney and Michelle had found at Terra Costa in North Dallas, the last-minute shopping proved wonders for Michelle's glow. Michelle looked breathtaking. A simple flower in her hair set off the straight but tucked material-filled dress.

"You look amazing." Keithe offered his right arm, leaning in for a kiss on the cheek.

"Mom, you are gorgeous." Stoney offered her left hand.

With a sincere smile and nod, Michelle looked to Keithe as her borrowed because she knew sooner or later her ex-husband would do right by Kenya if she allowed him the honor. Stoney was no doubt her something blue with the blue corsage her daughter had around her wrist. Having Stoney in her life now brought out a whole other meaning in living.

And down the aisle toward her future husband, Michelle was about to walk to her something new. With a wink toward Deek, Michelle was ready.

The church could actually seat hundreds of people. Now, no more than ten people gathered in the large, beautifully lit sanctuary. And that was perfect enough.

Michelle saw that Kendra had raced to her seat after doing Michelle's makeup. Gracie and Marcus were there for support to their extended family and to witness the union. And of course, Bishop, Stoney's dad, was officiating.

"You sure about this?" Keithe whispered out of the side of his mouth as they made their way down the aisle.

"Are you sure?" Michelle whispered back as she turned her eyes toward Kenya who stood in a row alone.

With a smile at Kenya and a nod of agreement, Keithe said, "Oh yes. I'm sure."

It was amazing how Michelle knew in her heart that everything was just right. There was no guilt behind it. She hadn't stolen anyone's man or husband. She hadn't connived in order to get Deek to love her. She was just at the right place at the right time. Michelle knew all things happened for a reason and in order to get where they both were, they had to go through what they'd experienced.

"I'm sure too," she said as she released her family and held out her hand to Deek.

As Bishop asked who would give her away, Michelle looked back to see Keithe and Stoney hugging one another and offering her to her future.

"We do," they harmonized.

After his duties, Keithe turned and walked to sit next to Kenya. Without thought, Keithe grabbed for Kenya's right hand and intertwined his fingers through hers.

Bringing her small and delicate hand to his mouth, Keithe gave her the softest and most gentle and respectful kiss. He hoped she liked it because it was definitely a church kiss. He'd do their official first kiss afterward.

EPILOGUE

A year and three months had passed from the chaotic day at the church; the day that was supposed to be Mercy and Grant's wedding day. Instead it was an abrupt end for some and the beginning for others.

In the year, things were progressing for Mercy. Her healing process took a toll on her at first, but realizing she still had Grant Jr. to take care of, Mercy used her energy to be the best mother she could be.

For a while, and unfortunately for her son, Grant had disappeared all together. Not wanting to counsel to at least remain friends in order to be the family unit Grant Jr. was used to, the senior Grant decided he wanted to live his life by his own terms, saying he'd deal with his child in his own way and time. At first Mercy thought that was just that. But God was still working behind the scenes.

Under what he thought were his own terms, Grant found his way back to church, back to God, and eventually back into the arms of his son. There wasn't much he wanted to talk about of his personal life; he just knew he couldn't leave his son behind no matter the cost. Much prayer, much power was what Bishop and Kendra had poured into Mercy, with the results being evident.

Stoney had been the best sister and godmother to Grant Jr. With one graduation under her belt, Stoney was less than another year away from graduating from the master's program that would put her in clinical. Accepted in a program in the area of Houston where home was, Stoney was able to spend even more time with her mother and Deek in between her own blossoming relationship. It seemed as if her time would be coming soon.

On her trips back to Dallas to visit with her dad and stepmother, Stoney always made it a point to drop in and visit with her other father figure, her pops, Keithe, and his wife, Kenya. From the smiles that always preceded them, Stoney could tell the two were still honeymooning.

It hadn't taken them long to know they wanted and needed one another in their lives. It was just that simple. Just as soon as Keithe brought up marriage, the proposal wasn't far behind. Keithe then put his condo on the market and the two hadn't looked back. During the coming weeks leading up to their nuptials, the two had closed on the home of their dreams. Because he wanted and needed to let Kenya know that she was indeed pure in his eyes, before they moved in together, they asked Pastor Peters if he'd do the formalities and marry them in his office. The wedding was just the icing on the cake.

"Happy birthday, honey." Keithe walked in with a tray full of breakfast goodies for his wife of almost a year.

"Aww, Keithe." Kenya eased up in bed. "Honey." She perched her lips so that her husband's lips would have a smooth landing.

Rolling her pajama top sleeves up, Kenya picked up a piece of bacon and bit into it. "I would say you didn't have to, but I'm starved." She giggled and took another bite. "Want some, before you go?" she offered.

"No. I drank a glass of orange juice. I wanted to save my appetite for breakfast with Stoney."

Nodding her head, happy she'd get to sleep in a bit longer, Kenya didn't know if she should give Keithe the news she had for him now or later.

"I'm surprised she wants me to meet this joker who calls himself crushing hard on her." Keithe pulled his polo-styled shirt over his head.

"Be nice, dear. She's excited about him. He might be the one." Kenya loved love.

Turning around while fastening his watch, Keithe said, "You're right. Just like I was the right one for you." He walked in close for another kiss. "I love you," he said. "And I love you too." He placed his large hand on Kenya's protruding stomach.

They had wasted no time in starting their family. The day Kenya came home with the news she was with child, the two had only been married for five months.

"I love you too, honey," Kenya said. Then she decided to give him his present now, rather than later. "Your son loves you too, Keithe."

"Oh, I know. I can't wait . . ." Keithe stopped in his tracks and turned back to his wife. When he did, Kenya held out the sonogram for him.

"Here you go," she said in a beautiful hush, handing her husband what she was sure would add brightness to his day.

Slowly taking the thin paper from his wife, Keithe held back tears.

God knew his heart's desire. He wanted a child with his wife. A child born from him; a male child.

"You sure?" Keithe asked as Kenya pointed to the details. A tear fell as he looked through blurry eyes at the 3-D photo. "Yep, that's my boy." Keithe laughed, wiping his eyes.

With an overwhelming feeling of love for his wife, Keithe placed the photo on the nightstand and removed the breakfast tray as fast as he could.

At that very moment, Keithe wanted, no, needed to hold his wife.

Over the last few years, God had allowed him to be used in some of the most unusual circumstances he had ever encountered.

His journey was for an appointed purpose of helping Michelle, his ex-wife, to receive her child she had once abandoned. But most of all, he was there to help lead her back to Christ.

Keithe was able to be the true friend his best friend Mike had wanted and needed. Even with their views on Mike's homosexual lifestyle, Keithe was able to love Mike unconditionally with no plans of ever leaving his side.

And with Kenya, God had moved him from Houston to Dallas to find a wife. With her own bout of confusion and running from what God had already ordained, Keithe was right where he needed to be: able to stand and wait for God's purpose, his purpose, to be revealed in her life.

And in all of that, God had not forgotten him.

By being a Christian, a believer, though not perfect, Keithe was simply . . . redeemed.

Discussion Questions

1. If you've read *Keeper Of My Soul,* do you agree with Keithe divorcing Michelle after she had finally given her life to God?

2. Did Keithe move too slowly when it came to Kenya? Instead of talking to Mike about her, should he have let her know his feeling from the beginning?

3. Do you feel Kenya was too hard on herself?

4. Kenya blamed Charlene for the advances, but does women's intuition work in discerning the motives in other women?

5. When Kenya felt God had forgiven her, should she have forgiven herself?

6. Do you feel as though Kenya was indeed gay?

7. Is it possible to give into an instinct, yet still be against the very act?

8. If Keithe was so against Mike and his gay lifestyle, do you believe he will actually be able to look beyond Kenya's past?

Discussion Questions

9. Mike said repeatedly he didn't want to be who he was; he didn't like being homosexual. Is it possible to let go of a lifestyle you don't believe in if you've been involved in it for many years?

10. Is it possible for Kenya to be once again productive in her ministry, even though she gave into the wilds of temptation?